And I Am You

Judy Mackie

Dedication

For my dear family and friends

Epigraph

Strangers passing in the street
By chance two separate glances meet
And I am you and what I see is me
'Echoes', Pink Floyd ('Meddle', 1971)

Contents

Prologue

Blackbirds sing me awake, their fluty song as familiar as a nursery-rhyme.

I lie, comforted by the ancient melodies dancing from twig to branch in the beech-tree canopy outside. My head is clear now and I know where I am.

It's who I am that might be the problem.

Feeling eyes on me, I turn, slowly, in the starched sheets of my institutional bed. I know I'll never be prepared for what's lying in wait, so I face it head on.

From an identical bed nearby, a dark-haired woman is watching me. My stomach clenches as I recognise her features but her fascinated, almost predatory, expression is unfamiliar.

Is it really you?

I sit up, and as I do so, I see our beds reflected in the ornate cheval glass across the room. I lift my hand – is this my hand? – in a tentative wave and the movement is mirrored by a frightened-looking woman with white-blonde hair.

I gasp. You laugh. Our eyes meet again and the acknowledgement is unspoken.

The experiment has worked – and I am you and what I see is me.

Part One: Pre-op

Chapter 1
One Month Earlier: March
Cairnacraig House, Buchan Coast, Scotland

Layla released a shaky breath as the baronial-style mansion came into view.

'See! It's hardly the Hammer House of Horror,' she chided herself, trying to relax her white-knuckle grip on the steering wheel.

An inexplicable dread had crept over her as she'd driven through the pillared gateway of the forested estate and negotiated the winding driveway. Yet the pink-and-grey building she now glimpsed through the trees appeared entirely benign, basking in the early spring sunshine that made tiny, flashing mirrors of the mica embedded in its granite walls.

Still she didn't feel reassured.

Slowly, she nosed her silver Mini over a series of speed bumps – and screamed as a rusty streak shot across her path. She stamped on the brake. The car stalled. Breathing deeply, she shook her head at her overreaction to a fleeing squirrel. *Get a grip,* she told herself, as she restarted the engine. *Remember, you don't* have *to go through with this.*

And so, nerves jangling, she completed her journey, arriving with a crunch of gravel before the impressive edifice of Cairnacraig House.

Professor James Blunstone looked different on his home territory. Framed by the ancient hardwood doorway, dressed in jeans and a pink oxford shirt, the white-haired man appeared younger and more relaxed than on the previous occasions they'd met. Then, he'd been very much the professional: suited, serious and softly spoken; his sharp grey eyes assessing her as he laid out his incredible proposal.

Now, he was marching towards her, grasping her leather holdall and shaking her hand firmly.

'Layla – marvellous to see you again!' he said warmly. 'I trust you enjoyed your short trip into the Shire on such a beautiful morning? Come away in!'

Returning his greeting, she followed him into a spacious hall floored with slate and lined with granite blocks brightened here and there by vibrant wall hangings. She shivered in the cool air, hoping the rest of the house would be a little less chilly.

Blunstone led her off to the right, into a large sitting room, where she was relieved to see a log fire crackling away at one end. The room was dominated by a pair of enormous brown leather couches which faced each other across the hearth. They looked faintly familiar. A few faded old paintings of horses, dogs and landscapes graced the walls, and Layla noticed some good antique furniture: a couple of ball-and-claw occasional tables; an ornately-carved bookcase full of leather-bound volumes, and a grand sideboard supporting a large silver tray with two half-full decanters and an assortment of glasses.

She sat down, as bidden, on the edge of one of the couches. Her right leg started twitching involuntarily and, dismayed, she tried to hide it by crossing the left one over it.

'So, how are you, Layla?' the professor beamed, sitting opposite her. He leaned forward and clasped his hands between his knees. 'Nervous? Well, who wouldn't be! But I can assure you there's nothing to worry about.'

How many patients had he said that to during his long career?

She felt she needed to assert herself and shake off the shyness that had overcome her upon entering the house. She cleared her throat and looked directly at him.

'I'll be honest: I am nervous. Terrified, in fact. I still haven't finally decided, you know. But I'm here, and I'm willing to take it to the next stage, at least.'

That was better. More like the confident academic, and less like the lost little girl she had been regressing into in recent months.

'Of course, I understand. And I'm delighted you're here. Now, how about a hot drink while we chat?'

'Tea would be lovely, thanks.' She needed the comfort of a warm cup.

'Back in a tick.' Blunstone rose and left the room.

Layla had half-expected him to ring a bell and for a crusty old servant to appear. She wondered if he did have help and, if not, how he could possibly manage such a large house on his own.

After a few minutes, the professor reappeared, carrying a battered tin tray laden with a modern glass teapot, a cafetière, three spotted mugs and a plate of shortbread. 'I fend for myself at the weekends,' he explained, 'but a local lady comes in during the week to do the cooking and light cleaning.'

Although he'd answered her unasked question, there were dozens of others bubbling to the surface. She needed to know more about this virtual stranger who had asked her to trust him with her life. But before she could speak, he looked up from pouring the tea and said: 'I don't see much point in diving into things until Stevie gets here, so why don't you tell me what you've been up to at work recently? As you know, I'm very interested in your research into personal identity.'

Layla couldn't help but smile. 'Yes, I'd kind of guessed that... but your discovery is really going to shake things up in my field of expertise. It'll do away with arguments about consciousness that have kept us philosophers busy for centuries.'

He grinned at her. 'Oh, I think there will still be plenty of argument to come! But yes, when my breakthrough becomes public, it will at least clear away the clutter of theories that are no longer valid. And that will allow philosophers, scientists – and indeed anyone with a natural curiosity about consciousness – to focus on the really important questions concerning what I call the "new reality". What's more –'

Interrupted by the sound of a car, he leapt to his feet.

'That'll be Stevie!'

Layla's stomach flipped and, feeling her right hand start to tremble, she tightened her grip on her mug.

There was so much she was both looking forward to and dreading.

Meeting her body-swap partner was the first such experience.

Chapter 2
Six Months Earlier: October
The University, Aberdeen, Scotland

The first time Layla met the professor, she was struck by two things: he had kind eyes and he had beautiful hands.

On that occasion, she was more excited than nervous; keen to find out more about the research project she had expressed an interest in, and curious about the man leading it.

When James Blunstone walked into the campus café – formerly a bland student common room whose walls were now radiant with blocks of primary colour – he looked every inch the newly-retired neurosurgeon. Tall, straight-backed and confident, he beamed at the young waitress who welcomed him and gave her a reassuring pat on the arm when he spotted Layla in a window seat overlooking the hall of residence gardens.

He strode across the room and she stood to greet him.

'I recognised you from your academic profile pic,' he smiled, as they shook hands. 'Websites are wonderful things!'

'I looked you up, too,' laughed Layla. 'Congratulations on your recent retirement.'

'Thank you!' The kind eyes twinkled, then turned serious. 'But it's really just the beginning of a new phase of my career, as I'll explain in due course.'

They sat down on two colourful cubes masquerading as chairs, and Blunstone ordered a black Americano from the waitress, who had followed him over.

'I see you're not a fan of froth, either,' he said to Layla, indicating the large mug of dark liquid sitting in front of her.

'Well... I do ask for hot milk on the side,' she replied, lifting the small white jug she had been just about to pour from when he arrived.

This man could transform my life and we're discussing hot drinks, she thought.

But the professor seemed in no rush to get to the heart of the matter. Instead, he chatted on about the ancient beauty of the university campus, with its crowned, fifteenth-century chapel and wealth of mature trees, now in full autumn splendour.

'I did my first degree here,' he said. 'I went back home to Edinburgh after graduating, but I've long had a hankering to return to the North-east. I'm sure you know that this area has always punched well above its weight in pioneering medical miracles that have transformed lives worldwide. That's something I intend to do myself, by the way, but we'll get to that shortly... Anyway, suffice it to say, I was drawn back to the region and a few years ago, I bought a house and some land on the Buchan coast. That's where I've retired to.'

If he had noticed Layla's look of astonishment at his casual hubris, he didn't acknowledge it. Instead, he thanked the waitress as she placed a steaming mug in front of him, and asked Layla: 'Do you enjoy living here? I know from your profile that you come from further north – Easter Ross, isn't it?'

'Yes, I'm a true Highlander "right enough",' she replied, ironically using the catchphrase associated with folk from her native region. His chuckle showed he'd got the reference and she continued: 'I love this place, though. I've always had a connection with Aberdeen – my maternal grandparents lived here and when I was growing up, we'd visit regularly for holidays.'

She paused to sip her coffee, then added: 'Sadly, all my grandparents are gone now and none of my immediate family lives in Scotland anymore.'

Seeing his questioning look, she explained: 'My parents and younger brother emigrated to California when I was a student, then both sets of aunts and uncles followed suit. I had intended to do the same once I'd graduated, but then I met my future husband and decided to stay...' She shrugged. 'It was probably not the best choice I ever made.'

He nodded seriously. 'Yes, you said in your email that you'd recently separated from your husband. I'm sorry to hear that.'

She smiled sadly and he continued: 'And there are no children?'

Layla had anticipated this, but still felt the prickle of tears.

'Yes, that's correct,' she said tightly.

He nodded again, seemingly satisfied. 'Well, I expect you want to hear more about this research of mine. I take it you've read about my medical background?'

Of course she had. He was a great man: umpteen letters after his name; a long and successful career as a neurosurgeon in two of the country's top teaching hospitals; a member of several UK and international medical committees – she remembered one of them was concerned with ethics – and a patron of a Scottish children's cancer charity. His brief personal biography had revealed that he was born and brought up in Edinburgh, the son of a GP, and that he was a widower with no children.

Seeing her nod, he went on: 'What's important about my past is that it should reassure you that I'm not a quack. I have deep, practical knowledge of the human brain and nervous system, and literally hundreds of people have put their lives in my hands throughout my career.'

He looked down now at his hands, resting on the table top. Layla saw he had long, slender fingers and perfectly–manicured nails. 'Of course, not every operation I've carried out has been a success,' he said softly. 'I have lost patients, whose faces I will never forget.'

He lifted his head and added: 'But it was never due to any malpractice on my part – these were people for whom surgery was a last resort. Some brain tumours, when they are removed, can cause fatal haemorrhaging, and that is not something that can be predicted or prevented.'

Why is he telling me this? she wondered. *Where does* surgery *come into the equation?*

Masking her confusion, she said: 'Given what I've read, I have no worries about your track record and professionalism. But I'd really like to hear more about what this project actually involves.'

She felt she'd waited long enough. Three weeks previously, irritated by the deluge of junk mail that had gathered in her inbox over the weekend, she had very nearly deleted the short message sent as an alert from an academic website she subscribed to. But, as a specialist in the philosophy of personal identity, she'd found the header *'Research subjects required for "body-swap" study'* too intriguing to resist, and so she'd read on.

'Retired neurosurgeon Professor James Blunstone seeks two adult females to assist in his groundbreaking research into the transposition of human consciousness. The successful applicants – preferably living and working in the North-east of Scotland – will receive substantial remuneration for their participation. Interested parties

12

should apply by email to the address below, briefly stating why they would like to be considered for the project.'

She'd laughed aloud. 'My god, this has to be a joke!' she cried, startling the young PhD candidate who shared her office. 'David – come and have a look at this! Can you believe it?'

The ever-serious David had instantly dismissed the message as a hoax and returned to his computer, clearly irritated by the interruption.

It was one of Layla's less vulnerable days; in fact, she'd been feeling rather reckless that afternoon, having spent her lunch break venting to Morven, her friend and colleague, over Calum's insistence on returning to the house that evening to collect 'some more stuff'.

'What the hell, I'm going to reply,' she'd muttered to herself. If it was a hoax, she would complain to the web master. But if it was genuine, it might be just the opportunity she was looking for. So, without thinking too much about it, she'd rattled off an email, providing brief details about herself, explaining her professional interest in the study's subject, and asking for more information.

The traumatic evening that followed had erased all thoughts of Professor Blunstone's mysterious project. Calum – her Calum – tousle-headed and dressed in jeans and an unfamiliar blue cashmere sweater, had shown up in a rented van. After a curt greeting and without meeting her eyes, he'd brushed past her and begun to remove what he called 'my half of the furniture and contents' without even trying to negotiate with her.

Her husband of ten years had always been self-possessed, but the coldness with which he now treated her still came as a shock three months on from the night he'd walked out.

She'd discovered his affair with his young marketing colleague, Darla – she could hardly bear to even *think* the name – after checking through their own shared credit card statement from the previous month. Calum had charged a hotel bill to the card, which was not suspicious in itself – she remembered he'd been in Glasgow on business that night – but the amount had seemed overly expensive to Layla. When she'd asked him about it, he'd shrugged it off, saying it didn't matter, as he had already claimed it back on expenses. But she'd instinctively known something was wrong. He'd been behaving differently towards her recently: more introverted and impatient; less loving, somehow. And so she'd called the hotel to query the bill.

'Double room; champagne, flowers and fruit as extras; room service for two,' the receptionist had read out in a nasal monotone.

Layla had rung off, feeling sick to her stomach. When confronted, Calum had been furious, but had to admit the truth: he and Darla were having an affair and had been for some time. She'd cried and raged at him as he threw some clothes into a suitcase, and then, incredulously, she'd watched as he simply walked out.

She was the wronged party, but since that dreadful night, in their brief email exchanges and in his previous visit to collect more of his belongings, he'd made her feel as if she were to blame. Was it guilt, or was he still angry that he'd been found out and that his comfortable existence had been shaken up? Whatever it was, it had hardened him beyond recognition.

'I'm taking the HD TV,' he'd said haughtily, the evening he'd arrived with the transit van. He had already carried out the rest of his books and clothes. 'I bought it, and you hardly ever watch it, anyway.'

'You are NOT taking the TV – you bought it with OUR money, and for your information, I DO watch it nowadays. There's little else for me to do in my spare time,' she'd retorted, shaking with rage.

She'd stood blocking the lounge doorway and for a horrible moment it looked as if he was going to barge past her. Then he turned on his heel and, without saying another word, marched out of the front door.

It was a small victory for her, but she really couldn't have cared less about the TV. It was the thought of Darla watching it with him, all cosy in her flat – which they now shared – that had made her dig her heels in.

After the van roared off, she'd spent yet another lonely evening crying until her throat felt raw. But later, lying in bed with a pounding headache, she'd felt the steel set in.

I will make him suffer for this, she'd vowed.

The next morning, on checking her inbox, she'd been greeted by a cheerful email from Professor Blunstone. He had read her message with interest and would be in touch in due course. Three weeks later, when she'd just about given up hope of hearing from him again and was still feeling at a low ebb, he had sent a follow-up email asking if she would like to meet with him to discuss the project.

She didn't need to think about it. But as she'd pressed the "send" button to confirm her interest in a meeting, she had experienced a tiny frisson of fear.

Just what am I letting myself in for?

Chapter 3
March: Cairnacraig House

Stevie was stunning.

As the professor showed her into the sitting room, Layla felt something akin to awe. While she, herself, stood five feet two in her socks, Stevie must have been at least eight inches taller. The woman's straight white-blonde hair was a sharp contrast to Layla's own dark brown curls, and those sculpted cheekbones were to die for. Casually dressed in skinny jeans, tan leather boots and a long oatmeal-coloured sweater, she looked like a Scandinavian model.

Layla had always known she was pretty, in a Celtic, girl-next-door way. Over the years, she'd been complimented on her slight figure, shiny hair and Delft-blue eyes. She had always despaired of the pale skin of her Highland heritage, but others seemed to find it attractive. Stevie, however, was in a different league. At Layla's school she undoubtedly would have been head girl – and not just because of the obvious fitness of her tanned physique; those unsettling green eyes now trained on her sparked with intelligence and a superior self-awareness.

Determined not to show her feelings of inadequacy, Layla got to her feet and smiled warmly at the newcomer.

'Layla, Stevie – it's an absolute pleasure for me to introduce you,' James Blunstone said grandly, beaming from one to the other.

'How's it going, girl – good to meet ya!' Stevie's broad Australian accent was another left-fielder. *Oh, my days*, Layla thought, feeling a bubble of hysteria rising in her chest.

'Um, fine, thanks – and likewise!' she managed to say in her natural voice, shaking Stevie's – rather large, she noted – outstretched hand.

'You have no idea what a monumental occasion this is for me,' the professor enthused. 'My two research subjects meeting for the first time! You do realise, of course, that if our project goes ahead – and I very much hope it does – you ladies will get to know each other *inside out!*' His sudden shout of laughter was a little too loud for Layla's liking. Her cat-gut nerves were at snapping point.

'Ha-ha! Good one, Prof,' Stevie guffawed and Layla managed a weak smile, sitting down again in case her knees gave way.

The next few minutes were filled with the professor's activity as he bustled around, stoking the fire, pulling over the other occasional table and serving Stevie, who was sitting beside him, with her requested 'long black' from the cafetière on the tray.

'Will I have to stop adding milk to my coffee, I wonder?' Layla found herself saying. A thousand infinitely more important questions were flapping around inside her skull, but this was the one that had found its way out first.

The other two laughed again and this time she joined in. The tension eased, and her latent hysteria morphed into a tingling excitement that took her by surprise.

Blunstone cleared his throat. 'Now, ladies, as you know, the purpose of this weekend get-together is for us all to become acquainted with each other away from the distractions of everyday life, and for you to find out more about the practical implications of my project. I hope that by the time you leave, you will have enough information to help you to make a final decision about whether or not you wish to go ahead.'

With his quietly authoritative manner, he could have been introducing a seminar, Layla thought. The dark wood panelling and antiques added to the impression that they were in deepest academia, poised to discuss an ancient philosophical conundrum that time had failed to untangle. Except that the conundrum they were currently entangled in: *can human consciousness survive beyond the body?* had, apparently, been solved.

'... so, I thought I could show you your rooms just now and when you're ready, we could go out for lunch, if you like?' he was saying.

'Sounds good to me!' Stevie said loudly, and Layla nodded. She was back to feeling oddly shy again.

Blunstone led them out of the sitting room and up a wide, red-carpeted staircase with ornate oak balustrades. After several steps, the staircase branched to the left and the right, the landing overlooked by a magnificent stained-glass window depicting a hunting scene. The professor took the right-hand stairs, leading them up to a narrow gallery. Layla saw that it formed three sides of a square, ending at the top of the other staircase, directly across from where they were now standing.

The wall side of the gallery was lined with oak panels and several closed doors. Blunstone opened the first one, revealing a sunlit chamber, spacious enough to be both bedroom and sitting room. It held a double bed, two bedside tables, a wardrobe and a chest of drawers, all in beautiful glowing rosewood. The bed was topped by a peony-patterned duvet and in the large bay window space sat a rose damask sofa and matching armchair, which Layla immediately fell in love with.

As if guessing her thoughts, Blunstone said: 'Layla, this is your room. I hope it's okay?'

'Oh, it's lovely!' she cried, hurrying over to the window, which offered a spectacular view over the estate's ancient, still-leafless beech trees, across the muted patchwork farmland beyond, and ending in Rothko stripes of cerulean sea and duck-egg sky. 'What a marvellous outlook.' She turned in time to catch a flash of steel in

18

Stevie's eyes, which was so quickly masked that she thought she must have imagined it.

'That's grand — glad you like it.' The professor beamed at her and turned to Stevie. 'You're just next door.' He swept along the corridor and opened the neighbouring door. 'This side of the house is east-facing, so you may well be treated to a lovely sunrise over the sea tomorrow, weather permitting. The coast is only a quarter of a mile away,' he explained, as Stevie strode into the room ahead of him. It was the mirror image of Layla's, but the colour scheme featured a vibrant Amazon green: the exact shade of the Australian woman's eyes.

'This'll do,' she said casually, opening a door that led to a modern, white en-suite. 'I'll go and fetch our kit bags from the hall.' And she squeezed past the others in the doorway and disappeared down the stairs.

Layla smiled at her host. 'You've chosen well — for me, at least. Pink is my favourite colour.'

'I'd gathered that from your clothes and accessories; it wasn't exactly brain surgery to guess,' he laughed, and in that moment, she decided that she liked him. He seemed genuinely kind, good-humoured and courteous. She also needed to be able to trust him but knew she hadn't yet reached that stage.

Stevie had made short work of the stairs and now handed Layla her holdall. 'If you don't mind, guys, I'd like to freshen up before we go out. Can you give me fifteen?'

'Good heavens, yes,' Blunstone said. 'There's no rush at all. I'll meet you downstairs when you're both ready.' He smiled at them and headed back towards the staircase. Layla turned to say something to Stevie, but the other woman had already entered her room and shut the door with a dull thud.

What was that about? Layla thought. *Did she want my room? Or was she annoyed that I was shown mine first?*

She sincerely hoped Stevie didn't live up to her head-girl image, as she had never got along with competitive women. With a little sigh, she returned to her own room and was again instantly enchanted by its cheerful, rosy glow. Drawn back to the window, she gazed out, still experiencing the low buzz of excitement she'd felt downstairs. A phrase of the professor's, from their first meeting, entered her head:

'This project is going to be life-changing...'

Chapter 4
The Previous October: The University

'... you need to understand that very clearly, Layla.' He stared at her, his grey gaze unwavering. 'But before I explain further, I'd really like to hear what your interest is in this study and what you think might be involved.'

She sighed inwardly at his use of the old power ploy: find out what the other person knows or expects before you reveal your own hand.

'Okay...' she began. 'Well, as I mentioned in my email, as an academic, I specialise in the philosophy of self, or personal identity. This involves asking questions such as: what makes the essential "me" persist through time, when my body goes through so many fundamental changes from birth through adulthood? Is it my perception, or consciousness, of being the same person? And what exactly is consciousness? I'm sure you'll be familiar with all this.'

Seeing Blunstone nod, she continued: 'In my field, the concept of body swapping has long been used to help us explore the nature of consciousness and the idea that consciousness could somehow exist outside the human brain. For centuries, philosophers have conducted thought experiments, imagining what it might be like if we could swap our own consciousness, or inner self, with that of another person, so that we can "live" in their body and see the world from their perspective. Obviously, potential survival of the self beyond the body leads to all kinds of possibilities, not least life after death.

'But,' she added, 'putting philosophy aside and straying into psychology, computer technology and a few other areas of applied science – nowadays, we can discuss more practical examples of "body swapping", thanks to the use of virtual reality technology. The VR studies I've read about most recently have had some quite amazing results; apparently, our senses and perceptions can be very easily manipulated and the brain confused as a result.'

His raised eyebrows encouraged her to go on. 'You'll probably be familiar with the research? The most fascinating study for me involved a man and a woman who were each given VR headsets in a controlled set of circumstances which apparently made them see, hear and actually *feel* themselves as the other person. The researchers spoke about how the technology could be used to help to foster a deeper empathy with other people, as well as to explore issues such as sexism and gender identity.'

'Yes,' he interjected eagerly, 'I've been following progress in that area, too. It's also an exciting time for neuroscience, which feeds very strongly into these studies. The research has demonstrated that if we are fed false, ie virtual, information involving video and sound, our brains can be fooled into perceiving all kinds of weird and wonderful things; for example, that we are invisible, or that we have rubber limbs – even that we are inhabiting someone else's body!'

He went on: 'I know the experiment you're referring to: the two research subjects stood facing each other and when they put on the VR headsets and looked at each other, they saw themselves! When they looked down, they saw the other person's body; when they spoke, they heard the other person's voice in their ears – and when they both moved and touched things at the same time, they had the overall sensation that they were inhabiting the other person's body.'

'*I am you and what I see is me*,' Layla smiled. Seeing his quizzical look, she added: 'An old Pink Floyd lyric I like to trot out from time to time.'

He chuckled. 'Yes, very psychedelic and highly appropriate! But do go on.'

His interest was flattering, but she wanted to get to the point. 'I was just going to add that these kinds of practical study can help philosophers better imagine a real-life body-swap scenario and therefore talk more meaningfully about what such a scenario could tell us about the true nature of consciousness... Och, I could rabbit on for ages, but to get back to your question, I'm wondering if your own project will take this kind of experimentation even further – perhaps involving more advanced VR technology and monitoring changes in the subjects' brain activity...?'

She tailed off, looking at him expectantly. To her surprise, he slowly shook his head.

'Oh, it's far more revolutionary than that, Layla,' he said quietly. 'My project involves *actual* body swapping.'

She almost choked on her coffee. '*What?* Impossible! Surely that would mean swapping people's brains!'

Her outburst attracted a few glances and she lowered her voice. 'Look, I don't pretend to know anything about neuroscience and organ transplants, but I do know medical science hasn't advanced nearly as far as that – never mind whether or not the procedure would ever be allowed from an ethical point of view.'

The professor leaned closer to her, his expression serious. 'Leaving ethics aside for the moment, what would you say if I told you I have discovered a way of surgically transposing people's consciousness without exchanging their brains?'

I'd say you were mad, was what she wanted to tell him. She felt horribly disappointed. She had been really interested in this project. Now, she would have to extricate herself from what was threatening to become an embarrassing situation, and she'd also have to ditch her dreams of taking part in some pioneering "applied

23

philosophy" – *an oxymoron, if ever there was one*, she thought glumly.

'Actually, don't answer that and just hear me out,' Blunstone said. And, before she could say anything else, he began his fantastical tale.

'For years, Layla, I concentrated on being a "fixer". As a neurosurgeon, I specialised in surgical procedures involving the brain and spinal cord, removing tumours and aneurysms; clearing blockages caused by stroke – you know the sort of thing?'

'Yes,' she replied in a flat voice.

Undaunted by her lack of enthusiasm, he continued. 'Anyway, needless to say, I've always been fascinated by the complex architecture of the human brain – the billons of neurons whose electrical activity makes us who we are and what we do. As technology has progressed, our neurosurgical techniques have become increasingly sophisticated, and in recent years, I have been able to sit in my high-tech surgeon's chair, in front of a monitor, and navigate my way through the inside of a live brain, just as if it were the landscape of a video game. The high-resolution camera allows me to see how the land lies with far greater clarity – and then to work on the problem with greater precision – than ever before.'

In spite of herself, Layla was getting interested. She nodded to the waitress, who had come over to ask if they wanted more coffee, and the professor continued.

'In my "fixer" days, I was a staunch materialist. For me, human consciousness began and ended with the workings of the brain. As far as I was concerned, when the brain died, so did the person – end of story. But, as I performed more and more operations, particularly those that relied on the patients being conscious throughout – allowing us to monitor their reactions during surgery – I also became increasingly interested in new research being carried out into human consciousness. I wanted to understand just how and where consciousness develops in the brain.

'Of course,' he went on, 'pressure of work didn't allow me to conduct any experiments myself; experienced neurosurgeons and the sophisticated equipment they work with are a very limited resource and, after all, my job was to treat sick patients. But in any spare moment I had, I would read up on the latest research, and the exciting work being carried out made me wish I could play a more proactive role in that field.'

The fresh mugs of coffee arrived, along with another jug of hot milk for Layla. Blunstone paused a moment to sip at his drink.

'Then several things happened which radically changed my life, both professionally and privately.

'My wife, Lydia, was one of the most pragmatic people you could meet. She stood no nonsense from anyone! She had a brilliant mind and became a university physics professor at a very early age.

'Sadly, she also suffered from congenital heart disease. She had her first heart attack, in her office, at the age of fifty-one. Thankfully, one of her students arrived for a tutorial a few minutes after she was taken ill and paramedics were able to resuscitate her. But Lydia told me later that she had been clinically dead for a short while. How did she know? Because she had found herself looking down upon her own body, lying on the floor.'

Layla had to suppress the urge to roll her eyes. *Here we go*, she thought.

'I know, I know,' the professor held up his hand. 'I was sceptical, too, and explained to her that it was lack of oxygen in the brain that had caused her to hallucinate the experience. But Lydia was adamant – and then it happened again.'

'Oh no!' she cried. 'Your poor wife!'

His eyes clouded. 'Yes, she had one more cardiac arrest from which she recovered, before her heart gave out completely. She was on the waiting list for a new heart for many years, but she died long before her name came anywhere near the top. She was only fifty-eight.'

'I'm so sorry to hear that,' Layla said.

'Thank you,' he said quietly. 'But to get back to what I was saying, Lydia had another near-death experience two years after her first. "NDE", as it's commonly known, is a fairly widespread phenomenon across all countries and cultures.'

'Yes, I've read about it,' she said. 'It's quite fascinating; but as you say, that kind of experience is an illusion produced by the oxygen-starved brain.'

'That is what I believed until Lydia persuaded me otherwise. It was so unlike her to subscribe to such mumbo jumbo, you see. She had always been a dyed-in-the-wool atheist, but after that first NDE, she said she now believed in an afterlife. For her, it wasn't a matter of faith; it was a proven fact. And when it happened again – this time she saw herself lying in the A&E ward, where she had arrested after being admitted with chest pains – it reaffirmed her conviction.'

He sipped his coffee and continued: 'I started reading up on the subject, focusing on the scientific perspective. I was astonished to discover that there is hard evidence to prove that several patients who had been resuscitated had claimed to have had a near-death experience *after all electrical activity in their brain had ceased*. They reported becoming aware of themselves looking down upon their own bodies and they described the activities and conversations of the medical staff attending them. Being temporarily brain dead, they couldn't possibly have seen or heard these things unless they – ie their consciousness – had for that short while existed outside their bodies.

26

'This peer-reviewed scientific data, together with Lydia's steadfast belief in the reality of her personal NDEs, forced me to review my own thoughts on the matter. As you might imagine, the idea of there being some kind of survival of consciousness beyond death brought great comfort to both of us when Lydia was dying.'

Layla didn't know what to say. The man had clearly taken a leap of faith that had helped him cope with both the thought and the reality of losing his wife, and she had no wish to gainsay such a strategy. But she also had no intention of accepting at face value the authenticity of near-death experiences.

'I don't expect you to believe me,' Blunstone said gently. 'But please just keep an open mind while I tell you the rest. I know you philosophers are good at that!'

She nodded slowly, and he continued his story.

'Now, I'm not going to tell you that Lydia contacted me from the spirit world, although, like many grieving people, I was sorely tempted in the months following her death to find a reputable medium, just to see what transpired. In the end, I couldn't bring myself go down that path. I feared I might get lost.'

He paused, his expression wistful. Then he said: 'Instead, I realised I had to focus my energies elsewhere: on trying to prove once and for all that consciousness is not in fact generated by the brain, as mainstream science would have us believe.'

This had Layla sitting up straight.

'How could you possibly do that?' she asked. The origin and nature of consciousness was the 'hard question' philosophers had been puzzling over for centuries, and it had consumed most of her academic life.

'It happened by accident – or perhaps it was serendipity. In any case, it was uncannily timely,' the professor replied. 'Six months after Lydia passed away,

27

during a challenging exploratory operation, I discovered for myself the precise location of consciousness.'

He said this so simply that the profundity of his claim was almost lost on her. She put down her mug.

'What exactly are you saying?'

His grey eyes gleamed. 'My patient was a woman with a very severe form of epilepsy and I was trying to find out what was causing her seizures. But I discovered something much more interesting instead.'

'Wait a minute – are you talking about finding the *seat of consciousness*? The modern equivalent of Descartes' pineal gland?' She laughed incredulously.

Blunstone smiled. 'Descartes had the right concept, but the wrong location. Quite understandably, considering he was wrestling with the mind-body question during the sixteenth century and relied solely on the workings of his own mind to reach his dualist conclusion.

'In fact, the true location is the claustrum: a thin, relatively unexplored region of the brain that lies beneath the neocortex. I must clarify that I'm not the first person to make this claim. Unknown to me, not long before my breakthrough operation, US scientists had found, again by accident, that stimulating this part of the brain could switch a patient's consciousness on and off, even while the patient remained awake.'

'But don't most scientists now believe that consciousness is created by a vast network of brain cells all working together?' Layla interrupted.

He nodded. 'Most modern theories conclude that consciousness is likely to be created by a part of the brain that integrates information and activity from different regions of the brain into the single, holistic experience that is our awareness of ourselves and of the outside world. Current thinking is that the claustrum is this "director of consciousness". I should say that there are actually two claustra – one on each side of the brain, supposedly performing the same function.'

'Okay... I get that. So what are you saying that's different from the theories?'

'I'm looking at it from an entirely different perspective. Yes, I do believe that the claustrum "holds the consciousness baton", so to speak, but –' he leaned towards her, his voice lowered to a whisper '– I have discovered that one of these seemingly innocuous pieces of tissue is the very point at which consciousness *enters the body*. Consciousness is then integrated – by both claustra – with the body's own sensory perceptions, in a vast neural network which creates the full mind-body experience.' He sat back, as if exhausted.

'Professor Blunstone, do you really believe that our consciousness originates *elsewhere*? That the so-called "Simple View" is actually fact?' Layla's voice was loud and scornful.

'I know it is,' he said calmly. 'I have discovered that the claustrum is a form of "receiver" and that our consciousness is "transmitted" to it from somewhere outside our bodies. Think of a radio or television – it's the same principle.'

Layla shook her head and smiled. 'You know, part of me is really loving this conversation. It's just the kind of hypothetical discussion I like to engage my students in. But I just can't accept your claim that the claustrum receives cosmic rays of consciousness like some sort of spiritual radio. How can you possibly expect me to believe that?'

He smiled at her, put down his empty mug and stood up.

'Because I have proof – and I will show it to you next time we meet.'

Chapter 5
March: Cairnacraig House

Having quickly refreshed her makeup, brushed her hair and checked her phone for messages – surprise, surprise, there were none – she re-entered the sitting room and was startled to find Stevie and the professor arguing in terse whispers. They turned and Blunstone cut the exchange short with an abrupt: 'Right, then – shall we go?' His expression stern, he then stalked out of the room.

Stevie merely shrugged at Layla's enquiring look and both women followed their host into the hall.

'I'm taking you to my favourite restaurant; it's in a delightful little place with a central village green, which is most unusual for this part of the country,' the professor told them, his good humour evidently restored. Layla was hardly listening, so amazed was she at the wonderful cream convertible they were riding in. 'Professor...'

'Oh, please call me James,' he interrupted, looking quickly to right and left as they reached the end of his long drive.

'Er, okay – James, what kind of car is this? It's beautiful!'

Before he could answer, Stevie piped up from the front passenger seat: 'It's a 1952 Aston Martin DB2 drophead – am I right, Prof? Sorry, *James*.'

He turned to her. 'Yes, you are! Are you a classic car buff as well, Stevie?'

As well as what? Layla, taken aback at their sarcastic tones, felt she'd missed out on something. Then she remembered that the two of them would have met once or twice previously, just as she and the professor had. There would be plenty of time for her to catch up and get to know the other woman properly. Hopefully, Stevie's off manner was just a front for her nervousness. She knew that she, herself, was finding it hard to be natural in what she felt was an increasingly surreal situation.

Stevie was laughing, her long hair flapping around her face, as the car accelerated with a roar along the main road. 'No, you told me about it, remember? During our first little chat?'

'Of course; I'd forgotten,' he said loudly, expertly steering around a bend. 'I hope it's not too breezy for either of you? It's such a lovely day that I just had to put the top down.'

Perched on the red leather back seat, her own hair protected by a pastel-pink pashmina, Layla shook her head. In that moment, she felt almost happy. 'It's fun!' she cried.

Fifteen minutes later, they entered a small village whose traditional granite houses sparkled in the sunshine. Blunstone pulled up outside a restaurant facing the central green, which was bordered by beautiful old trees. 'Here we are!' he announced.

The restaurant was small and stylish: a cottage converted into a contemporary bistro, which had retained its original narrow passageways and snugs. A smiling man sporting a chef's white jacket and tartan trews greeted them in the tiny reception area.

'Professor Blunstone – great to see you again! I've reserved your favourite table.' The sandy-haired man led them through to one of the snugs, where he seated them by a window.

After some chat, during which Blunstone introduced his guests as his 'research assistants', the chef – who turned out also to be the restaurant owner – left them to study the lunch menus.

'Local lad, and a very talented cook, as you'll find out,' the professor explained, putting on his reading glasses. 'Anything you choose will be a delight, I can promise you. They grow most of their own fruit, veg and herbs in polytunnels nearby.'

Scanning the menu, Layla was relieved to see several vegetarian options. Feeling hungry, she decided on Thai chickpea broth, followed by snow pea risotto with carrot and kale mini cupcakes. When the waitress arrived shortly afterwards to take their orders, Stevie asked for a spring salad starter and corn-fed chicken with lemon, garlic and parsley.

Uh-oh, how is this going to work? Layla wondered, as the realisation of their dietary differences – and the implications – dawned on her. Across the table, Stevie was looking bemused, as if she were thinking exactly the same thing.

Oblivious to the silent undercurrent, their host cheerfully ordered spicy parsnip soup, followed by confit of duck with crispy kale potatoes. They all opted for sparkling spring water.

'Are you sure you don't want some wine?' he asked. 'I'm driving, but don't let me put you off.'

'Need to keep a clear head, I think,' said Stevie, and Layla agreed, feeling faint fingers of anxiety creeping up her spine.

He nodded. 'Understood. Now, I expect you ladies have a million questions for each other, but how about starting with a wee verbal pen-portrait of yourselves?'

Stevie flicked back her hair. 'I'll go first, then, shall I?' Without waiting for a response, she said: 'Stevie Nightingale. Born and brought up in Sydney, Australia. Age thirty-eight, divorced, with no children or pets. I'm a freelance investigative journalist and I'm over here taking time out to try to write a novel. She looked at the professor, her glance almost sly, as she added: 'I'll have plenty material to work with before too long!'

Blunstone smiled thinly and looked at Layla, eyebrows raised expectantly.

She cleared her throat. 'Okay, yes – Layla Sutherland, from the Black Isle, which is further north from here, past Inverness,' she said for the other woman's benefit. 'I'm the same age as you, Stevie, likewise with no children or pets, and I'm separated from my husband.'

How weird it still felt to say those words. She quickly added: 'I'm a post-doctoral philosophy research fellow, with teaching commitments, at the University of Aberdeen, and if this project works for me, I'll be taking a sabbatical to write my thesis on personal identity. And like you,' she said to Stevie, 'I should have no shortage of material.'

The Australian bared her too-white teeth in a grin. 'No guessing why you're interested in this project, then.'

'Hobbies and interests?' the professor encouraged.

Stevie was first to reply. 'I like to keep fit: running, tennis, squash... I'm a karate black belt and a regular at my local gym. When I do sit still, I read novels: anything well-written is fair game.'

Layla said: 'I enjoy walking and I attend a weekly yoga class. I'm a member of the university choir and I do some watercolour painting when I'm in the mood. I love reading, too – in fact, it's my real passion.'

Stevie sighed. 'Apart from being bookworms, we're not exactly compatible, are we?' she said to Blunstone. Inwardly, Layla had to agree.

'Aha, but that's deliberate,' he smiled. 'As I'll explain in due course, it's all part of the experiment.'

The experiment... Layla's anxiety notched up a level, dispelled only slightly by the arrival of her aromatic soup.

33

As they ate their starters and the smiling chef approached the little group to ask if all was well, she couldn't help wondering what he would say if he knew the true relationship between the two "thirty-something" women and their avuncular companion.

Chapter 6
The Previous October: The University

She hadn't intended meeting him again. After he had left her in the campus café, she'd sat on for another half hour, mulling over what he had told her and finally deciding he must surely be mad. Then later, back at her desk, the thought struck her that perhaps his tale was some kind of weird psychological screening test. Either way, Layla didn't like it. The experience had left her feeling edgy and uncomfortable, and this, she told herself, she didn't need right now.

Yet... the philosopher in her was deeply fascinated by his story and she couldn't help but wonder what possible proof he could have to show her. She'd searched online for details of the claustrum breakthrough in the US that he had referred to and had found several references: '... *Scientists discover the on-off switch for human consciousness deep within the brain ... When the claustrum was stimulated, the patient stopped speaking and moving and stared into space; when the stimulation stopped, she continued her activity with no memory of what had just happened... The claustrum seems to bind together all of our senses, perceptions, and computations into a single, cohesive experience...*'

Something was niggling at her, but it wasn't until she was lying in bed that night, unable to sleep, that she realised what it was. If the professor really did read everything he could find on consciousness research, surely he would have known about the claustrum breakthrough *before* he carried out the operation he spoke about. It would have been big news for the brain science community at the time. And if he did know, did this mean he had intended from the outset to experiment on his epileptic patient? That was not how he had presented it to Layla; he had made it sound as if he'd made the discovery by accident and that he had read about the US research only afterwards. Just how ethical was it for someone in his position to conduct his own consciousness-seeking experiment when he was meant to be searching for the cause of a serious medical condition?

Then she'd finally allowed herself to consider what she'd been repressing all day: what her own role in this project might be. He wanted her to be a guinea pig, of course. He wanted to experiment on her brain! Well, that wasn't going to happen. He might be crazy, but she wasn't – yet.

She acknowledged that the bizarre encounter had briefly distracted her from her relentless grief and anger over Calum and that that was a welcome development. She knew she also wanted to find out more. But should she travel any further down this strange new road if she didn't intend to finish the journey?

Next morning, in the cold grey autumn light, she'd decided the whole scenario was ridiculous and that she would have no more to do with it. Tired and disgruntled, she'd showered and prepared to face another day, trying not to think about how futile her work and everything else about her life now seemed.

The dreaded haar, blown in from the North Sea, had slowed the city traffic to a crawl and by the time she'd reached the university campus she'd felt as if the dank grey mist had permeated her soul. Her negative thoughts multiplied as she walked slowly towards her office building.

I am thirty-eight, alone, and have nothing to look forward to. My family are too far away; my few good friends are too busy with their kids, husbands and jobs. I desperately want a child of my own and there's no prospect of that happening in the foreseeable future. At

36

work, I feel as if I'm stuck in a rut, going around and around with the same old arguments and never breaking new ground.

Really, what is the point?

Reaching the office, she'd slumped down at her desk, relieved to remember David was on holiday that week. At least she wouldn't have to make the stilted small talk favoured by her buttoned-up colleague. She'd wished, not for the first time, that she shared space with someone upbeat like Morven; her cheery friend would soon have shaken her out of her self-indulgence. Morven, however, worked in the next building and was also away on leave. It was the October school holidays and half the staff seemed to be taking time off. If Calum had been less selfish and more like most men of his age, she'd thought peevishly, they probably would have had a couple of school-age kids by now and – who knew – perhaps they'd still be together.

She and Calum had agreed from the outset that they wouldn't think about starting a family until both their careers were established. But, over the years, her husband had grown less and less inclined to become a father and no amount of rational argument, tears and pleading on her part could change his mind. As her late thirties approached, she'd grown depressed and resentful. Their home life was heavy with sulky silences, and she'd felt herself withdrawing from him. It was her way of hitting back at his intransigence, and it was also the main reason he'd strayed; he'd made that clear before he left her.

Despite everything, she missed him. She still loved him and clung to the hope that he would change his mind about fatherhood. Darla was just a distraction, she'd told herself during those first few dreadful weeks on her own. Surely he would see sense and come home to her. But, three months on, there was no sign of that happening any time soon. And meanwhile, she was dragging herself through the days, outwardly composed, but feeling increasingly lonely and afraid of the emptiness that stretched ahead.

'Bloody hell! I'll be slitting my wrists before coffee time, at this rate,' she'd muttered, opening her email inbox and scanning the new messages.

One heading stood out as clearly as if printed in red ink: *'When can we meet again?...* *james.blunstone@hotmail.com'*.

Taking a deep breath, she'd read the body text.

Dear Layla,
I very much enjoyed meeting you yesterday. I knew right away that you would be perfect for the project, but I am aware that you will need a little more persuasion to come on board!
What I told you might sound far-fetched and absurd, but I assure you that every word is true. If you would kindly indulge me a little further, I will endeavour to prove this to you.
Can we meet at your office at your earliest convenience? I am sure you will understand that I am keen to progress things as quickly as possible and that if you are not interested in my proposal, I will need to continue my search for a second subject.
I look forward to hearing from you.
Warmest regards,
James Blunstone

In spite of herself, Layla had felt a tremor of excitement. 'Second subject' meant he had already recruited someone else! She tapped her pen against her teeth. What would be the harm in 'indulging' him, as he suggested? If they met in her office, she would be in control and could end the meeting whenever she wanted. Curiosity had always been a driving force in her life, and regardless of that morning's resolution, she now knew she couldn't give the professor the brush-off without at least finding out what he had to show her. At the very least, it would provide further escape from her grey and gloomy thoughts.

Her fingers hovered over the keyboard and she started writing.

Dear Professor Blunstone,
Likewise, I enjoyed meeting you – and many thanks for the coffees.
You are right about my reservations, but I am prepared to meet with you once more. As my colleague is away just now, I have the office to myself, so any time this week would be fine with me. Just let me know when would suit you best.
Kind regards,
Layla

And, before she could change her mind, she'd pressed "send".

Two days later, on a blustery, leaf-strewn morning, Layla showed James Blunstone into her office, each of them carrying a mug of instant coffee, brewed in the tiny kitchen along the corridor.

'Sorry it's a bit cramped in here; you can sit in David's seat,' she told him. 'As long as I remember to leave it tucked back under the desk, he'll never know.'

'A pernickety fellow?' the professor grinned.

She rolled her eyes. 'You don't know the half of it. Wait – let me give you a coaster for that mug! But let's look on

39

the bright side: his pernicketyness is sure to produce flawless thesis footnotes and appendices.'

He chuckled, placing his mug on the proffered coaster. '"*Hell is other people*", eh?'

'Och, David's fine, really,' she said. 'I just wish he wasn't quite so serious all the time.'

Guiltily aware that she had hardly been the life and soul of the office recently, she changed the subject. 'Anyway, you've certainly given me something to think about since we met on Monday. I really don't want to commit myself, but I would like to find out more – both about what you say you discovered and what your project actually involves. It's all been very cloak-and-dagger so far!'

She was pleased with this opening, feeling entirely in control – the opposite of how she'd felt when he'd left her so abruptly the other day without revealing anything about the research he was planning.

He seemed undaunted. 'I'm sorry it appears that way, but I felt I'd said enough for one day. As I'm sure you'll have gathered by now, my research is revolutionary and it flies in the face of most Western people's beliefs about human existence. Given your profession, I knew that you were a thinker and that you wouldn't take anything at face value. I wanted to give you a little time to process what I was telling you, so that you could decide whether or not you really wanted to learn more. I'm so glad you do – and thank you for giving me the benefit of the doubt so far.'

She looked at him levelly. 'Well, your Scheherazade trick worked wonders. Look, to be honest, I'm doing a Descartes and "suspending belief": I just want to hear the end of the story.'

'I appreciate your honesty,' he replied. 'Suspended belief will do just fine for now.'

They smiled at each other and he said: 'Right, then, I'd better get on with the next instalment!' He delved into his battered brown briefcase, pulling out a transparent plastic DVD case. 'I hope this will persuade you as to the truth of my story so far, namely that consciousness can survive – indeed, originates – outside the body. I've recorded a brief introduction, outlining my hypothesis and methodology, and the rest of the DVD consists of two films based on my practical research. I'll leave this with you so that you can watch it in your own time. It's all home-made, so please forgive the fuzziness.'

He handed her the case and, nodding her thanks, she casually set it on her desk, hoping he couldn't sense her excitement and impatience. *Talk about building suspense – Alfred Hitchcock himself couldn't have done any better!* She knew she would start watching the DVD as soon as he left the room.

'Now,' he continued, his expression serious, 'I must ask that you do not share either the contents of the DVD or what I am about to tell you, with anyone else. Do I have that assurance, Layla?'

Intrigued, she nodded. 'Of course; you have my word.'

'Thank you. Although we hardly know each other, I do feel that I can trust you. Trust is going to be such an important part of this project.'

He drank some coffee and continued.

'So, what is the project all about? Well, as you will have gathered by now, it involves an actual exchange of consciousness between two human subjects – namely, body swapping.'

He paused and Layla swallowed, desperately trying to keep an open mind.

'As you will see from the DVD, this involves an incredibly simple keyhole surgical procedure which I have already carried out – and reversed – one hundred per cent successfully on two separate occasions.'

She had felt unsettled by their previous conversation. Now, anxiety was making her heart race.

Blunstone continued: 'For reasons that will, again, become clear from the films, I now need two healthy subjects to help me expand my research. I intend to extend the exchange period from mere hours to several months. I have already recruited one research subject, Layla, and I would like you to be the other.'

He sat back, surveying her, his expression inscrutable.

A feeling of unreality washed over her. Her face started to feel numb and she hoped she wasn't about to have a panic attack. 'I can't believe we're having this conversation,' she said nervously. 'It's like something out of a horror story!'

He laughed. 'It's a party trick of mine: from Scheherazade to Dr Frankenstein in sixty seconds.'

She didn't laugh back. 'I'd kind of guessed you might be proposing to do some sort of surgical brain experiment, but *this* – can't you understand how preposterous it sounds? Me? Exchange bodies with another person? And live like that for several months?'

She felt light-headed. The room darkened, as black clouds scudded across the sun. Looking out of the window, she took a deep breath and tried to focus on the reassuringly normal ebb and flow of academic life, as students and staff hurried between lectures, muffled against the wind in woolly hats and scarves.

When she turned back to him, he was watching her, his eyes full of concern and sympathy.

'I know exactly how preposterous it sounds. Believe me, had you come to me with a similar proposal a few years ago, I would have laughed you out of my office – and then locked the door!

42

'That's why I'm going to leave you now with the DVD. Please watch it, and you will have a deeper understanding of what this is all about. I can't promise you'll be any less shocked or incredulous, but at least you'll be better informed. And then you can finally decide whether or not you want to proceed.'

'Professor, I can tell you right now that I don't want to be part of this!' Layla almost shouted. His proposal had frightened and disturbed her.

But he merely rose to his feet, carefully tucked David's chair under the desk, and nodded at her gravely. 'Please just watch the DVD, Layla. I'll be back in touch soon.'

He left her sitting alone, her anxious thoughts whirling in a frenzied vortex.

After a few minutes, she slotted the DVD into her computer.

Chapter 7

It had all the hallmarks of a home movie.

First, a close-up of Blunstone's face came into shaky focus and then the professor crossed to a chair opposite the camera and settled himself into shot, but not quite in the centre of the frame. Dressed in his grey suit, a lavender shirt, and with matching handkerchief peeping from his jacket top pocket, he appeared calm and confident. But evidently he hadn't realised that a large, abstract painting behind him was fighting for the viewer's attention, garish in large splashes of scarlet, mustard and orange.

Numbly, Layla stared at the screen as he cleared his throat and began.

'If you are watching this, you will already be aware of what my project involves. You will no doubt be feeling sceptical and perhaps angry that I am wasting your time with what you believe are ridiculous claims about human consciousness.

'Let me tell you that I completely understand and sympathise with how you are feeling. But please bear with me while I explain further.'

He sat forward a little and continued: 'For the purposes of this film, I am using laymen's terms, as it is not intended for medical professionals or scientists, but for the benefit of my research subjects only.

'As I will already have explained in an earlier conversation, while stimulating the claustrum tissue of a brain surgery patient I chanced upon the precise location of the so-called "seat of consciousness". It is, in fact, a previously overlooked gland – a tiny, discrete node which nestles in a pouch of protective tissue that is linked by blood vessels and nerve cells to the rest of the right-hand claustrum. From what I could see – and remember that the camera technology I use is extremely sophisticated – I believed that, using the latest keyhole surgery techniques, this gland could easily be removed from, and even returned to, its protective pouch.'

Layla's eyes widened.

'In my professional capacity,' Blunstone went on, 'I obtained access to three preserved human brains that had been donated to medical science. In each case, I confirmed my theory was correct by successfully finding and removing the node – which, for now, I have perhaps flippantly called the "me-gland"– and then reinstating it, with no disturbance beyond a tiny slit in the pouch, in its rightful place.'

The "me-gland"! How appropriate for a megalomaniac, she thought angrily. The professor's next words only reinforced her conviction that he had completely lost the plot.

'Of course, I could only prove my theory that the me-gland is the receptacle for consciousness by conducting the same surgical procedure on living subjects. And here is where – I fully admit – I departed from my professional code of ethics.'

He looked earnestly into the camera: 'Please understand that this is not something I did lightly, but I knew I could proceed entirely humanely – even philanthropically – and so I began setting up my own private research project. You will shortly see a record of how this initial part of the project progressed, but first let me set the scene.

'In my role as a neurosurgeon, I meet people who are terminally ill. In some cases, all I can do to help them is to try to reduce the size of the tumours that will eventually kill them. Removing the entire tumour may be impossible but removing as much of it as I can will often help to prolong their lives and to relieve the many painful and distressing side-effects caused by a growing mass within the brain.'

He coughed and continued: 'Following my research with the preserved human brains, I identified four patients who had gone through this process and for whom surgery was no longer an option. At the time, each of them had only weeks to live.

'I approached patients A, B, C, and D privately, in their own homes. None had been hospitalised at that stage. I presented my plan to each of them and I offered to pay a very generous fee for their participation. Of course, by then, money was of little use to them, but they understood that it would benefit their families. More on that later. The procedures – the exchange of me-glands – were to be carried out in the strictest confidence, under the auspices of a final attempt on my part to operate privately, but free of charge, on their tumours.'

By now, Layla was horrified.

'All four patients agreed to participate. The consensus was that they had nothing left to lose and that their families had everything to gain. In case you are wondering, they were all in full control of their faculties and made the decision rationally, after careful consideration. The two films that follow will show you what happened next.'

She paused the DVD. She couldn't handle any more of this right now. Shakily, she returned to the kitchen to make more coffee.

As she stood waiting for the kettle to boil, she marvelled at the range of emotions the professor had managed to stir within her since he had appeared in her office that morning. Incredulity, anxiety, anger, horror and revulsion had all jostled for position, subsiding and resuming as the full scope of his shocking project had been revealed.

But it was curiosity that once again won the day.

How could she *not* continue watching his grotesque little film? She would watch it and then destroy it – and she would refuse any further contact with the man. In fact, she should consider reporting him for breach of professional ethics. But supposing he was psychopathic and came after her? Or supposing it was all a fantastical hoax? How gullible would that make her appear?

Exhausted by endless questions and suppositions, she sat back down at her computer and resumed watching.

The first film opened in what appeared to be a dining room. Two men – one in his thirties and the other a couple of decades older – were sitting side-by-side at a large, highly-polished mahogany table. It was clear that both of them were very sick: parchment-coloured skin stretched over their gaunt faces, and their casual clothes seemed to swamp them. Nevertheless, they were talking to each other animatedly, apparently comfortable in each other's company.

Professor Blunstone's voice cut in from behind the camera: 'Sorry to interrupt, gentlemen, but that's me ready to begin.'

They turned, both smiling, and the younger man quipped: 'Stephen Spielberg has spoken!' There was general laughter and the professor continued: 'The purpose of this film is to explain to others what this project is all about and to prove that such a phenomenon as body swapping really is possible. For the sake of confidentiality, I will refer to you as "Patient A" and "Patient B", and I would like you both to tell the camera what you have agreed to do as part of this study. Patient A – can you start, please?'

The focus switched to the elder of the two, who suddenly looked self-conscious.

'Er, well, it sounds daft, like, but I've agreed to have a bit o my brain swapped with Kevin's here...' his hand flew to

47

his mouth as he realised he'd revealed the other man's name. 'Never mind,' the professor's voice said patiently, 'please carry on.'

'Aye, okay,' he said in his broad Aberdeen accent. 'Me an Patient B here are gaun to be deein a body swap.'

'And do you understand what's involved?' Blunstone asked.

The man nodded. 'Aye, although I still canna get my head around it, like...'

'No pun intended!' roared Kevin, who seemed a little hysterical.

They all laughed again, the picture wobbling slightly. After a beat, the professor continued: 'Patient B, can you tell us what's going to be happening tomorrow?'

The younger man straightened his face and said in a Geordie accent: 'You'll be operating on our brains, removing those wee glands and swapping them over. Apparently, when we wake up, I'll be him and he'll be me, and we'll be all together... "*See how they run like pigs from a gun, see how they fly...*"'

His nasal rendition of the Beatles' hallucinogenic words was a good imitation of John Lennon's and suddenly Layla felt heart-sorry for the men, who both seemed full of life despite the death sentence that so obviously hung over them.

'Well, hopefully it won't turn out to be as complicated as that,' Blunstone said good-naturedly. 'But yes, basically, when you recover from the anaesthetic, you will find your selves in each other's bodies.'

'But you'll be swapping us back after a few hours, right?' asked Patient B, who seemed oblivious to the sheer absurdity of the situation. 'And all we'll need to do is answer some questions?'

'Yes, that's right. I'll be asking you all kinds of things during the time you're inhabiting each other's bodies, and then I'll reverse the procedure and return you to your own bodies.'

'Simple!' said Patient B, and then the picture went black.

Layla was hooked. She had to find out what had happened to the men who had so trustingly handed over their lives to a madman. She allowed the film to continue.

In a scene straight out of a hospital drama, a masked man in blue scrubs checked the camera and crossed a small operating theatre, to where two high-tech chairs were sitting, side by side. He positioned himself in one and swivelled it round to face the camera. Blunstone's muffled voice could then be heard saying: 'Right, let's proceed with Neurosurgery 101!

'As I mentioned previously, this particular procedure is carried out using what is popularly known as "keyhole surgery" and is clinically described as "minimally invasive endoscopic neurosurgery". Through a very small opening in the patient's skull, I can insert this endoscope,' – he held up a slim, tubular instrument with a bright light at its end, 'which allows me to see and remove the me-gland. To operate the instrument, I look into the viewfinder of this piece of equipment.' He tapped a plastic-wrapped package with what looked like binoculars sticking out of it. 'My route to the gland's location has been plotted out using this guidance system' – he indicated the large computer screen attached to his chair – 'which provides highly-sophisticated computer-aided neuronavigation, delivering pinpoint accuracy. So, it's a case of open up, dive in, grab the me-gland and slip out again – all with minimal disruption. As Patient B said earlier: simple!'

Layla snorted as the screen went momentarily blank. *He sounds so smug, playing God*, she thought.

The film resumed with Professor Blunstone standing between two operating tables, whose occupants, viewed from the top ends of the tables, appeared to be entirely shrouded in blue. Strange surgical instruments protruded from what were presumably their skulls, and, snaking out from under the covers, various other tubes and wires extended off-camera. She could just make out another masked figure at the foot of the left-hand table and assumed it was either a nurse or an anaesthetist. 'Partner in crime,' she muttered to herself.

The neurosurgeon spoke through his mask: 'The gland swap has been successfully completed and the two patients are fully conscious. I will now ask each of them a short series of questions.' He walked forward, picked up the camera and moved to stand at the foot-end of the operating tables. 'Nurse Murray, if you will continue to monitor the vital signs, please,' he said over his shoulder. Layla saw the other masked blue figure hurry to the opposite side of the room and move out of shot.

Now the film zoomed in to show the pale, skeletal face of Patient A, the older man. His expression was blank.

'Patient B, how are you feeling?' boomed the professor's voice.

The man licked his lips and croaked: 'Like I'm a hundred years old!' Then: 'Bloody hell, it worked!'

'Yes, it certainly did. Patient A, how about you?'

The camera panned over, showing a close-up of Patient B's younger, but equally gaunt features.

'Christ almighty, you're nae kiddin. I'm feelin fair swack – like a new man.' The Doric words sounded strange uttered in Patient B's Geordie accent.

'That's interesting; obviously, neither of you has been able to move about, so how can you feel so different, just lying there?'

Patient B said, off-camera: 'It's easy, man. I feel much heavier, with lots of aches and pains.'

Patient A, in the younger body, smiled broadly. 'An I feel wired – an hungry for the first time in weeks. I could fair dee wi a rowie an jam.'

Layla couldn't help smiling at his allusion to the popular salty roll unique to the North-east of Scotland.

The professor reeled off another few questions, focusing on how well they could move their fingers, toes and limbs – slowly, but with increasing confidence, as it turned out – and asking them to relate childhood and more recent memories, which they did quite easily.

After several minutes, he said: 'Well, gentlemen, I think we can safely say that our experiment has been a success. Congratulations: you have made history. You are the first human beings to inhabit another person's body!'

The film cut sharply to the next scene, in which Patient A and Patient B were sitting on a leather couch, beside a roaring log fire, sipping what appeared to be whisky. They were both wearing grey sweatshirts and jogging pants, which hung on their sparse frames. Layla was surprised to see, however, that their thin faces were bright and animated.

'That was absolutely mind-blowing,' Patient B said with a broad grin. 'One of the best experiences of my life. I can but thank you, Professor Blunstone.'

'Aye,' Patient A said eagerly, 'it was far better than ony o those computer games, wi atavars.'

'I think you mean "avatars"', his companion corrected, adding: 'Or any LSD trip.'

'If you say so, Kevin – I widna ken aboot thon hippy-dippy stuff,' Patient A retorted.

'How clearly can you remember the experience, *Patient B?*' asked Blunstone's voice pointedly from behind the camera, and Patient A mouthed a 'sorry'.

'Very clearly!' the younger man replied, and he proceeded to relate more or less all that he had been asked during the operation, and what his replies had been. His companion found it harder to remember some of the questions and answers, but when prompted by the professor, most of what he had experienced came back to him.

'Now, gentlemen, although you were conscious at the time, it was obviously impossible to allow you to move around. Do you think, from how your host body felt, that you could have managed to get up, walk about, make it work as if it were your own?'

'Well, I could move my fingers and toes, arms and legs... yes, I suppose I could have got up and walked about, eventually,' Patient B replied.

'I could have run a marathon!' said Patient A. 'I felt twenty years younger!'

His companion smiled sadly. 'Before the tumour, I was pretty fit. Believe me, the way my body feels now is nothing compared to how it felt then.'

'Well, it was good enough for an auld mannie like me! Best gift I could ever have wished for.' The elder man's voice cracked and he took a swig of his drink.

'I can't honestly say I would have wanted to stay in your body for any longer,' Kevin said to him carefully, 'but at least now I know how it feels to be twenty years older. Let's face it: it's not going to happen otherwise...'

'You've both been incredibly brave,' the disembodied voice cut in. 'What you have done will go down in medical history. You are true pioneers.'

The men said nothing as they let the professor's words sink in. As the final seconds of the film captured their expressions – a combination of wonder and wistfulness – Layla began to cry.

She paused the DVD and sat, hugging herself, allowing the tears to flow freely. She felt deep sorrow for the two cheerful men, who, by now, would surely be no more.

She was still furious with the professor, but this was tempered by a new feeling: the belief that he had *actually carried out a body-swap experiment*. It had to be true; why would he have gone to the trouble of setting up such an elaborate hoax, involving actors, an operating theatre, and all that sophisticated equipment? The skeletal men were quite clearly terminal cancer patients and they truly seemed to believe that they had, for a few short hours, swapped bodies with each other.

And now another sensation was taking hold: a slow-burning excitement that gradually quelled her tears and soon had her pacing around the office, fizzing with energy.

Consciousness really could survive outside its host human brain! The implications were mind-blowing. She had to find out more.

Chapter 8
March: Cairnacraig House

'Here we are: eating again,' James Blunstone said amiably, taking a bite out of a home-made cranberry scone which he'd lathered with cream and jam. 'Ah, delicious! Mrs Brodie, my housekeeper, is a first-class baker.'

They were back in his sitting room, the fire re-lit and the atmosphere country-house cosy. Layla and Stevie were also tucking into the scones, Layla marvelling at the three of them having any appetite left after the superb lunch they'd enjoyed only a couple of hours earlier.

When they'd returned to Cairnacraig House, Stevie had disappeared up to her room with a muttered 'Seeya later', and the professor had said he was going to read his newspaper for a while. 'If you fancy some more fresh air, why don't you have a wander through the grounds?' he'd suggested to Layla. 'There are some lovely spring flowers in the walled garden and dotted around the woods.'

Glad to escape their company for a time, she had walked round the outside of the house until she found the walled garden. It was charming: laid out in traditional style, with low, box hedges bordering beds radiant with the pinks, purples, oranges and yellows of primulas, winter pansies and early-flowering narcissi. Around the perimeter, in the herbaceous borders, a proliferation of azaleas and rhododendron bushes were still in bud. Behind them, the high redbrick walls were adorned with the delicate blush of cherry-plum blossom and supported the espaliered stems of later-flowering fruit trees and climbing roses.

She had followed the narrow pathway through the garden and sat for a while on a sheltered, south-facing bench, grateful for the beauty and stillness of the space. For that short interlude, relishing the warmth of the midafternoon sunshine, she had managed to push away her growing doubts about Stevie's suitability as a body-swap partner. Feeling an all-too-familiar exhaustion creeping over her, she had fallen asleep for a full hour.

'I'll have to work this off later,' Stevie said now, wiping cream from her chin. 'This is a great place for running, Prof, with all those woodland paths. Aren't you ever tempted?'

'Not at all! Golf is my thing,' he replied, enthusiastically. 'I don't know if you ladies know this, but there are seventy courses in the North-east: links and inland; new and historic. It's a true golfer's paradise! I'm a member at Cruden Bay, just down the road – it's more than one hundred and twenty years old and ranked one of the best in Scotland... a lovely, scenic links course, bordered by sand dunes – but I do also like to tour around for a bit of variety.'

Layla smiled politely and asked a question that had been bothering her since lunchtime: 'If Stevie and I are to swap bodies, will I need to start running? It's not something I've ever done.'

'Too right you will – you can't let my body go to seed!' the other woman exclaimed, giving her a challenging stare.

Before Layla could reply, the professor intercepted. 'That's a very good question, Layla, and it raises the important issue of personal responsibility: while you are living in a host body, how responsible should you feel towards its welfare?'

He put down his empty plate and looked at her keenly. 'You're the philosopher: what's your view on that?'

Layla thought for a moment, and then said: 'I don't think you need to be a philosopher to conclude that the answer is "totally responsible".'

He looked pleased. 'And why is that?'

55

'Well, for a start, you have no choice; if you don't look after your host body, you're endangering both it and your "self".' She hooked her fingers into air quotes as she said the last word. 'And secondly, isn't it simply the right thing to do to take care of someone else's body while you're inhabiting it? It's like house-sitting: you have a moral obligation to look after someone else's home if they've trusted you to do so.'

She looked at Stevie defiantly and continued: 'But how far do you go? I'm not a keep-fit fanatic and I have no inclination to go out running every day, or to attend the gym regularly.'

'But don't you see?' Blunstone said quickly, pre-empting the Australian's response. 'Stevie's body will retain its muscle memory and it will *want* to continue its regular exercise. You will "inherit"' – it was his turn to do air quotes – 'her desire to work out and it won't be hard for you, as her body is already fit and well accustomed to it.'

Stevie looked relieved. 'Well, hallelujah to that.'

Layla still wasn't convinced. 'But surely I – as in my consciousness – will have an influence over Stevie's body? And if *I* am not inclined to run or work out in the gym, then that disinclination would override the muscle memory, don't you think?'

The professor frowned. 'No, I really don't agree. You will inherit the physical sensations of your host body, and that body will crave exercise. And the *you* part will therefore want to satisfy that craving – why wouldn't you? It will feel almost as natural as breathing or eating.'

'So, by the same token,' Stevie broke in, 'I, in Layla's body, will take to her hobbies just as easily? Will I be able to sing, for example? I'm tone deaf!'

'Yes, I do believe you should be able to sing like Layla,' he replied. 'After all, you will be in possession of her voice box. But, of course, we won't know for sure until you're *in situ*, so to speak.'

'Meanwhile, I will be trying to sing and failing miserably,' Layla said. 'It's just as well that I'd have to take time out from the choir.'

She paused as an earlier thought struck her. 'If I have to keep up the exercise, Stevie will need to become a vegetarian,' she said.

'And you will need to start eating meat!' Stevie retorted.

Over my dead body, thought Layla and she repressed the urge to laugh at the absurdity of it all.

'Seeing how you cope with the differences between you will be one of the things that will make the experiment so interesting,' Blunstone said. 'As I hinted at during lunch, what's the point in having body-swap research subjects who like and do the same things?'

'But what if we feel trapped in these bodies that want to do things *we* don't necessarily want to do?' Layla cried.

'My head hurts,' groaned Stevie. 'Look, we could tie ourselves in knots supposing this and supposing that. As you say, Prof, we won't really know until it's actually happening. Why don't we just get on with it?'

'But it's important to think through the implications!' protested Layla. 'It's far too serious a business to rush into blindly. I, for one, want to know what I'm letting myself in for.'

The other woman laughed. 'Why don't you just live a little, girl? Exploring the unknown is one of the best parts of the whole project.'

Layla flushed at the rebuke. But Stevie was right. Hadn't she decided she wanted to be a pioneer in her own field of personal identity? And didn't she also have some other very good reasons for getting away from her life for a while?

'Stevie is right, Layla,' Blunstone said gently. 'While we can make endless suppositions, and while I, as a neurosurgeon, can make predictions based on medical research and experience, it really will be a voyage into the unknown, in so many ways. Ultimately, you have to ask yourself if you're willing to take that first step.'

'"Leap" is how I'd choose to describe it,' she replied wryly.

'If it is any help at all, I truly believe from the research I've carried out to date that you will each be mistress of your host body and that you won't be *forced* into doing anything your own consciousness doesn't want to do. The phrase "We are the authors of our own being" appears to be true: ultimately, we can choose whether or not to follow our physical impulses – regardless of whether they originate in our own bodies or in a host body.'

Layla thought about that. It presupposed freewill, of course – something she firmly believed in, but just for fun often liked to argue against with her students. Somehow, freewill felt intuitively *right*. She hoped it was, for her own sake. But then it struck her that if she could override Stevie's physical impulses, Stevie could do the same to hers...

'One thing *I'd* like to know is, if consciousness is not generated by the brain, where the hell does it come from?' Stevie was looking at the professor.

'Another very good question,' he said with a small smile, 'but I'm afraid I haven't a clue as to the answer.'

Layla saw her own surprise reflected on the other woman's face.

'To put it in very basic terms,' he continued, 'all I know is that the me-gland acts as a receptor for a particular person's consciousness, which is "transmitted" from elsewhere – and that when the gland is transplanted into

58

another host brain, it continues to act as a receptor for the original consciousness.'

'So, you're saying that the externally-transmitted consciousness "follows" its receptor gland?" asked Layla. 'But how do you know that consciousness doesn't just grow and develop within the me-gland in the same way the rest of the human body grows and develops? Your body-swap experiment doesn't prove that human consciousness comes from somewhere beyond the physical world; only that it exists as a self-contained entity that can be transferred between brains!'

Blunstone ran his fingers through his snowy hair, but said patiently: 'Remember what I told you about near-death experiences? I believe that there is sufficient scientific evidence around NDEs to prove that consciousness survives the death of the body; therefore, logically, it must originate elsewhere. But where that might be, I simply do not know.'

Seeing the doubt on their faces, he continued: 'Yes, it's a staggering concept; goodness knows, I've struggled with it for long enough.'

'And presupposing the existence of these spiritual "cosmic rays",' Layla went on, 'we still have the problem Descartes came up against with his theory that the pineal gland was the seat of consciousness: namely, how can something that is non-physical interact with and influence something that is physical, ie the me-gland? Or is consciousness actually physical in a way we don't yet understand?'

'Oh, for crying out loud,' Stevie said derisively. 'Who cares *how* it happens – it obviously happens; end of story.'

The professor was more diplomatic. 'I can understand your need to get to the truth of the matter, Layla, but in essence, Stevie is right. For the purposes of this project, we have to move beyond all the whys and wherefores and focus on the practical.'

He sat back in his chair and steepled his fingers.

'I have a clear goal: I have already proved that it's possible to transfer human consciousness between living subjects and now it's time to explore the longer-term effects of the process. I will share my results with the rest of the world in due course, and it will then be up to other minds to speculate on the bigger picture of where consciousness comes from and what it consists of.'

There was a silence as his words sank in. 'I can see a whole new philosophy syllabus opening up,' mused Layla eventually. Then, steeling herself, she said: 'There's something else we need to speak about. The elephant in the room.'

Stevie made a face and Blunstone crossed his arms. 'Go ahead,' he said in an amused tone.

'Okay, well, this whole project – it's unethical, isn't it? Don't you feel guilty about what you've done, and are planning to do?' Layla's heartbeat picked up speed, but she was determined to confront him about this.

He nodded slowly, his face serious now. 'Yes, of course you're quite right to broach the subject of ethics. And yes, strictly speaking, the project is unethical, in that I have neither applied for nor received any legal authorisation to proceed. It is an entirely private and confidential matter, but I have no doubt that should the authorities discover what I am doing during the research phase, they would do their utmost to shut it down.'

Layla saw that he was looking pointedly at Stevie, whose expression was now blank.

'However,' he added, raising an index finger, 'We are all consenting adults here, as were my four previous patients. If we proceed, we will be doing so with our eyes wide open; we will be causing no harm to others, and we will be playing a crucial part in a truly revolutionary experiment that will forever change humankind's view of existence. I, for one, do not intend to wait around for years while ethical committees debate the matter and other researchers hijack the project for their own glorification. It's my discovery; I don't feel guilty about it; I intend to proceed with it, and I will deal with the consequences.'

'Nice speech, Prof,' muttered Stevie.

Layla sighed. 'There's no going back for you, is there?'

'No, indeed,' he replied. 'And if you want to accompany me into what is, after all, an amazing adventure, you will have to set ethics aside, as I have had to do. For me, the value of the knowledge to be gained more than justifies the fact that the project is unlicensed.

'Now, I already know that Stevie has no problem with the ethics of the project.' Again, he stared pointedly at the Australian, who simply stared back. 'But what are your own thoughts on the matter, Layla?'

'Much as I dislike the subterfuge, I suppose I have to agree with you,' she said, shrugging her shoulders. 'I wouldn't have come this far if I hadn't already reached the same conclusion, but I had to raise the subject. It's a massive risk to do this illegally, and I can't help wondering how it's all going to end.'

'No doubt, when I go public, there will be an outcry and I could well be taken to task,' he said shortly. 'But I will already have opened Pandora's Box, so to speak, and the results will have been released into the world for others to absorb and take forward.'

Layla nodded. 'I suppose we would have to take the rap, too, for being willing participants,' she mused.

'Nah, we won't get the blame; we'll be celebrities!' said Stevie, joining the conversation at last. 'As I already said, I'll be writing a book about my experience.'

'I hadn't banked on being a celebrity,' said Layla glumly. 'I just want to boost my career.'

'And so you shall,' said Blunstone hastily. 'Look, let's not worry too much about what happens further down the line. We need to take this a step at a time, and we can discuss and manage the "going public" side of things as and when appropriate. Agreed?'

Both women nodded, but Layla felt a prickle of fear at the thought of what might happen when the project was exposed to the full glare of publicity.

Their host grinned. 'Excellent! Now, why don't we have a break from the heavy stuff, while I show you around the rest of the house? I want you to see the full setup.'

Chapter 9

'My library,' he announced unnecessarily, opening the door on a room packed floor to ceiling with books.

Both women stepped forward eagerly, wandering along the rows of mahogany bookcases lining three of the walls. The fourth was centred by an ornate fireplace, at either side of which squatted a burgundy leather chesterfield armchair. In the alcove behind the right-hand chair, an antique roll-top desk faced the wall, a slim, silver laptop sitting incongruously on its surface. Layla recognised from the DVD the large, garish print on the wall above the desk. Now she knew why the leather couches in the sitting room had looked so familiar: the film truly was a home movie.

The professor's hardback collection was impressive and wide-ranging. She spotted ancient medical texts; art and photography books; volumes dedicated to philosophy, history, psychology, science and natural history, and a whole bookcase holding five hundred years of classic and modern European literature. There was even a couple of series of twenty-first-century Swedish detective novels.

'What a treasure trove,' she gasped.

'Wowee, this little lot will certainly keep us occupied while we're recuperating,' Stevie said, grinning.

'I thought you would both be pleased with this room,' smiled their host. 'I'm rather pleased with it myself. It's a bit of a cliché, I suppose – the classic country-house library, with all the bells and whistles – but I'd always wanted one just like this.'

'Me, too,' breathed Layla, eyeing a chintz-cushioned window seat wedged between two of the bookcases at the far end of the room. The tall window above it overlooked a large lawn bordered by a beech hedge, which ran along the west-facing side of the property. She could imagine herself spending a lot of time reading in this place: whether in here, in her charming pink guestroom, or – weather permitting – in the peaceful walled garden.

The professor was giving them the 'domestic' tour first. They had already peeked into the small downstairs cloakroom and admired the morning room next door to the library: a formal chamber tastefully decorated in soft blues and greys, with damask sofas, a Victorian tiled fireplace and elegant vases of white calla lilies in the three large front- and side-facing windows.

'I think you'll like the kitchen, too,' he said now, leading them through the slate-tiled hallway, beyond the central staircase and down a few steps into a huge room at the back of the house. Layla had been expecting a traditional kitchen, but this space was purely contemporary: fitted-out in dazzling white and gleaming chrome; floored in warm, polished oak, and accessorised in red and black. A sparkling black granite-topped station dominated the centre of the room, combining a five-burner glass hob with a sizeable breakfast bar accommodating six high stools.

'I like it!' Stevie said, opening the enormous walk-in fridge-freezer to reveal well-stocked shelves. 'Lots of goodies in here.'

Embarrassed, Layla looked at the professor, who seemed unabashed by the woman's forwardness.

'Please feel free to help yourselves at any time over the weekend,' he said casually. 'Mrs Brodie has left us a few dishes to heat up at mealtimes, but there are plenty of snacks, too.'

'Great – hey, I love this,' Stevie said, wandering over to the curtain-glazed far wall with sliding patio doors. Outside, they could see a decked terrace, furnished with several rattan seats and a large glass-topped table.

Beyond that lay what Layla surmised was the kitchen garden. Its raised box beds were bare just now, but she saw a greenhouse and some small polytunnels nearby and could picture the rows of vegetables and herbs which would no doubt be planted-out very soon.

'Are you a gardener?' she asked Blunstone. 'The grounds are beautifully kept.'

'Good heavens, no! There's an old boy in the village who has looked after the estate for years. Jimmy McCallum... a real character. His grandson, Murdo, helps him out with the heavy work. He's a rather – how can I put it – *introverted* young man, but he's a keen enough gardener. The place would be a wilderness without the pair of them. They keep the rabbit population down, too: both have licenses for shotguns, so don't worry if you hear shooting in the woods!'

Layla made an involuntary moue of distaste at the thought and was glad that the professor didn't notice. He ushered them out of the kitchen and opened a door on the left, revealing a grand, but austere dining room, panelled in oak and furnished with antique mahogany. Below an exquisite crystal chandelier sat a big oval table which, again, she recognised from the DVD.

'I tend not to eat in here when I'm on my own – it's much cosier dining off a small table at the fireside next door – but the room will seem much friendlier with your company this weekend,' he said gallantly. Then, rubbing his hands together: 'Right, it's time to show you where it's all going to happen: the hospital wing!'

Layla felt a shiver as she and Stevie exchanged apprehensive glances and turned to follow their host upstairs.

On the first landing, they took the left-hand staircase up to the gallery, where the row of closed doors mirrored that of the guest wing opposite. When he opened the first door, however, Layla could see that that was where the similarity ended. This room was the size of Layla's and Stevie's rooms knocked into one – the two large bay windows hinted at the renovation – and it was indeed reminiscent of an infirmary ward. There were only two beds, but they were proper hospital ones, with veneered locker-style cabinets alongside. Spotless white tiles covered the floor and the windows were uncurtained but had cream pull-down blinds. Bizarrely, a handsome walnut cheval mirror stood opposite the beds, next to a matching large wardrobe and a three-mirrored dressing-table.

A ward, but not a ward, thought Layla.

'I've tried to make it as homely as possible, while keeping hospital hygiene in mind,' explained the professor, striding across the room to a door in the far wall.

'We won't go into the theatre, but you can look through here,' he said, stepping back to allow them to peer through the reinforced glass window in the top half of the door.

'Amazing,' said Stevie. 'This is where you filmed yourself operating, for the DVD?'

He nodded. 'The very same. It's the part of the house that I'm most proud of. There's a wee scrub-up ante-room on the left and then, through that set of double doors, you can just see the operating theatre itself. It's small, but it's fully furnished with state-of-the-art equipment that is not yet available in most NHS hospitals across the country.'

Peering through the glass, Layla recognised the space, her stomach clenching at the sight of the sealed, sterile room.

Turning back to the ward, with its empty – somehow ghostly – hospital beds, which also were familiar to her,

66

she thought of the two women in the professor's second film.

Chapter 10
The Previous October: The University

It was well past lunchtime, but food was the last thing on her mind as she clicked on "play" to watch the final part of the professor's DVD.

Two women sat at the same oval table as in the previous film. One, petite and pinched-looking, was nursing a mug between bony hands, her dark hair straggly; her brown eyes dull. The other woman, larger and plumper, wore a colourful cloche hat and was smiling sweetly at the camera. It was impossible to tell their ages – with the dry, sallow skin of the seriously sick, they could have been anything from thirty-something to mid-fifties – but the second woman's eyes radiated laughter lines that confirmed her seniority.

'Ladies, I'll be referring to you as "Patient C" and "Patient D" in this film – not because your names are not important, but simply to protect your anonymity,' the familiar voice of James Blunstone rang out. 'Now, Patient D, please tell the camera why you are taking part in this project.'

The cloche-hatted woman nodded, still smiling. 'This is the opportunity of a lifetime,' she said in a fluty voice, the inflection pure Western Isles. 'I've always wondered what it would be like to stand in someone else's shoes, and now – at the end of my life – here's my chance.'

Layla felt humbled by her composure. It was a very special kind of person who could stare death in the face so calmly – never mind sign up for a science fiction-style experiment while she waited for it to claim her.

'Patient C,' Blunstone said gently, 'why are you taking part?'

The other woman stared at the camera. 'My family needs the money,' she said hoarsely, in a North-east accent. 'It's as simple as that.'

'But you are doing this willingly, with no coercion whatsoever?' he prompted.

'I understand what I'm letting myself in for and nobody is making me do it,' she replied.

The atmosphere of this interview was vastly different from that of the preceding film, and Layla felt vaguely uneasy. But she kept on watching.

'And you both understand that following the operation tomorrow, you will be inhabiting each other's bodies for a period of twenty-four hours and that during that time you will be required to stay within this house and grounds, and be available to answer my questions?'

Both women nodded and Patient D said: 'Oh yes, I'll be happy to. It's such a beautiful place you have here.'

The screen went momentarily blank. The next scene was also familiar: the scrubbed-up professor at work in the operating theatre, assisted by, she assumed, the same masked nurse. This time, however, the two reclining patients were apparently unconscious, and Layla saw that another man – presumably an anaesthetist – was also present, stationed between the operating tables and monitoring some kind of equipment.

Blunstone spoke over his shoulder as he settled into his neurosurgeon's chair. 'On this occasion, the operation will be much shorter. It is simply a case of removing and switching the patients' me-glands via keyhole surgery, while they are under anaesthetic. The study proper will begin after they have regained consciousness in their new host bodies.'

He pressed a remote control and the screen once again went blank.

Layla half-expected to see the women sitting by the fire, where the male patients had been, but the film resumed in a different setting. It was a large, sunlit room, furnished with two modern hospital beds, positioned on either side of a bay window that revealed the tops of mature trees in full leaf.

The beds were occupied by the two patients, now wearing white towelling turbans and matching dressing gowns. They were sitting up and looking straight at the camera. Their expressions couldn't have been more different: the petite woman was smiling broadly, while her older neighbour looked unhappy.

'I won't disturb you for long, ladies; I just want your initial thoughts now that you've come around from your operations. How are you feeling, Patient D?'

He'll be addressing the one who looks happy, Layla thought.

Sure enough, the smiling woman – with the body of Patient C – answered him.

'Oh, this is just amazing,' she said brightly, in Patient C's hoarse voice and local accent. 'I feel so small and light – like a wee bird! And it's unbelievably strange to see myself as others must see me.' She looked across at her own body in the next bed.

'Any ill-effects from the op?' Blunstone asked.

'I do have a bit of a dull headache,' she replied. 'But, my goodness, it's nothing to complain about, considering.'

'The headache has nothing to do with the operation,' the other patient said sharply, not looking at her neighbour. 'It's my illness; it's what I have to live with all the time.'

Layla noticed that what had previously been a sweet face had soured considerably. *Fascinating*, she thought. *Patient C's mental state is already affecting the physical appearance of her new body.*

70

Patient C had more to say: 'But the headache in this body is much, much worse. I don't know if I can stand it for the best part of a day.' Her lilting voice rose to a whine. 'I need strong painkillers – now!'

'I'm so sorry to hear that,' said Blunstone. 'Nurse Murray will bring you some right away. Nurse?'

Someone off-screen said 'Yes, of course,' and within seconds, a white-sleeved arm was holding out a cup to the patient, who immediately swallowed the contents, sipping from a water glass that had been sitting on her nightstand.

'I must say, you both seem to be in very good command of your new bodies already,' the professor said cheerfully. 'It won't be long before you're up and walking around.'

But Patient D had turned to Patient C, a concerned look on her face. 'You must have a very low pain threshold, C; I can usually get by without taking too many pills. You get used to the pressure of the tumour. Mind you, I'm glad to get away from it for a wee while. Your body's headache is different: more like a very mild migraine.'

Patient C muttered something inaudible and looked down at her plump new hands, which were fiddling with the bedcover.

James Blunstone coughed and said briskly: 'Okay, well, I'll leave you both for now and come back later, once you're up and about.'

The next scene opened on the same room, where both women were now shuffling around with the aid of walking frames. Patient C – in her larger new body – seemed to be slower and more disorientated than her diminutive companion, who was moving across the room with a cheerful confidence that increased with every step.

'Ladies, you're doing marvellously,' the professor's voice encouraged. 'Tell me, how does it feel to be walking around in different bodies?'

Patient C glowered at the camera and said, reluctantly: 'I don't like it. It feels weird, as if I'm drugged or something.'

'How do you mean?' he asked.

'Well, my body feels heavy and my arms and legs are moving too slowly, as if I've been taking Valium.'

'Oh dear, I'm not that overweight, am I?' laughed Patient D. 'I know what you mean, though – it takes a bit of getting used to.' She turned to the camera. 'Being smaller, I'm seeing the world from a slightly different perspective. But the overall experience is very pleasant. I feel as if I can see and hear more clearly and I don't have any of the usual aches and pains.'

'No, because I have them now,' Patient C said angrily. 'This is going to be the longest twenty-four hours of my life.'

The film cut suddenly to a sunny terrace, where the patients were sitting at a glass-topped patio table, eating under the shade of a candy-striped umbrella.

'I'm interested to hear how you're finding everyday tasks,' Blunstone's voice said.

'Well, as far as eating and drinking are concerned, this body seems to know that I need to favour the right side of my mouth, as a couple of the teeth on the left are very sensitive,' Patient D told the camera, brown eyes twinkling.

'How do you mean "seems to know"? Did you feel you had to override your body to find out that the teeth *are* sensitive?' he asked.

'Yes! "Override" is good way of putting it. I really had to force myself to bite down with the left side of my mouth, because my body must already have known that it would be sore. And it was!'

'Welcome to my world,' sighed Patient C, who was eating what looked like a quiche and salad, with good appetite.

'How's the head now, Patient C?' the disembodied voice asked.

'Fine at the moment... I'm actually feeling much hungrier than I normally do,' she volunteered. 'This tastes really good.'

Layla found herself feeling pleased that the younger woman had cheered up a little.

'Splendid!' The professor evidently felt the same, because he ventured to ask: 'This may seem a strange question, but do you feel that you are still *you*?'

She chewed for a moment, then said decisively: 'Yes; inside, I'm still the same person I was before the operation.'

'Me, too,' said Patient D. 'Apart from the different physical feelings I'm experiencing, I don't think the real me has changed at all!'

'Fascinating!' he exclaimed. Then: 'I'd like to do a wee experiment now. I want you both to recall a happy memory that gives you a real tingle of excitement – you know, that flutter in your chest and stomach that comes with remembering something thrilling.'

Patient C grimaced but put down her knife and fork and tilted her head upwards, as if in thought. Patient D nodded and shut her eyes. Layla felt her own flutter of excitement. She thought she understood what the professor was doing: he wanted to see the extent to which the women's emotional memories could provoke the same reaction in their host bodies as they would in their own bodies. She had read that happy memories were believed by psychologists to be less potent than negative or traumatic ones, causing less powerful physiological effects. So, if the two women's host bodies were able to experience physical feelings of pleasure and excitement when the patients recalled a happy memory, it would be a pretty good measure of how well-embedded their consciousness was within their host bodies.

After a moment, Blunstone said: 'Okay, did it work? Did you physically feel the way you usually do when you conjure up that particular memory?'

'I did!' said Patient D happily. 'It's the very same feeling.'

'Yes, same here.' Patient C looked more sad than excited. Layla couldn't help wondering what they'd both been thinking about.

'Fantastic! You are truly in control of your host bodies,' he boomed. Then, in a softer voice, he added: 'Now, I have one last favour to ask of you. Tomorrow morning, before your reversal operations, I'd like you to record a video diary in private, sharing your honest feelings about the experiment. I want to know what has struck you most about the experience – both positively and negatively – and I also want you to try to describe any dreams you may have tonight. Will you do that for me?'

'Yes, of course,' beamed the smaller woman.

Patient C, her borrowed face expressionless, merely nodded and carried on eating.

After a short break, during which Layla wolfed down a takeaway sandwich and yet more coffee – wondering all the while what it would be like to eat and drink with a different mouth – she was ready to continue watching the film.

74

Chapter 11

It resumed with the first of the video diaries.

Layla was glad Blunstone had switched to this new format, rather than continuing to film the women himself. It was bound to be more revealing than his previous, rather clumsy attempts to engage them both together.

Patient C was first up. Her plump face filled the frame, then returned to normal size, as she settled into an armchair opposite the camera. The plain white background gave nothing away as to her location.

'I feel as if I'm on *Big Brother*,' she began nervously, adjusting the towelling turban she still wore from the previous day.

'Okay, well, honest opinion? This has been a mostly horrible experience. I've really missed my own body. In fact, I've been feeling homesick for it ever since I woke up from the operation.'

She paused, then said bluntly: 'I can't stand to look in the mirror. Patient D's body is too big and it's quite fat. I've never been fat in my life! I hate the hot flushes that come out of nowhere. Her joints ache all the time and her headache is horrible – far worse than mine. I don't know how she can stand it, never mind be so cheerful all the time!'

Then the woman's indignant expression softened. 'The only good things are that her sense of taste is better than mine – I've enjoyed my food for the first time in months – and the fact that I'll be able to leave so much money to my mum and kids. It'll help them a lot when I'm gone.'

Her voice faltered on the last sentence and she stood abruptly, making as if to switch off the camera. Then she sat down again heavily. 'I forgot about the dreaming bit... Well, I had a terrible night; couldn't sleep for hours. First, I was too hot, then too cold – those bloody flushes again.

When I finally did drop off, I had a nightmare that I was dead, but that a mad professor was trying to bring me back to life using electricity, just like in *Frankenstein*... Hey, no offence,' she added in an ironic tone. Her cynical expression didn't sit well on Patient D's amiable face.

'I also had a horrible dream about a little girl who called me "Mummy". I have two teenage boys, so it had nothing to do with my own kids. She was just a toddler and had dark, curly hair. One minute she was playing on a swing and the next she had fallen off. I went to pick her up and saw that her neck was broken! God knows where that came from – it was really disturbing.

'Anyway, you asked me to be honest and I have been. I can't wait for the operation this morning. I never rated my body much before, but I'll be so glad to get it back, headache, death sentence and all.'

When she switched off the camera, the screen stayed black for a full minute.

Well, I suppose she learned something from the experience – even if it's only to make the most of being inside her own skin again, thought Layla, as she waited for the next instalment. She suspected Patient D's take on her own body swap would be very different.

She was right. Despite her fragile-looking frame, the woman now sitting in front of the camera was the picture of contentment.

'My, what a wonderful experience this has been!' she began, her small face radiating joy. 'I can't tell you what a privilege it is to have taken part in this experiment.

'I must admit, though, that C's body here is a little too skinny for my liking: no padding where it counts! But it's been fascinating seeing the world through her eyes. Her vision and hearing are sharper, as I said before, and it has felt like a holiday to be free of the usual aches and pains – oh, and the hot flushes!'

She leaned forward and said in a confidential whisper: 'I hope she now realises how fortunate she is.'

Hear, hear, thought Layla.

Patient D continued: 'Living inside a host body is like driving a new car... Och, that's not a very good analogy, but it's the nearest experience I can think of. You have to get used to all the new equipment at first, but it's not long before you feel you're back in control. And I think that's helped by the fact that so many movements seem to happen automatically.'

She shifted in her seat. 'One thing I *have* found unsettling is how weirdly intimate it feels to be living in someone else's body. For instance, I felt really shy going to the loo for the first time! But luckily my nurse's background came to the rescue: I decided to treat C's body as if it was just another patient's and I soon got over the embarrassment factor.'

She smiled and continued: 'You asked us to tell you about our dreams last night. Well, I had the best sleep I've had in ages, thanks to the lack of hot flushes. The duvet stayed in place all night; usually, I wake up umpteen times, having to throw it off, or pull it back on again...

'But, my goodness, the dreams I had! I can't recall the details, but I do remember there was a very bad man in all of them who wouldn't leave me alone. He was a stranger, but for some reason, he was living in my house. He was really angry and I knew he wanted to hurt me. He was the complete opposite of my husband, Ron, who's a gentle soul, even with his early onset dementia...' She tailed off, her peaky face now pensive.

Then she added: 'You know, I had another reason for taking part in this experiment. Yes, I was mad curious to find out what it would be like to escape from my own body for a while, and to experience the world through someone else's. But to be honest, as C said yesterday, the main reason is the money. When I'm gone, it will pay for Ron to go into a lovely care home – not the shabby place he's having respite care in while I'm here.'

She paused, before continuing: 'I know you said you have no idea where consciousness comes from – or goes to, for that matter. But this whole experience has confirmed my suspicion that there is some form of life after death. I can only hope that Ron and I will meet again at some point, and that, being free of the brain diseases we're suffering from just now, we'll be our true selves again.'

Eyes shining, she added: 'So thank you, Professor Blunstone, for giving me the precious gift of hope. I only wish I could share it with Ron, but he's too far gone. Thanks to you, though, I now have hope enough for both of us.'

And with that, she leaned forward and switched off the camera.

Once again moved to tears, Layla paused the film and went to make herself a mug of tea. She no longer had any doubts that the extraordinary experiment was genuine – and its implications were electrifying.

After sitting quietly at her desk for a while, deliberately blanking out the frenzy of thoughts that threatened to overwhelm her, she reached for the mouse to watch the final segment of the DVD: James Blunstone's summing-up.

Now back in his original study setting, he began: 'I am indebted to Patients A, B, C, and D for their bravery and fortitude in participating in the world's first body-swap experiments.' Despite the melodramatic statement, his voice was quiet and serious. 'This humble film is dedicated to the memory of those four fine people, all of whom, sadly, are now deceased.'

Although she had expected as much, she still felt the hammer-blow of dismay.

'Their deaths, in the ensuing weeks and months following their operations, were natural and entirely due to the terminal brain illnesses they were suffering from. Each of their families has since been very well provided-for, by "an anonymous donor", whose bequest was made "in gratitude for a past kindness" shown by their deceased relatives.'

There was a respectful pause and he continued: 'I hope that by now you will believe in the authenticity of my project, and that this DVD has given you plenty of food for thought.

'Of course, I have learned far more from these first two experiments than I have captured on film, but I think there is enough here to give you a flavour of what these patients experienced, warts and all. Quite clearly, body-swapping is not for everyone. But for those of a certain mindset, the opportunity to occupy someone else's body is surely the most profound experience a human being could have.'

He leaned forward and looked earnestly into the lens. 'The full effects of transposing human consciousness will become apparent only as a result of a longer-term study. That is where you come in.

'My aim now is to carry out a three-month study, in which my research subjects, after a short period of recuperation, will go back out into the world and live as normal a life as possible. I will require regular updates – online, if not in person – and I will ask you to keep a daily log to record your experiences as fully as you can.

'To provide a level playing field and avoid unnecessary complexities at this relatively early stage in my research, I will ensure that your body-swap partner is of the same gender and age as yourself.'

He sat back and drew a deep breath. 'If, after digesting all you have witnessed in this film, you feel you would like to proceed to the next stage, that is, meeting your fellow research subject and talking through the process with me in more detail, I will be more than delighted to hear from you.'

The screen went black for the final time.

Chapter 12
March: Cairnacraig House

'You're looking very thoughtful, Layla,' the professor said, bringing her back to the present.

'Hmm, yes, sorry.' She turned to him, another question occurring to her. 'The other two medical staff in your DVD... who are they?'

'Ah, I was just coming to that. Let's go back to the sitting room and get comfy and I'll explain all.'

Stevie, who had been pacing around the ward, left the room ahead of them and almost galloped down the stairs.

Sitting beside the newly banked-up fire, the professor asked if either of them wanted a hot drink or something stronger.

'Maybe in a little while?' said Layla, keen to keep the conversation going. Stevie merely shrugged.

'Okay, so the people you saw assisting me in the DVD are loyal and trusted colleagues with whom I have been working for many, many years. Allan Cameron is a very talented neuro-anaesthetist, and Susan Murray is a discreet and highly-capable nurse with a master's degree in advanced practice nursing.'

'How the hell did you persuade them to take part in the experiments? Surely they'd lose their jobs if their NHS bosses found out?' Stevie quizzed him.

'They're both now working part-time in private practice and what they do for the rest of the time is entirely their own affair,' Blunstone replied.

Except when it contravenes medical ethics, thought Layla.

'Allan and Susan are intelligent professionals with keen, enquiring minds,' the professor continued. 'Over the

81

years, the three of us have had many conversations about the brain and human consciousness. Once I knew for certain that I could safely and successfully perform the me-gland operation, I took them into my confidence and they both readily agreed to help me out. They trust me implicitly, you see.'

'And I bet you pay them well, too!' laughed Stevie, once again embarrassing Layla.

But, again, Blunstone seemed unfazed. 'I do – and that brings me on to the subject of your fees.'

Stevie leaned forward eagerly, her hair swinging into her face. Layla couldn't pretend she wasn't interested in the financial aspects of the project – of course she was – but she tried not to look too keen as she waited for him to continue.

'If you choose to participate in my project, you will obviously need to take time out from your professions. Layla, in your case, as an employee, it would be in the form of a sabbatical; Stevie, as a freelance journalist, you could probably resume your normal routine more or less right after the operation, but you may not wish to do so. Ideally, I would like you both to stay here for up to two weeks following the operation. Not so much to recuperate, as you referred to earlier, Stevie – it's a very straightforward procedure, after all – but to give you a chance to acclimatise to your new bodies and also to let me monitor you at close quarters before you return to real life.'

Seeing both women nod, he went on. 'I propose to pay you each the sum of £100,000 for your time as research subjects during those three months. Obviously, you will be free to follow your own chosen pursuits for most of that period, so you may well still be earning, in any case.'

Layla and Stevie looked at each other, their shock mirrored in their respective expressions.

'Wowee!' Stevie was the first to recover. Her green eyes narrowed. 'But how can you afford that, along with everything else involved in this project?'

Layla nodded and looked at him, momentarily speechless.

'I am a very rich man,' he replied quietly. 'I inherited rather a lot of money from my parents, and via Lydia, who also was from a well-off family. Add to that my savings from a long career as a top surgeon, and there you have it. I can afford it, and it will be money well spent.'

The three sat in silence for a moment, before the professor added: 'Now, cash is obviously a great motivator. But, as you will have no doubt gleaned from Patient C's experience, it should not be the only one. Patient C found it hard enough living in another body for twenty-four hours; think how she would have felt after three months.'

'She would have gone off her rocker,' said Stevie.

'She simply could not have borne it,' Blunstone agreed. 'That is why I must be convinced that each of you is not motivated solely by financial gain.' He stared pointedly at the Australian as he said this.

'For your own sanity's sake, you must truly want to take part and know within yourselves that you have the emotional strength and stamina to stay the course. As I said in the film, it takes a certain mindset to embark on such a groundbreaking journey.'

He clasped his hands and leaned towards them. 'I've been looking for subjects who have the intelligence, curiosity and capability of coping with such an experience. I believe each of you possesses these qualities, along with many others that will help you to not only manage, but also relish your temporary new reality. There is no doubt that it will change your outlook forever afterwards, and so you need to be sure that, for you, this will be a positive, life-enhancing development.'

'But how *can* we be sure?' Layla asked. 'I have a pretty good idea of my own feelings, motivations and capabilities, but nothing in my experience has prepared me for occupying someone else's body!'

'Back to that again,' snorted Stevie derisively. 'We've had this conversation already.'

'So, *you're* quite sure, are you?' Layla challenged, her face flushing.

'I am!' the Australian said triumphantly. 'I know I can do it, and I just want to get on with it.'

Layla gave a deep sigh. The woman's impetuosity was beyond her comprehension.

Blunstone looked from one to the other and said quickly: 'That's good to hear, Stevie, but I really think you and Layla need more time to get to know each other before you make your final decision.'

He glanced at his watch. 'Five-fifteen already! Why don't I leave you two together for a wee while? I could nip along the road and fit in a quick nine holes before it's time to fix our evening meal. It only needs heating up, after all. Let's reconvene in the kitchen at seven-thirty. If you're peckish in the meantime, feel free to help yourselves to snacks and drinks.'

Layla felt the now-familiar prickle of anxiety as she watched their host sweep from the room, leaving her alone with Stevie for the first time.

Chapter 13

The women eyed each other cagily for a moment before Layla took control. She moved across to the sofa the professor had just vacated and sat down opposite Stevie.

'Okay, I'm really interested to know: what makes someone like you want to swap bodies with someone like me? Honestly?'

Stevie stretched out her long legs, resting her blonde head against the back of the sofa.

'It's nothing personal, I can tell you,' she said at last. 'Practically any body would do.' She gave Layla a sly look and then grinned. 'Don't look so shocked. I'm really keen to do this, and it's only for three months. You're not exactly Mrs Shrek, are you? I'm sure I'll get by just fine in your body. The question is: will you manage to cope with mine?'

Layla said nothing. It was a good question, and she'd need to give it more thought. She changed tack. 'Let's assume for the sake of argument that we both agree to this. How are we going to work it following the operation? Do we go back to our own homes, pretending to everyone that we've done a house swap, or do we exchange homes as well? James hasn't raised the subject, but I think we need to decide for ourselves up front, don't you?'

Stevie looked thoughtful. 'How about we do both? I mean, stay in our own places to start with, and then, when we feel more comfortable, do a swap. That way we can really make the most of the experience. What's the point of swapping bodies, but carrying on living in the same old spot the whole time?'

The suggestion both thrilled and terrified Layla. She started thinking aloud. 'So, first we pretend to be house guests in our own homes... that'll be the easier part. It'll be weird – and, let's face it, dishonest – duping the folk who know us, but we won't be doing them any harm, as they won't know what's really going on.'

'Never in a million years,' chuckled Stevie.

'But then,' Layla continued, 'things ramp up a level and we pretend to *be* each other and start living each other's lives. That's going to be a whole lot trickier – and it carries far more risk.'

The other woman rolled her eyes. 'Well, duh – that's the exciting part! Imagine the buzz of having to wing it like that.'

'"Winging it" is not really part of my skills set,' Layla replied wryly.

That wasn't exactly true, though, was it? Wasn't it just what she did when fielding questions fired at her by a lively group of students? From her quizzical expression, Stevie was evidently thinking along the same lines, so she quickly added: 'But I hear what you're saying. I'm not against the idea in principle; it's just that there's so much that could go wrong.'

She sat forward in her seat. 'Look, we can do all the preparation under the sun, but either of us could still be caught out by friends or family at any time. Supposing we're asked about people or memories we should know about, but don't? Think about what that might mean: worst case scenario, they could start to believe we're losing our minds. And we could really upset people without meaning to, leaving a horrible tangled mess for me or you to have to deal with when we swap back. That's the risky part.'

'Ordinary life carries huge risks as well – get over it,' Stevie retorted, stifling a yawn. 'We're intelligent human beings and we'll each find a way of adapting to and managing the situation. Anyway, I have no family over here and not that many friends yet, so you'll have it easy. Stop worrying so much; it'll be fun!'

Feeling like a stick-in-the-mud, but determined not to be intimidated, Layla said quietly: 'If we're going to go the whole hog, as you suggest, we'll need to find out a great deal more about each other. I'm talking personalities, lifestyles, families – even if they are all abroad – friends, practical living and working arrangements... We'll need to share every last detail we can think of. Are you prepared to do that?'

'Yeah, I'm cool with that,' Stevie said. 'We'll have plenty of time to get up to speed when we're staying here after the ops, but we can start now, if you like?'

Taken aback, Layla found herself agreeing. 'Okay... where do you want to begin?'

During the next hour she forgot her reservations, as she and Stevie swapped basic information about themselves. Animated and chatty now, the Australian seemed happy to open up about her daily routine. While most working hours were spent sitting in front of a computer, writing, her leisure time was taken up with running and sporty pursuits, along with regular noisy nights out with a small crowd from the gym. When Layla found out that she was renting a house in Footdee, or Fittie – a charming heritage fishing village near Aberdeen Beach – she squealed with excitement: 'I love that wee place!' The proposed house swap suddenly sounded a much more attractive idea.

In turn, Layla described her own work and domestic circumstances, realising how utterly monotonous her quiet life must appear to someone as active and gregarious as the woman sitting opposite her.

'We really should be taking notes,' she said eventually, suddenly feeling exhausted. 'There's still so much to find out – and work out – but I can't handle any more right now. I think I'll go and have a shower before James gets back.'

'Fair enough,' Stevie said, jumping to her feet. 'I'm off to raid the fridge.'

Layla couldn't remember the last time she'd eaten so well. Since Calum had left her, she'd subsisted mainly on sandwiches, cheese on toast and microwave meals, barely interested in what she was putting in her mouth. Now, she was eating the second delicious home-cooked meal of the day: a thatched lentil and vegetable pie, with green salad and garlic bread. Her dinner companions had decided to go vegetarian as well, and they all ate with relish.

'Your Mrs B also knows her way around a cooker,' said Stevie to the professor, shovelling cheesy potato topping into her mouth. Layla was quick to agree.

'Yes, she really is the archetypal "treasure",' Blunstone replied happily, topping-up their lead-crystal glasses with a fruity Rioja.

As they ate, relaxed for the moment in each other's company, Layla felt that some ground had been gained with her late-afternoon chat with Stevie. The other woman seemed far less confrontational this evening, and Layla found herself wondering what it would be like to inhabit such a fit and fearless body.

Inevitably, the conversation turned from lighter subjects back to the project, and Layla, emboldened by two glasses of wine, decided to press for an answer to her earlier concern.

'I would still like to know what happens if one or both of us want to back out before the three months are up,' she said. 'Obviously, I would do my best to make it work, but I would feel better knowing there was a "get-out clause" if need be.'

Her host put down his fork and wiped his mouth with his napkin. 'And quite right, too,' he said, ignoring Stevie's heavy sigh. 'Once again, it's all about trust. If either of you is truly unhappy with her temporary situation, we must all agree to a reversal of the procedure as soon as possible. Is that acceptable to you, Stevie?' He asked the question firmly.

'Yeah, yeah – whatever,' the blonde woman conceded, mopping up the last of her tomato sauce with bread. 'Just as long as you agree to pay us the full fee regardless of how long the project lasts.'

Mortified, Layla hardly dared look at the professor. Despite his earlier stipulations about motivation, it was pretty clear where Stevie's priorities lay. However, he seemed unaffected as he replied: 'Of course; I was just about to come to that. The fee is not in any way time-sensitive.'

Does nothing rile this man? Layla thought.

'Will we get that in writing?' the Australian asked. 'Trust is fine, but I've been shafted in the past and I don't want to go there again.'

'Good point,' he said mildly. 'I'm sure you will understand that I can't bring lawyers into this, but I will draw up a contract, which, if we all sign it, will be legal and binding under Scots Law. We'll need witnesses to the signing, but that's easy enough to arrange with my colleagues Allan and Susan. Will that work for you both?'

'Yes, that sounds fine,' Layla said. Stevie shrugged and nodded, then said: 'We've decided what we want to do when we leave here after the procedure.' Ignoring Layla's cautioning look, she went on to tell the professor about the living arrangements they'd discussed while he was out.

He raised his eyebrows and said: 'Of course, you must do whatever you feel most comfortable with. I must say, though, I'm surprised that you're prepared to swap homes as well. It wasn't what I'd anticipated, but if you're happy to go ahead with that, it will certainly add an interesting new dimension to the project from both a sociological and a psychological perspective!'

Warmed by the wine, Layla allowed herself to acknowledge the excitement that had been growing within her throughout the day. As the practical details were fleshed out, the project was becoming more feasible by the minute and she was starting to believe that escaping from her own body and living someone else's life for a while really could be the solution she was seeking.

Four months previously, such a prospect had seemed unimaginable.

Chapter 14
The Previous December: Aberdeen

Just as she had done in the days after Calum left, Layla sought refuge in denial.

She threw herself into her work, cleaned the house with dervish-like energy, contacted friends she'd lost touch with, called her parents to confirm her visit to California at Christmas, and watched hours of boxed-set drama series which she'd previously had neither the heart nor the concentration to view on her own.

Night-time was a different matter. If she wasn't dreaming about Professor Blunstone, his now-deceased patients, or of being trapped in someone else's body, she was lying awake, unable to stop his home-made recordings replaying in her mind.

At a fundamental level, she had accepted the reality of Blunstone's breakthrough. To have proved that human consciousness could survive beyond the body was revolutionary on a par with – what? Other earth-shattering discoveries paled in comparison. In terms of its implications – for science, philosophy, religion – it opened a portal on an entirely new dimension with infinite possibilities.

If she allowed herself to even start thinking about this "new reality", it would give her own research into personal identity an energy boost beyond anything she could ever have imagined. But was she brave enough to go down that path?

And what was she going to tell the professor when he got back in touch?

It took a full two weeks of subconscious processing before Layla finally felt ready to face her demons. She woke on a Friday morning feeling refreshed and resolute.

And that evening, sipping tea on her sofa, she began to think things through.

The discovery about consciousness was a given. So, her first decision was whether to: a) ignore it and continue as if her encounter with the professor had never happened; b) embrace it – but only theoretically – focusing her research on the exciting philosophical implications of the discovery *without* becoming a subject in the body-swap project; or c) go the whole hog and become a research subject.

Considering option a) in more depth, she realised that turning her back on the discovery would lead to another dilemma: whether or not to report Blunstone for professional misconduct.

If, for whatever reason, she decided not to report him, he would proceed with his experiment and, eventually, would share the results with the wider world. In that case, she would miss out on the unique career opportunity that direct involvement with the project would have given her.

So, could she bury the knowledge? Did she feel outraged enough to report him and ruin his research? And did she want to see her own, new career prospects wither and die?

Parking option a) for the moment, she turned to b). It was highly attractive: it meant she could piggy-back on to the professor's research without getting personally involved. But would he allow her to do that if she wasn't going to take part in the project directly? Could she do it, anyway, without his consent? Already, she had enough information to set out on a highly-rewarding philosophical journey of her own. But then, if she wanted anyone to take her work seriously, she would have to wait until the professor published his evidence. No, she would really need to keep him on side.

She sighed and rubbed her eyes. So many decisions!

It was time to confront the third – and scariest – option: could she really become one of the professor's guinea pigs? What would it take for her to choose that path?

A longstanding fan of quality crime fiction, Layla realised that the three criteria for murder always considered by her favourite detectives could also help determine her own, very different, course of action. *Do I have the means, motive and opportunity to take such a life-changing step?*

Opportunity was not a problem: for some time, she'd been thinking about taking a sabbatical in order to try to write up her research as a non-academic book with wider appeal. The crisis with Calum had put this on hold, as she'd needed the work routine and daily contact with colleagues to help her function normally. But she was sure the break from work could be easily arranged: she was the only person in her department who hadn't taken time out, and it wouldn't come as a surprise to any of her colleagues.

"Means", in this case, meant financial security during the three-month period of the project. Again, that wouldn't be a problem: if she took the sabbatical, she would still be entitled to part of her salary, and she would also be paid by the professor.

It was motive that was the trickiest part of the equation. *Why* would she want to change bodies with someone? And what would prevent her from doing so?

Scrambling for her notebook, Layla keyed in her password and opened a blank document. Within half an hour, two short columns had taken shape on the screen:

Pros
1. It's the opportunity of a lifetime to carry out pioneering, practical research in my professional field of expertise
2. This could make my career

3. I need a new challenge
4. I want to feel passionate about my work again
5. I need to take my mind off my personal problems
6. It will literally change my outlook on life – hopefully for the better

Cons
1. It might be dangerous – life-threatening, even
2. It's unethical
3. It's unnatural *(where did that come from? So is* normal *brain surgery, so what's the big deal?)*
4. It's frightening: I'm scared I might go mad!
5. My family and true friends wouldn't want me to do it
6. Supposing I somehow get trapped in the other person's body?

Reading through the lists, she sighed heavily. They were pretty fairly balanced. Her fear, revulsion and the possibility of hurting those closest to her were strong enough to dilute her desperate need to change her life and to revitalise her career.

She felt frustrated, knowing that before she could finally decide which of the three main options to pursue – ignore, piggy-back, or participate – she had to break the stalemate over motive. Something else was needed to tip the scales.

It arrived, quite unexpectedly, the following day.

Chapter 15

Once, Layla had looked forward to Saturdays, when she and Calum could sleep late and luxuriate in not having to be at anyone else's beck and call. They would eventually get up and potter around in their dressing gowns, enjoying the cosy home they'd saved so hard for in their early years as a couple: a 1930s granite-built detached villa in the city's Midstocket area.

Nowadays, she dreaded the weekend, and, despite the uncharacteristic lack of energy that now seemed to haunt her, she rose early on Saturday mornings so that she could fill the first half of the day with mindless chores and food shopping, before settling herself for long, lonely hours of reading or watching catch-up TV.

Sundays were even worse: she would usually end up working in her small home office to pass the time, playing loud rock music to block out the devastating silence permeating the house. Unless she made a real effort, she could sometimes go a whole weekend without speaking to another living soul.

But this Saturday morning brought a visitor. Polishing her coffee table, idly wondering why she was even bothering, she suddenly spotted Calum's Audi pulling up outside. Frantically, she dashed through to the bedroom, dragged the scrunchie out of her hair and quickly changed from her scruffy sweats into a cerise long-sleeve t-shirt and half-decent jeans. She had no makeup on, but there was no time to do anything about that, as the doorbell was already ringing.

The moment she saw his face, she knew something had changed. The cold, haughty expression had been replaced by a nervous grin. Her heart leapt. *Has he left her?*

'Sorry to bother you so early – can I come in for a minute?' Calum asked, running his hand through his thick blond hair.

'Er – yes, that's fine.' She let him precede her into the lounge, where the beech-wood furniture was illuminated to an amber glow by a low December sun.

'Ignore the mess – I was cleaning,' she said awkwardly, moving papers and books from the cream leather sofa to the coffee table.

'No worries. Look, can I sit down? I've something to tell you.'

Yes, he was definitely nervous. Calum never usually asked before doing anything.

She waved a hand at the sofa and sat down in a nearby armchair. Her stomach was in knots. Was he going to ask if he could come home? Despite the simmering anger she felt towards him, she knew what her answer would be.

'This is really awkward,' he began. 'There's no easy way to say it.'

'Just say it,' she said quietly, trying to sound calm. She wouldn't make it difficult for him. It would take time to mend their shredded marriage, but they could get through it.

He looked down at his hands, clenched into fists in his lap. When he glanced up again, half his face was lit by sunlight, the other half was in shade, his familiar features transformed into a sinister, chiaroscuro mask.

'Darla is pregnant and we want to get married,' he blurted out.

She almost laughed. He was saying the wrong words, trotting out a sick joke instead of getting to the point. But, searching his face for a sign of humour, she saw only dread, embarrassment and – worst of all – pity.

She couldn't breathe. She tried to swallow the invisible lump that was choking her.

'Layla?' He half-rose from the sofa. 'Are you okay?'

Finally able to suck in air, she put up her hand to stop his approach, her own face a bleached-out mask of shock and disbelief.

He sat back down again with a thud.

'I'm sorry – it wasn't something we'd planned, but now it's happened, we want to be a proper family,' he said almost imploringly.

Speechless, she could only stare back at him. Then shock transformed into a searing rage.

'You *bastard*,' she hissed venomously. 'You *utter bastard*. You've *never* wanted a baby – you wouldn't hear of it! And now you're telling me that little *cow* is pregnant and you want to play happy families?'

'I understand how you must be feeling, but there's really no need to get nasty,' he said, eyes narrowing.

She leapt to her feet and he did the same, backing towards the door. Her voice rose to a scream as she advanced on him: 'You *understand* how I'm feeling? For years, I've had to live with the pain of being denied having children. You have NO idea how that feels, you selfish bastard!'

Hands up in a defensive gesture, he backed into the hall. With the prospect of escape, his self-confidence returned. 'Look, I could have done this the easy way, but I didn't. I came here to tell you face to face. I know you're angry and upset – you have every right to be. But it shouldn't come as a surprise that I want a divorce. I've made it perfectly clear that our marriage is over.'

'GET OUT!' she howled, lunging at him, but he had already opened the front door and was down the shallow steps in an instant. Hurrying towards his car, he turned briefly. 'I'll be back in touch when you've calmed down', was his parting shot.

'You smug, self-centred FUCKER,' she screamed after the retreating Audi. 'I'll NEVER give you a divorce! Your baby can be a BASTARD – *JUST LIKE ITS FATHER*!' Then she slammed the door and collapsed on to her knees on the unforgiving hardwood floor, years of bottled-up grief and rage wracking her body.

'... and it's a wonder the neighbours didn't call the police,' she sniffed, half-laughing through her tears. Morven, sitting beside her, made a sympathetic face and hugged her closer.

Layla's friend had dropped everything when she'd received the almost unintelligible call that morning. Within half an hour, she had arrived on the doorstep, armed with two large take-out coffees and a bag of salted-toffee muffins. 'Emergency comfort food,' she'd announced, laying her purchases on the kitchen table and enveloping Layla in a big, soft hug.

'But what about the kids?' a raw-eyed Layla had croaked when she eventually pulled away. 'I'm so sorry for spoiling your Saturday.'

'Don't worry, it's absolutely fine. Davy will take them out for a pizza and then to the cinema. They'll be happy to have him to themselves, for a change,' Morven had smiled, dimples forming in her rosy cheeks. Layla, feeling a rush of gratitude, had once again dissolved into tears.

'I feel so humiliated. I really thought he'd come to ask me to take him back,' she said now, her grief momentarily spent. They were still in the kitchen, empty coffee cups and half-eaten muffins on the table before them.

'Of course you feel humiliated; who wouldn't?' her friend soothed. 'How could he have told you in such an unfeeling way? Did he expect you to be happy for them?'

'Typical Calum: he hasn't a shred of empathy,' Layla replied. She felt exhausted, despite the hefty dose of caffeine.

'And you're one of the most intuitive people I know,' marvelled Morven. 'How did that work out for you both?'

'Well... we loved each other... we made each other laugh... we were good friends. Those things were important to me.'

'And so was having a baby, but you had to hide that from him, didn't you?'

Layla shrugged miserably. 'When I started feeling broody, in my early thirties, I did hide it, because I knew he wasn't ready. But when I tried to talk to him about it last year – we were both thirty-six, for goodness' sake – he didn't want to know.'

'What a bastard,' muttered her friend. 'No wonder you're in bits now.'

The ache in Layla's chest was becoming almost too much to bear. Tears coursed down her face and her friend hugged her close.

'I thought nothing could be worse than Calum leaving me,' she wailed into Morven's shoulder. 'But that cheap little bitch having his baby? It's intolerable!'

'I know, honey, I know.' After gently rocking her for a while, the younger woman said: 'You know what you need to do, Layla? You need to get away from this mess for a while. Take a holiday. You haven't had a break in months.'

Pulling away, Layla fished for a tissue and blew her nose. An outrageous idea was starting to take shape. 'Ye-es – actually, I'm planning to, she said eventually.

'Oh, that's right! You're going to visit your folks soon, aren't you? Christmas in California will be lovely: a complete escape from real life.'

Layla looked at her friend blankly. 'What? Oh, yeah – it can't come soon enough,' she muttered.

The escape she was thinking about was far more radical.

'That's marvellous news, Layla; I'm so glad I haven't scared you off.'

Blunstone's voice was warm and reassuring. She relaxed a little and said into the phone: 'So what happens next?'

'Well, I'm afraid I'm going to have to ask you to bear with me for a few weeks,' he replied. 'The other research subject I had in mind has backed out due to illness in the family. Such a pity, as she and you would have got on so well. Now I need to recruit someone else and that might take a little while.'

'Oh, I see.' Layla felt utterly deflated. It had taken all her courage to make the call.

'Don't worry; I'm planning to advertise again right away. I'm sure another suitable candidate will come forward soon!'

Was his voice a little too hearty?

'Okay, well, I'm going to be out of the country, anyway, for the next two weeks,' she said, trying to sound equally upbeat.

'Going anywhere nice?'

'California – for a long overdue family visit.'

'How wonderful! Well, have a lovely, relaxing break and I'll be back in touch as soon as I can in the new year.'

And that was it.

Despite the turn of events that had tipped the scales in favour of "option c", she had forced herself to wait a couple of days before contacting the professor, wanting to make the decision with a clearer head. But her mind was already made up. She had nothing left to lose.

And now the project was seemingly still a mere concept, hovering tantalisingly just beyond reach.

Did he really have to find a new subject, or was it all part of his convoluted recruitment plan to make sure she was not only ready, but hungry, to take part? Whatever the truth of the matter, he was the one in control and she would simply have to wait.

In the meantime, at least she could find temporary respite with her family, more than five thousand miles away from her fragmented existence in Aberdeen.

Chapter 16
Early January: Santa Barbara, USA

'I don't know what you ever saw in that man. You wasted thirteen years of your life with him, when you could have been over here with us, living the dream.'

Morag McIver raised her sunglasses and looked sharply at her daughter, who sat next to her on the deck, enjoying the balmy warmth of the Santa Barbara winter sunshine.

'Mum,' Layla sighed, closing her Kindle. 'Not this again. We've been through it already. I hear what you're saying, but I had a choice and I chose to stay in Scotland, to make a life with Calum. I don't regret all those years we had together; we had a good marriage!'

'Nonsense! You've been unhappy for ages, and don't try to tell me otherwise.'

'Only latterly,' she mumbled, feeling the familiar prickle of tears.

Seeing her distress, her mother softened her tone. 'It's not too late, my pet. There's still time to meet someone else and have those children you've always wanted.'

'Where and when, exactly?' Layla burst out. 'I don't go anywhere to meet anyone! At my age, it's practically impossible to meet an unattached man, other than over the internet – and I'm not that desperate yet!'

Morag looked horrified. 'I should think not! You could fall prey to a serial killer... No, don't look at me like that – it has happened, you know.'

Exasperated, the younger woman had to laugh. 'You've been reading too many crime thrillers.'

'And who recommended them?'

Mother and daughter smiled at each other, tension gone. They knew how to push each other's buttons, and how to make amends.

After a pause, Morag said tentatively: 'Daddy and I are wondering... how about staying on here a little longer this time? Get some roses back into your cheeks and some meat on your bones – you're looking much too thin and peaky. Maybe even meet a nice man...'

'Mother!'

'Okay, okay – the last bit was wishful thinking, but I mean it about staying on. You need the rest and the change of scene.'

Layla was silent for a moment. It was a tempting offer. She had enjoyed every moment of the past week-and-a-half. The small, gated community her parents lived in was quiet and beautifully kept, and the neighbours had welcomed her back with genuine warmth, including her in festive brunches and barbecues. She had watched college football with her sports-mad father; shopped with her mother in the colourful, Spanish-styled downtown; admired the pelicans diving off East Beach, and walked for miles along the palm-lined Cabrillo Boulevard, dodging gorgeously-tanned joggers, skateboarders and rollerbladers gliding along with pushchairs and panting dogs. On Christmas Day, her beaming brother, sister-in-law, nephew and niece had arrived laden with goodies and she had relished the noise and hilarity that had resounded throughout the red-pantile villa over the next few days.

The Californian sun had warmed her bones and her family's love had helped to ground her, restoring her sense of self.

It would be so easy to stay on. She knew she could wangle another couple of weeks of holiday leave if she wanted. Despite all the rest and good food, she still lacked energy and felt oddly shaky at times. Yet, she said to her mother: 'Aw, that's lovely of you both to ask, but I really do have to leave at the end of this week... I-I have an interesting project to get my teeth into this year.'

Seeing the spark of interest in her mother's eyes, she was quick to add: 'No, I'm not ready to share just yet. All will be revealed in good time.'

She felt deeply guilty about what she was planning to do, knowing her parents would be horrified and would try to stop her – if they ever reached the stage of believing her.

But what they didn't know wouldn't worry them.

Morag sniffed huffily and picked up her paperback. 'Well, as long as whatever it is takes you out of yourself, because that's just what you need.'

Mum, you have no idea, thought Layla.

Chapter 17
Early January: Cairnacraig House
James

From: James Blunstone
To: Stevie Nightingale
Subject: RE: My role in your "body-swap" study
Sent: ... 09:51

Dear Ms Nightingale,
I thought I made it clear at our last meeting, in December, that
for various reasons I did not think you would be a suitable
research subject for the above study.
I have not changed my mind about this.
I urge you to accept and respect my decision, and to refrain from
contacting me again.
Yours sincerely
Professor James Blunstone MBBS (Hons), MSc, MD
(Neurosurgery), FRCSI, FRCS (Neuro.Surg)

From: Stevie Nightingale
To: James Blunstone
Subject: RE: RE: My role in your "body-swap" study
Sent: ... 10:00
Nice try, Prof – but I don't accept or respect your decision. I know
too much about your "study" for you to give me the brush-off.
Let's meet up for another cosy chat, when we can discuss terms
and conditions.
Stevie x
Stevie Nightingale
Freelance Journalist

James Blunstone sat at his desk, his head in his hands. He had no choice but to offer her the job.

Chapter 18
Mid-January: The University
Layla

The phone call came sooner than Layla expected.

She had returned to work following her restorative holiday, determined to proceed with the project. Her distress over Calum's double betrayal still burned and tormented her, and she knew it would drag her down into a very dark place if she didn't regain control and try to bring new purpose to her life.

Keen to do something constructive while she waited for Blunstone to contact her, she had sounded-out her head of school about a possible three-month sabbatical that year. As she had anticipated, Professor Bruce Black – a quiet, well-respected academic in his late-fifties – had been supportive. 'I think it might be just what you need,' he had said, smiling at her over the rims of his half-moon glasses. 'You did more than your required quota of teaching last year, when you filled-in during Robert's long-term sick leave. A sabbatical will give you the chance to regroup and to weave all those interesting thoughts and ideas that I know you have into coherent theories. Just keep me posted, so that I can find a stand-in in plenty of time.'

A week later, when her desk phone rang during her lunch break, Layla sighed in exasperation. It had been a morning of interruptions and distractions, and all she wanted was half an hour to enjoy her egg salad sandwich in peace. But she picked up, all the same – and was surprised to hear the professor's cheerful voice.

'Happy New Year, Layla! I hope you had a lovely holiday with your family?'

She managed to respond sensibly enough and, after a couple of minutes of chat about the festive season – he had spent his in Edinburgh with two old friends – he said, in an even heartier tone: 'Well, I'm very pleased to tell you that the original research subject who stepped down has now changed her mind and is going to be participating in the project after all!'

'But what about the family illness...?' Layla's heart rate had increased.

'Yes, well, it turned out not to be the serious diagnosis they had anticipated, so all can go ahead as planned.'

'Oh, okay... that's good news, I think!'

'You haven't changed your mind, I hope?' His voice faltered a little.

'No... but there are lots of things I would like to know before I commit myself.'

'Of course there are!' the almost-false heartiness was back. 'That's why I'd like to propose an informal get-together for the three of us, so that we can address all the questions and issues and allow you both to make a final decision.'

Without waiting for a response, he continued: 'We'll need a good bit of time for this, so how about spending a weekend as my house guest? I have plenty of space and I'm sure you'll enjoy the surroundings. I think I've mentioned already that I live on a country estate? It's very quiet and peaceful.'

'When – oh *shit*!' She had sloshed tea on to her desk. She leapt to her feet, grabbed tissues from her drawer and started to mop up.

'Er, Layla?'

'Sorry! I've just had a spill here... When would you like this meeting to take place?' She dabbed angrily at her beige trousers, which had fallen casualty to her carelessness.

'Oh dear! Ah, well, the other research subject won't be available until early March, I'm afraid. She is relocating from overseas.'

'Do I get to ask where from, and – more to the point – who she is?'

'I'd really rather not divulge that information at the moment. I know you would be straight on to the internet to research her, and I would like you both to meet without having any preconceived ideas about each other.'

'More cloak-and-dagger stuff!' she said tartly.

'Afraid so. Can you bear with me for just a few more weeks?'

She sighed and sat down, her legs shaky. 'I guess so. Is there anything I can be doing in the meantime, Professor? By way of preparation, I mean?'

'Not really, but I'm sure you'll still have a lot of thinking to do and questions to formulate,' he said lightly. 'Now, let's pencil in a date for our March weekend get-together...'

Chapter 19
March: Buchan Coast

'You may or may not know that Slains Castle was one of the inspirations for Bram Stoker's *Dracula*,' James Blunstone said loudly, his words instantly whipped away by the gusty wind that had greeted them on arrival at Cruden Bay.

After tramping through a small patch of native woodland and a gully overshadowed by red granite rocks, where the track ran parallel with a fast-flowing stream, the professor, Layla and Stevie had emerged into flat, open countryside. Now they were walking a straight path – bordered by fields on the left and by the rough ground of unprotected clifftops on the right – heading towards an impressive, sprawling ruin which dominated the coastal landscape. At James's side trotted a panting black Labrador: a surprise companion they'd picked up en route.

'I must just stop here to collect my dog,' he had told them, steering his Aston Martin – the top up today – off the main road and down a farm track. Stevie, who was sitting in the back, let out a shriek. 'What? You have a *DOG*?' Surprised, Layla turned around in time to glimpse a fleeting expression that held both fury and fear before it was quickly replaced by an insincere grin. As she turned back, their host had said quietly: 'Don't you like dogs, Stevie?'

'Got bitten by one when I was a kid... but I'm more of a cat person, anyway,' the Australian had replied grumpily. That certainly hadn't come as a surprise to Layla, who had said to Blunstone: 'I love dogs! I didn't realise you had one. What kind is it?'

'Buller is a black Lab. He's been on his holidays,' he'd smiled, pulling up outside a converted farm steading and prompting a cacophony of barking from inside. 'I was visiting my friends in Edinburgh this week and didn't get back until just before you arrived yesterday afternoon. When I'm away, Buller boards here with his two brothers, Bo and Brad.' Opening the car door, he'd said: 'I'll just nip in to fetch him, as we'll need all our time.'

The professor was greeted at the door by a casually-dressed woman, who'd peered over his shoulder and given a friendly wave to Layla and Stevie. Then they'd disappeared inside.

'What kind of a name is *Buller*?' Stevie had muttered sulkily. Without turning, Layla said mildly: 'It'll be after the Bullers of Buchan – you know, the cliffs we're going to be visiting this afternoon. I've heard they're amazing.'

When Stevie didn't answer, she'd added: 'Look, I can swap seats with you, if you don't want to sit next to the dog.'

The woman had sighed heavily and said: 'OK, thanks. I really don't fancy being slobbered over by a great big brute.'

Now, on their way to Slains Castle, Layla and Buller were already the best of friends, the dog trotting between her and Blunstone and occasionally looking up at her as if delighted by the extra company. He and Stevie, however, had avoided each other on sight.

'I didn't know that – how marvellous,' the Australian replied to Blunstone's remark with what appeared to be genuine enthusiasm. 'Did Stoker live here?'

'Eventually; he was a regular holiday visitor to this area for many years before retiring to nearby Whinnyfold. Several of his other books were also inspired by the Buchan coastal environment.' He looked sideways at Layla. 'Have you been here before?' he asked.

She shook her head, her brown curls flying around her face in the turbulent air. 'I'm ashamed to say I haven't,' she cried. 'What a fantastic place!'

Heavy black clouds had bowled in from over the sea, providing a suitably sinister backdrop to the ruin. The damp air was full of the screams of herring gulls and kittiwakes as they rose and swooped above the invisible water far below.

'I hope the rain stays off, as there's no shelter out here,' said Blunstone, quickening his steps. This encouraged Buller to bound ahead, but a sharp rebuke from his master soon brought him back to heel. 'We'll need to keep him close,' the professor announced, snapping on a short lead. 'These cliffs are treacherous.'

'Oh yeah?' sneered Stevie. 'I can't see much evidence of that so far!'

The man eyed her coolly. 'Just wait,' he said shortly.

Soon, they reached the castle, which Layla could now see stood sentinel above a steep grassy slope. Beyond it, layered slabs of granite formed a jagged cliff edge that sheared steeply down hundreds of feet, into the churning grey sea.

'Absolutely spectacular!' she shouted, peering downwards and then across at giant rock formations which rose from the ocean like megalithic monsters.

'Isn't it just! Those great brutes are the Scaurs of Cruden,' James said loudly at her side. 'According to local folklore, during a full moon, at the Lammas tide – that's in August – people with "the sight" may witness the rising of all those mariners who lost their lives on the reef during the preceding twelve months. And in days gone by, between fishermen and smugglers, that could have meant many poor souls. Bram Stoker referred to just such a ghostly procession making its way back to the cliffs, in his novel, *The Mystery of the Sea*. They were on their way to St Olave's Well, to be directed to either heaven or hell.'

'Wow, how atmospheric!' she laughed, thrilled by both the story and the natural wonder that lay before her.

The rocks, streaked white with guano, were noisily populated by thousands of seabirds, balancing and jostling for position on the narrow ledges that jutted all the way up from sea level to peak. Further out, on smaller outcrops, she spotted colonies of cormorants, their heraldic wings held proudly aloft.

Seeing her delight, the professor added: 'At this time of year, apart from the ever-present gulls, we have eiders, cormorants, fulmars, razorbills and guillemots all nesting and displaying – and next month, the puffins will return to add a touch of colour and comedy!'

Layla smiled and turned to see Stevie examining a nearby fence post, which was covered in bunches of dead flowers. As she joined her, she realised it was a small shrine. Pinned to the post and flapping in the wind was a plastic-wrapped sheet of paper carrying a photograph of a long-haired teenage girl and a sad caption obliquely referring to her death at the site.

'Did she jump, or was she pushed?' mused Stevie.

'Or was it simply an accident?' said Blunstone briskly, coming up behind them. 'This is a notorious place for both accidents and suicides. I believe this poor girl was fooling around with some friends, when she slipped and fell off the cliff. Such a terrible waste of a young life.'

Layla's heart clenched as she imagined the horror of the scene: the shocked, bone-white faces of the girl's friends; the frantic rush back to the village; the suffocating dread of having to break the news and bear the brunt of adult grief and censure.

'Why are these cliffs so easy to access?' she asked, having noticed several people – visitors like themselves –

picking their way across the uneven ground, precariously close to the edge. The professor made a face. 'You can't fence-off an entire coastline. You have to rely on folk being sensible and looking after themselves. Unfortunately, young people are attracted to all kinds of dangerous places, fenced-off or otherwise.'

Layla sighed, bent down to pat a patient Buller, and turned towards the ruined granite edifice.

Stevie said: 'What's the story with this place, then? It doesn't look much like a castle to me.'

Blunstone turned to face the building. 'Believe it or not, this is actually New Slains Castle; the last remnants of the original, thirteenth-century fortress lie nearer Collieston, further up the coast. New Slains was built by the ninth Earl of Erroll in the late fifteen-nineties, but various extensions were added over the centuries, which accounts for its half-manor house, half-castle appearance.'

He began walking, the women and dog following suit, as he continued: 'Dr Johnson and the ever-patient Boswell stayed here as part of their Scottish tour, in August 1773. Boswell gives a marvellous insight into the house and family of the time in his *Journal of a Tour to the Hebrides*. I can show you a copy when we get back.'

'You'd make an excellent tourist guide,' Layla told him, as they headed through an open archway into the great roofless ruin.

'Thank you,' he smiled. 'I'm very passionate about this area, but unfortunately, it's rather a hidden gem, overlooked by tourists and locals alike.' He stopped to allow Buller to sniff at a dense patch of nettles. Nature had long since carpeted the flagstones with tussocks of grass and weeds, and the group had to negotiate around muddy puddles as they wandered through the damp, crumbling brick ruins of formerly grand rooms. Despite being open to the elements, the interior was gloomy, courtesy of the lowering March skies.

'Spooky, eh?' said Stevie with a wicked grin. 'This would make a great setting for a Halloween party. I must bring your body back here again, Layla – maybe in the dark!'

Layla suppressed a shiver at the sinister remark but pretended to take it as a joke. How odd it sounded, particularly in this place. She couldn't help wondering what Bram Stoker would have made of the bizarre pact the three of them were hovering on the brink of. Something ghastly, without a doubt.

'I'm going outside again,' she announced, foregoing the chance to climb up to the floor above, where loud, echoing laughter told her another group of visitors had already gathered.

She wandered out through the open far end, glad to be free of the dank, dingy building which, to her, held the despairing atmosphere of an ancient prison.

Looking north, she marvelled at the scene before her: the rugged cliffs zig-zagging up the coast; the whipped-up sea a restless palette of greys and greens, and above it all, the moody, hovering storm clouds which in the city would have seemed oppressive but were so fitting in such a desolate setting.

Standing amid the tangled undergrowth, relishing the invigorating North Sea ozone, she reflected on her first morning at Cairnacraig House.

Chapter 20
March: Cairnacraig House

She wakened early, the room still dark, the house silent. Her mind was tangled with fleeting memories of the kaleidoscopic dreams that had twisted through her sleep. They hadn't been nightmares, as such – more exaggerated highlights from the previous day – but they'd been accompanied by an underlying uneasiness which still lingered.

Activating her phone, she saw it was only six am. She was just wondering if it was too early to rise when she heard muffled noises from the next room. A few minutes later, a door closed and there was the sound of footsteps galloping down the stairs. Stevie, on her first run of the day, no doubt. Layla sighed at the thought of having to adopt such an energetic routine after a lifetime of refusing to join the jogging brigade, despite the number of unlikely friends and colleagues who had surprised her by signing up for fun-runs and even marathons, over the years. *Well, I won't do it if I can possibly get off with it*, she thought defiantly. Then she realised she was thinking about the body swap as if it were a *fait accompli*.

Wasn't it, though? Wasn't she kidding herself by believing she still had a choice in the matter?

Unable to lie still any longer, despite the warm comfort of her bed, she decided to get up and have a shower. Annoyingly, her limbs felt stiff, and she all but staggered into the en-suite, hoping the hot water would soothe away both her physical and mental discomfort.

For all its hard surfaces and sharp, contemporary lines, the kitchen was cosy, thanks to the slim vertical radiators that were already pumping out heat. Having made herself a mug of tea, Layla, now dressed in jeans, ankle boots and a pale blue cable-knit sweater, decided to stay for a while. She settled herself in the comfy red leather recliner that faced the curtain wall and gazed out upon the apricot-tinged garden, heavy with dew, where the long shadows of shrubs and trees gradually shortened as the peaceful scene brightened into daylight.

'Good morning, Layla!'

The professor's cheerful greeting from behind her almost made her spill her tea. Carefully swivelling around, she smiled up at him and made as if to rise.

'Don't get up; I'm the self-appointed breakfast chef today,' he said, rolling up the sleeves of his shirt – a denim Oxford – and donning a red plastic apron he'd grabbed from a nearby hook.

An hour later, the three of them were sitting at the central counter, finishing off a breakfast of scrambled eggs on toast. Layla had been unable to eat all of her huge helping, but Stevie had fairly shovelled hers in, announcing that she was 'starving' after 'a ripper run around the estate'.

Still haunted by faint echoes of her dreams, Layla dabbed her mouth with a paper napkin and turned to Blunstone. 'I've been wondering about something the two ladies touched on in your DVD,' she began.

A flash of wariness crossed his face, quickly replaced by a questioning look.

'You asked them to record what they remembered about their dreams on the night of their operations. Each of them seemed puzzled by what they had dreamt so vividly. Were they dreaming each other's dreams, do you think?'

The professor coughed and pushed away his empty plate.

'Good question,' he said. 'I did wonder that myself... whether some residual part of their consciousness – or sub-consciousness, rather – had remained in their own brains after their me-glands were exchanged. But when I asked each of them afterwards about the subject matter the other had described, neither of them recognised the characters concerned – the dead child, and the abusive man, if you remember. And so I dismissed the idea.'

Layla nodded slowly. 'Good... because that particular scenario would complicate things far too much. Imagine "inheriting" someone else's subconscious!'

Stevie made a mocking face across the counter. 'Yeah, imagine what deep, dark secrets would be revealed...'

'Indeed,' Blunstone cut in, smoothly changing the subject. 'Now, although it's a lovely spring morning again, the weather is set to change late afternoon. How do you fancy a bracing tour of the Buchan coastline? We could pack a picnic lunch and round off with an early supper in my favourite hotel at Cruden Bay.'

'Sounds good to me,' was Stevie's reply, while Layla nodded enthusiastically, swallowing the last of her tea.

'Right you are.' He looked at his watch. 'Let's aim to leave around eleven. I'd like a quick scan of the morning papers before we set off.'

'And I'm going for a shower,' Stevie said, slipping from her stool and leaving the room.

'I'll do the picnic, then,' offered Layla. She had spotted a packet of cheese-and-onion pasties in the fridge and was sure she could pull together some other bits and pieces for lunch. 'I take it there's a thermos around here somewhere...'

Chapter 21
March: Buchan Coast

They had eaten their packed lunch, all of them well wrapped in weatherproof jackets, scarves and beanies, at a picnic bench on the Forvie National Nature Reserve, where both Layla and Stevie had marvelled at the wild and beautiful landscape. The River Ythan estuary was shriekingly alive with myriad flocks of seabirds, and the reserve's colossal sand dunes bristled with gorse and spiky marram grass.

After hiking one of the shorter trails with an ecstatic Buller pounding ahead, they'd returned to the visitor centre car park and driven to nearby Collieston – an attractive heritage fishing village, where small, white seamen's cottages and minimalist modern houses rubbed shoulders all the way up the staggered cliffs that towered above the small working harbour.

Now, having seen Slains Castle, Layla was keen to experience the famous Bullers of Buchan, which lay further up the coast, nearer to the professor's home. She walked quickly back towards the ruin, peering into the dim interior to see where Stevie and Blunstone might be. Hearing angry voices echoing above, she realised with a jolt that they belonged to her weekend companions, who evidently had climbed the crumbling staircase to the first floor.

'You have no choice, and you know it!' Stevie was practically shouting. 'Get used to it, old man.'

Shocked by the woman's venomous words, Layla strained to hear Blunstone's reply, but his voice had dropped and she could only just make out '... more respect...' and '... must understand the implications...' before a yelled 'Whatever!' and the stomp of feet told her Stevie was on her way downstairs. Quickly, she retraced her steps into the overgrown grounds and started sauntering back again, pretending to look at her phone.

'We're going back to the car park,' the Australian announced abruptly from the entrance; then she turned on her heel and disappeared back inside. Following her, Layla met the professor and his dog at the foot of the stairs. His expression was mild enough to make her think momentarily that she'd overheard someone else's conversation, but Stevie's accent had been unmistakable. Flustered, she bent to accept Buller's enthusiastic licks and hugged the dog close. The smell and feel of his briny black fur were comforting in the unsettling circumstances.

Before Blunstone could move away, she stood up and touched his arm. 'Professor – James – I need to know what's going on between you and Stevie,' she said firmly. 'I couldn't help overhearing what sounded like a row just now, and I know the two of you were also arguing yesterday afternoon. I may be about to trust my entire life to this woman, so I think I have the right to know if she means trouble.'

He sighed and looked at the ground. 'I understand your concern,' he said eventually. 'Stevie, as you will no doubt have gathered, is a temperamental and impetuous young woman. She is very keen that I should allow her to share my discovery with the rest of the world rather sooner than I would like. She is a journalist, so I can hardly blame her. Unfortunately, she wants to write a series of newspaper features during the body-swap period.'

Layla felt her stomach lurch. 'But I thought she was planning to write a *book* about the experience – after it's all over,' she cried.

'Yes, yes, she will do that as well.'

'But surely,' Layla continued, 'if you don't agree to participate in the features, she'll have no chance of

119

getting them published? No one will believe her story without your corroboration.'

'And that's why she is so angry with me: I refuse to agree to her proposal. It would be sheer madness to do such a thing!'

Buller, ears flattened at his master's strident tone, let out an impatient whine.

'Poor boy, have you had enough of this damp, depressing place?' Blunstone said to him gently. He turned to Layla, his expression earnest. 'Please don't worry about this. I have no intention of letting Ms Nightingale's tantrums bully me into going public before I'm ready. I sincerely believe she will settle down and realise that it is in all of our interests to keep the project completely private until its conclusion.'

'I hope you're right,' she said unhappily.

'And I don't think you should have any concerns about trusting your body to her,' he continued, *sotto voce*, looking around to ensure no one was nearby. 'Stevie will be feeling equally as nervous about what you will be doing with hers. Both of you have every reason to be careful; it's a very even balance. Now, shall we go?'

'I *hope* you're right,' Layla muttered again, following him outside into the grey and blustery late afternoon.

Stevie hadn't waited for them, but by the time they caught up with her in the car park she was in a different mood altogether.

'All right, guys?' she greeted them brightly. 'Time to move on?'

Layla and the professor exchanged a meaningful glance.

'WOWEEEE!' screamed Stevie into the skirling wind that blasted and buffeted them on the clifftop. She stood, feet planted wide apart, peering down into a deep cauldron of tempestuous seawater that boiled and spumed hundreds of feet below them.

Beside her, Layla was speechless. If the scenery had been sensational at Slains Castle, it was nothing short of superlative at the Bullers of Buchan. They were standing on the grassy lip of The Pot: a massive circular collapsed cavern carved out by eons of relentlessly-pounding waves. Opposite them they could see a huge natural archway which ushered in the stormy sea, whose rumbling roar combined with a cacophony of screeching from the hundreds of birds wheeling and diving in the turbulence below.

She turned to James Blunstone, who stood a few steps behind her, restraining an enthusiastic Buller on a short leash. 'This is amazing!' she yelled. 'I've seen some dramatic natural landmarks in California, but I had no idea we had *this* so close to home!'

He smiled broadly at her, his lean body swaying in the wind. 'That's exactly what I was talking about earlier!' he cried. 'Folk don't know what's on their own doorstep.'

After leaving the car at a roadside carpark, the small party had made their way in single file past quaint clifftop cottages and along the grassy track leading to the Bullers. '"Buller" is derived from "boiler",' Blunstone had explained on the way, 'and you'll soon see why.'

Once again, Layla was struck by how dangerous and unprotected the cliffs were. As they'd passed the cottages, she had wondered if any young families lived there. *Surely not; you couldn't let a child out of your sight around here*, she'd thought.

Now, they continued their precarious walk around the edge of the cauldron until they reached the top of the archway. Layla gasped when she saw the path ahead of her. It was only a few feet wide, with a sheer drop to the sea on either side.

'We're not walking along *there*?' she gasped, sudden vertigo sinking steely claws into her skull.

'Of course not!' laughed the professor, slowing to a halt. 'On a day like this? It would be madness. I have walked it in fine weather, although even then, it's not for the faint-hearted.'

Ignoring his words, Stevie strode on to the narrow path, arms outstretched like a tightrope walker.

'STEVIE, COME BACK!' shrieked Layla, horrified at her recklessness. Beside her, Blunstone roared out furiously.

'Only kidding, guys!' the Australian cried, quickly retracing her steps. 'Even *I* wouldn't be so crazy as to walk along there in this wind.'

Layla's heart was thudding and she started to feel nauseous. Blackness ate at the edges of her vision and she staggered a little, before her right leg gave way completely. She cried out as she felt herself falling sideways... then she was jerked back violently by a strong grip on her arm.

'Christ almighty, girl – what's got into ya?' Stevie's face was blanched with fright. And little wonder, Layla's clouded mind slowly registered: the woman had saved her from falling into the abyss!

'Here, sit down a minute.' Blunstone's voice was full of concern, as he and Stevie helped her to lower herself on to a flattened thatch of wild grass. Instinctively, she put her head down between her knees until she felt the dizziness recede.

'Are you all right, Layla?' the professor asked, crouching beside her, Buller trying desperately to lick her face. 'What on earth happened?'

'Adrenaline surge, I think,' she managed to say. 'I got such a scare that it made me feel faint. And I'm not very good at heights,' she added sheepishly. 'I'm fine now, though.'

She looked up at them both. 'Sorry to give you such a fright. And Stevie... how can I ever thank you?'

'S'alright,' the other woman said soberly. 'I guess I shouldn't have run on to that path.'

The professor nodded grimly and for a moment there was silence, as Layla allowed Buller to head-butt her playfully. Then, slowly, she got to her feet and dusted herself down.

'Did you mention something about an early supper at Cruden Bay?' she asked Blunstone with a forced smile.

'Why, yes,' he said with surprise, clearly relieved at her quick recovery. 'And I think we're more than ready for it now!'

Several hours later, Layla lay in bed in her rosy room, trying unsuccessfully to fall asleep. A hearty meal of battered North Sea haddock for Stevie and James, battered halloumi cheese for her, and a mountain of chips, at Blunstone's – and Bram Stoker's – favourite local hotel had revived them all, but she was paying the price with indigestion.

Worse still, now she was alone, the memory of her near-death experience on the clifftop kept playing on a continuous loop in her mind. She knew she owed Stevie her life: the woman's lightning reaction had saved her from The Pot, whose dangerous attraction had claimed so many lives – deliberately or accidentally – over the centuries. It made her feel dizzy all over again to think about the noisy horror of such a demise, amid the Harpy-

123

like screams of the seabirds and the churning boom of giant waves.

Turning over on to her back, she took a deep, calming breath. It was time to acknowledge what she had repressed all evening while the three of them chatted in the hotel bar. The conversation had been light-hearted – a reaction to their earlier scare – and the research project hadn't even been mentioned. But the dramatic episode at the Bullers had galvanised something in Layla.

It had helped her to finally make up her mind.

'I'm going ahead,' she now whispered to herself. And then she drifted into a deep and, for once, dreamless sleep.

Part Two: Post-op

Chapter 22
April: Cairnacraig House

Layla's Log – Week 2, Monday
Blackbirds sing me awake, their fluty song as familiar as a nursery-rhyme.

I lie, comforted by the ancient melodies dancing from twig to branch in the beech-tree canopy outside. My head is clear now and I know where I am.

It's who I am that might be the problem.

Feeling eyes on me, I turn, slowly, in the starched sheets of my institutional bed. I know I'll never be prepared for what's lying in wait, so I face it head on.

From an identical bed nearby, a dark-haired woman is watching me. My stomach clenches as I recognise her features but her fascinated, almost predatory, expression is unfamiliar.

Is it really you?

I sit up, and as I do so, I see our beds reflected in the ornate cheval glass across the room. I lift my hand – is this my hand? – in a tentative wave and the movement is mirrored by a frightened-looking woman with white-blonde hair.

I gasp. You laugh. Our eyes meet again and the acknowledgement is unspoken.

The experiment has worked – and I am you and what I see is me.

It's a full week since I opened the eyes of my borrowed body and saw "myself" lying in the bed next to me.

James Blunstone has asked us to keep a log. Mine is a concise, deliberately academic account of my

127

experiences, literally as another woman. I'm sharing it with him daily while I'm staying here, at Cairnacraig House, and then it'll be weekly, when I return to the real world next Sunday.

But I'm also writing this more personal "secret journal", and I find myself addressing you, Stevie, because for the next three months I *am* you.

Will those first few "awakening" paragraphs end up as the introduction to my life's work? I hope so, but who knows? Right now, I don't feel certain of anything. This new body of mine is all I can focus on and the future is a fuzzy concept.

I still find it inconceivable that one moment I can be myself, little Layla Sutherland, lulled into unconsciousness by the soothing words of a kindly nurse, and, seemingly the next, awaken in the alien body of the Amazonian Stevie Nightingale!

The first question the professor asked us, of course, was: 'How does it feel?'

How can an experience be both unnatural and normal at the same time? Yet, that's how it feels. You are the only other person on Earth who understands this. Isn't that mind-blowing?

Sceptics – and I'm thinking of some of my colleagues – would argue that the tiny glands transposed between our brains, though undoubtedly our physical "seats of consciousness", have yet to be proven to be the receptors of spiritual consciousness that James Blunstone believes they are. It remains a matter of faith, and each of us has our own beliefs. You, I know, prefer not to 'waste time' speculating. You are a person who lives in the moment, in the material world.

And me? I'm with the professor on this. Intuitively, I now believe that Descartes' concept of the 'ghost in the machine' is correct: that our physical bodies are inhabited by non-material souls.

But back to the practicalities, or else I'll disappear down the rabbit hole!

Learning to live in someone else's body is a frustrating and humbling experience. For me, the initial shock and wonder of discovering that the operation was a success were quickly superseded by a roiling wave of dizziness and nausea.

You told me – *in my voice* – to lie back down, that you'd experienced the same feeling a few minutes earlier, and that it would soon wear off.

'Isn't this a blast?' you added, resting on your elbow and grinning across at me, for all the world like some excited teen on her first sleepover. 'Everything about me is tiny! I have the dinkiest hands now.'

In dull response, I lifted "my" hands again, marvelling at the length of the fingers and absurdly irritated by the ragged cuticles and unkempt nails. Arms outstretched above me, like a baby asking to be lifted from its crib, I lay and gazed for a moment at the jutting wrist bones and at the unfamiliar patterns of moles dotting my forearms. I felt heavy and stupid; like a modern-day Frankenstein's monster with so many basic lessons to learn – or, rather, re-learn – about how to move and behave. It all seemed too much. Wearily, I let my arms fall, shut my eyes, and allowed tears of self-pity to run down my face.

But after a minute or two, curiosity won through, and I opened my eyes again.

'Got over yourself, have you?' you said, sardonically. 'Hey, don't look so glum! Millions of women would kill to have my body, and don't you forget it.'

The preposterousness of your statement – of the whole situation – made me laugh, in your loud, braying style (which made me laugh even more) and after a beat, you

129

joined in. And that's how Nurse Murray found us when she bustled into the room a few minutes later: two patients lying prostrate, helpless with laughter, in the starched, clinical surroundings of a home-made hospital wing.

There were many similar bouts of laughter and, on my part, lots of tears, in those first few hours following the operation.

With only a small dressing covering the shaved, surgical point of entry at the base of our skulls, the immediate post-operative phase was more a case of recovering from the anaesthetic than dealing with the localised pain, which was easily controlled with medication. And so, as with Patients C and D in the video, it wasn't long before we were up and tentatively negotiating the ward with the help of walking frames and the infinitely-patient Nurse Murray (that woman is a saint!).

Just like C and D, we found that the unwieldiness of our new limbs started to wear off very quickly. My Frankenstein's monster fears soon subsided as I realised that our new bodies' muscle memory had kicked in, just as the professor said it would, enabling both of us to move around almost automatically. After all, as the man himself pointed out when he arrived, beaming, to inspect his two latest guinea pigs: 'you must remember that, in physical terms, your me-gland is only a minute element of your host brain, which has been running your host body successfully for thirty-eight years.'

No, our biggest challenge was not so much physical as psychological.

Chapter 23

Anyone reading yesterday's entry might be astonished that I focused so much on my physical feelings after coming round from the operation.

'But how about *emotionally*?' they might ask. 'What goes through your mind when you wake up to discover you're now living in someone else's body?'

Eight days on, I'm just about ready to answer that question.

The truth is that I, a professional philosopher, have not yet allowed myself to confront the full reality of living through one of the most profound experiences imaginable.

Denial is an incredibly powerful defence mechanism, and it's one I've relied on once or twice in the past. Yesterday, I mentioned my fear of disappearing down the rabbit hole. I was talking, of course, about madness, and that's what I've been struggling against ever since I regained consciousness that nightmarish morning.

But I also know that the protective bubble of denial, in distorting the reality beyond, is a kind of madness in itself. The longer I rely on it, the greater the danger of trapping myself within it – and if I don't break through the membrane, I might as well call myself "Alice" and be done with it!

Does this sound melodramatic, Stevie? From your own reaction to our new circumstances, I suspect that it might.

Okay, I've waffled on long enough. It's time to revisit those initial emotions.

My tears of self-pity were nothing compared to the meltdown I had when I got out of bed for the first time.

I had just watched Nurse Murray help you walk to the en-suite. I was amazed at how quickly you'd managed to get going, and it spurred me on to rise, too.

'I want to look at myself close up,' I told the nurse firmly, as she shut the door behind you. Raising her eyebrows, she got me to my feet and patiently waited until I was ready to use the walking frame.

'Now, be warned, dear,' she advised in her genteel Edinburgh accent, as, shakily, I shuffled across to the large, freestanding mirror. 'It's going to take some time to get used to seeing yourself as you now are.'

I was amazed at the calm way she seemed to accept the reality of our circumstances. Of course, she'd been through it twice before, but at what point does it become normal to nurse patients who have exchanged bodies?

Because I was concentrating so much on moving one foot in front of the other, I had my head down as I approached the mirror. Reaching it, I looked up and saw... you.

Well, duh, I hear you say. But even though I knew what to expect, and despite the fact that we'd already seen ourselves in the cheval after coming round from the anaesthetic, it was still shocking to view my new persona close-up. Earlier, with two across-the-room reflections to process, our brains had probably compensated by dismissing the body swap as an optical illusion. Now, seeing only your figure in the frame, I had the strangest experience: it seemed to me that I was wearing a Stevie rubber costume. Yet, moving closer and examining the face, I could see it was made of real flesh. It was familiar, and it was coldly beautiful; but it was horrifying, because it wasn't me!

Heart pounding, I saw fear ignite in your green, looking-glass eyes as I searched them for myself. Aren't the eyes the window on the soul? There was no sign of *my* soul.

132

Where was I? Anxiety spiked in my stomach and a slow feeling of unreality washed over me. *Panic attack,* I thought. *Breathe,* I told myself. I gripped the walking frame as if my life depended on it, and, seeing my distress, the nurse put her arm around me and helped me back to the safety of the bed. I sat there, sobbing, grieving for the apparent loss of my own identity.

Then I saw you in the en-suite doorway, wearing a 'WTF?' expression on *my* face.

'How come *you're* not having hysterics?' I screamed at you. 'Don't tell me you didn't look at yourself in the mirror in there!' Then I turned to Nurse Murray and howled: 'This is a horror film come to life! I hate it! I want to swap back... I want to go home!'

Thinking about it now, I'm ashamed of my childish outburst. I'd believed that I was the mature one who'd thought everything through beforehand and prepared myself for the experience. But you're the one who's coped marvellously, right from the start. I can't say I like you, Stevie, but I do admire your ability to adapt so quickly to your circumstances, however bizarre they are.

Just over a week on, the horror and angst are still hovering in the background, but I've learned how to keep them at bay. James tells me I've suffered more, psychologically, because I have a highly-sensitive and imaginative nature, whereas you are much more pragmatic. I suppose he's right. Of course, he'd heard about my "episode" from Nurse Murray and had wisely waited until I'd calmed down before putting in an appearance. 'The secret,' he told me quietly, while you chatted to the nurse, 'is not to overthink. At this early stage, let your body lead you and focus your mind on the task in hand, rather than on the hand that's doing the task!' He grinned as he said this, and while I was hardly in a state to appreciate his wit, I could see the sense in his words.

And it does work. It's denial in practice. As long as I concentrate on what I'm doing – truly live in the moment – I can forget the fear. But as soon as I start thinking about my situation, about occupying this new body and how different it is from my own, the anxiety creeps up on me and I have the urge to escape.

Escape! That's hilarious. Where could I go?

Even in sleep, I can't get away from the weirdness. Thankfully, unlike mine, your body has the ability to sleep deeply and sleep well. But during that downtime, my subconscious goes into overdrive, creating the most vivid dreams I've ever experienced. Nightmarish and haunted by ghoulish characters who chase me through the darkness, they're the visions of Victorian opium addicts. You, on the other hand, say you never remember your dreams, but you do complain of restlessness and of constantly waking throughout the night. Well, Stevie, as Patient C said in the video: 'Welcome to my world!'

Writing down your thoughts is meant to be therapeutic, and it always has been for me. But today's session is taking its toll (my heart is racing, a preamble to panic), and I need to sign off. I think I've made some progress, though, and hopefully, for the sake of my book-to-be, I'll be able to reflect more deeply on the situation as time goes on.

For now, it'll be less frightening – although no less uncomfortable – to describe the physical aspects of getting to grips with a new body.

Chapter 24

Layla's Log – Week 2, Wednesday

You're fascinated with my body; you won't stop commenting on how tiny everything is. And it's incredible how shy I am about yours. It's golden and glorious, but I still can hardly bear to see it naked. As for bodily functions... let's just say they're taking a bit of getting used to!

The enforced intimacy is almost unbearable. I felt invaded when you asked me how heavy and painful my period gets; what kind of contraception I use, and whether my apparently 'low' sex drive is normal. I know I'm shy and inhibited – I'm from Scotland, after all – but I find your complete lack of embarrassment astonishing. I haven't felt so targeted or inadequate since I was at secondary school.

On a more positive note, even at this early stage, I find your energy levels exhilarating. Your body is glowing with good health and I can already tell that I'll need to give in to its demands for regular exercise. But if that includes the kind of casual sex you've told me you often indulge in, I'm afraid it'll be sorely disappointed. You might be shamelessly promiscuous, but I certainly am not.

The downside is, of course, that you're not happy about my body's lack of vigour and the fact that it's so easily tired, but I know you'll have plans to get it into shape. Thankfully, we've been forbidden to do anything more taxing than walking around the grounds for now, because I'm sure you'd make much more of a fuss if you tried to go jogging.

That's a showdown for later, I guess.

Chapter 25

Layla's Log – Week 2, Thursday

Back to the privacy issue: we are, of course, being closely monitored by Nurse Murray and the professor, who is quite obviously on a high. His constant filming and endless, enthusiastic questions at all hours about all sorts of things began to seriously grate on me after a couple of days, and I had to insist that we establish some sort of structure that would accommodate his research and also allow us some "me-time". He agreed, and so now we spend the mornings with him, while the afternoons are our own. We meet up again at mealtimes, the food cooked and served by Nurse Murray, who has replaced Mrs Brodie on housekeeping duties for the two weeks of our stay. 'I told Mrs B to take a well-earned holiday; gossip in the village is the last thing we need,' James told us the day before the operation. Cue visions of an angry mob storming the gates with flaming torches!

Our morning sessions are tiring, but I'm finding them interesting, now that we're sticking to a manageable routine. In the run-up to the operation, James asked us to fill out a comprehensive questionnaire, asking us for a motley collection of details from various times in our lives. These included: our most vivid childhood memories; awards and achievements; aspects of family history; favourite songs, and even former neighbours' names. We also had to complete a general knowledge quiz and an IQ test (needless to say, you scored higher than me).

Anyway, for the first couple of days following the body swap, he kept taking each of us aside, wanting to check whether we had retained all those recorded memories and bits of knowledge, as well as our intellectual ability. Hence the million and one questions that irritated me so much. I'm relieved to say that we passed with flying colours.

Next, James asked us about people, places and experiences we weren't familiar with, but which were in fact details from each other's lives. This was to check whether our host brains had retained any residual memories and knowledge (ghosts of a ghost in a machine!). Again, it was a relief to find that they didn't appear to have done so.

I suppose it shouldn't have come as a surprise that our conscious selves had survived the swap intact: the professor's previous experiments had proved that they would. Also, from all the reading I've done on the little scientists actually know about consciousness, it's generally agreed that conscious experience is an integrated phenomenon and not something that can be broken down into segments. But, all the same, I'm glad not to have bucked the trend.

As I'd envisaged during my first visit here, I spend much of my spare time reading books or writing my journals on the comfy window seats in my room and in the library, or rugged-up in the walled garden. April has come in like a lamb, although the daytime temperatures are still cool. Even on my most angst-ridden afternoons, I'm cheered by the beauty of the birdsong and the vibrantly colourful flowers, shrubs, and trees that surround me. The sheer optimism of spring is helping me through this strangest of times.

But there's always trouble in paradise, isn't there? And I think I came face-to-face with it today.

It was after breakfast and I was sitting, as usual, on my favourite seat in the walled garden. I didn't hear him approach; it was his shadow looming over me that caused me to look up from my Kindle. I got such a fright when I saw the burly stranger standing just a couple of feet away, his back to the sun, his face obscured.

'Oh- hi,' I said, feeling vulnerable in my new body. 'Can I help you?'

But he just stood there, looking down at me. I got to my feet and the fleece blanket fell to the ground, revealing my outfit of skin-tight leggings and fitted sports top. Shading my eyes, I saw that what I'd thought was a man was no older than a teenager, and he looked less comfortable than I did. Then I realised I'd seen him before, from a distance, helping his grandfather elsewhere on the estate.

'It's Murdo, isn't it? I said, trying to sound friendly.

He nodded and shuffled his feet. His hands were behind his back, but I could see that he held a spade in one of them.

'Did you want to work in here? I can move out of your way, if you like?'

Again, Murdo said nothing, but merely stared at me. He had the darkest eyes, and with his mucky face and mop of dirty black hair, appeared rather wild and frightening. Why was he looking at me like that? I wondered. Then I remembered I was now the archetypal blonde bombshell, and I understood, Stevie, the effect your radiant good looks might have on such an awkward lad. How did James describe him to us? 'A rather *introverted* young man'.

Before I could say anything else, he turned on his heel and, muttering to himself, shambled away. I wouldn't like to swear on it – his voice was low and his accent was thick – but I thought I caught the words: 'Bloody hoor'. Surely not!!

The experience fairly shook me up and it brought home the fact that for the next few weeks people will be looking at me in a very different way from what I'm used to. How do you handle the unwanted attention, Stevie? I guess I can answer that myself: rudely!

Anyway, moving on from that unsettling episode... when I'm outdoors on my own, I can't help feeling like a nineteenth-century character in a TV drama, caught up in some ghastly plot and seeking solace in a secret garden. Okay, I'm romanticising, but it's just another way of coping with our bizarre situation. And when I think about it, the acting analogy fits quite well. You and I are currently in rehearsals, literally "getting into part", preparing ourselves for a ten-week run in the most important drama of our lives.

How will we perform? Will we be convincing in our roles? And when it's all over, how well will we be able to shake off our disguises and return to "real life"?

Will the world believe us when we go public with this project?

And, most importantly, will those who love us ever trust us again?

Chapter 26

Layla's Log – Week 2, Friday

Only two days to go before we're let loose on the world!

I'm feeling much cheerier today, having had a full night's sleep, with no dreams that I can remember. I'm also starting to feel a little more comfortable in your skin, Stevie. It's incredible what strange circumstances we humans can get used to, but then I suppose being adaptable is a survival mechanism, and it's one we share with all living creatures.

Anyway, I'm feeling less self-conscious about living with your body, which (I'm sure you would agree) really is a fantastic piece of engineering. I'm so relieved that you're happy to continue my vegetarian diet: the thought of eating meat makes you feel sick, you say. And I'm delighted to find that I can override your body's carnivorous cravings and stick to my own ethical beliefs. Of course, we've swapped clothes and the necessary toiletries, and I'm starting to enjoy grooming and dressing myself in your particular style. Hey, I'm a life-size Barbie!

Seeing my own body as a separate entity is a very different matter.

Pre-op, I had no idea how I appeared to the world, in terms of my posture, the way I walk, my – frankly, embarrassing – idiosyncratic gestures (have I really always waved my arms around like that when I talk?)... but the curious thing is that the expressions I now see on my former face are not my own – they're yours! You, as the old Stevie, had a way of raising your eyebrows and curling your upper lip when you were being scornful or disbelieving, and that expression, along with many others, has followed you to your new host body.

We've talked about this, and you tell me you're seeing the same phenomenon in me. Apparently, I, as the old Layla, crinkled my nose when I smiled and you now see me doing the same on your former face. James tells us this is not surprising, as our faces quite obviously reflect our inner feelings and those feelings are strong enough to override the host body's facial muscle memory. He says he won't be surprised if we soon start to adopt our own bodies' particular gestures again, for the same reason. (I will make a conscious effort not to wave my arms around so much.)

If I'm brutally honest, I've also been experiencing some difficult emotions when I'm with you. At times, I'm achingly homesick for my own body. I'm jealous and resentful, and I hate the fact that you're in charge of it. My body is by no means perfect, but it's *mine*! I'm not ready to share these feelings yet, as I'm still trying to deal with them, but I wonder if you're experiencing the same thing. With a body like yours, you surely must be.

Talking of feelings, I seem to have developed a very strong connection with James. It's completely platonic, I hasten to add, and it reminds me of the kind of bonding I imagine people feel in a crisis situation, where they have to trust and depend on each other. I'm rather in awe of him now (a big change from thinking he was a lunatic only a few short months ago): he has achieved a miracle, and my life and future entirely depend on him. In turn, he treats me as if I am his favourite niece and protégée, who is doing everything just right.

By contrast, your relationship with the professor is stormy and unsettling. You are forever having rows, and you're increasingly sarcastic and disrespectful towards him. Is it just because he won't allow you to go public with the project earlier than he wants to? Or is there something else going on between you? If you were me

141

(ha, ha!), I'm sure you'd ask outright, but I don't want to do that. I don't think I could cope with any more complications.

Buller's reaction to our body swap was anything but complicated – but it was very surprising. When the big, soppy lump was allowed into the ward the day after the op, he made a beeline for me, in your body! How could he have known that we'd swapped? Surely he's guided by scent, rather than by being able to sense someone's "spirit"? Yet, even when I urged you to call him to you, he ignored you, just as he'd done from the first day you met. I've always thought that animals are far wiser and more in tune with the universe than humans give them credit for, and Buller's uncanny ability to identify me in a different body reinforces that belief.

Every day brings new discoveries and experiences such as the ones I've mentioned, and regardless of whether they're positive or negative, from a professional point of view it's all manna from heaven. I'll be drawing on this research material for years to come. Thankfully, now, instead of feeling completely overwhelmed by it all, as I have been to date, I'm starting to get excited. There's so much to explore in terms of the project's implications. It will change how the world thinks about consciousness and human existence, and I want to be at the forefront of the philosophical revolution!

But all that's for another day. Right now, I need to concentrate on the practicalities of returning home as another person.

Chapter 27
Mid-April: Cairnacraig House

On the second Saturday following the operation, Layla awakened early and stretched her long limbs luxuriantly. The air was already melodic with birdsong and shafts of spring sunlight striped the rose-coloured carpet.

Out of nowhere came a long-forgotten rush of happiness. She leapt out of bed and automatically began to prepare for her first jog in Stevie's body.

The run was as exhilarating as she'd hoped it would be. As she powered along the forest track, last autumn's beaten-copper beech leaves crackling underfoot, she was consumed by a feeling of wellbeing she hadn't experienced since childhood. *Now I understand why people become hooked on running. If you have the energy and motivation, it doesn't get much better than this.*

A frantic flap of wings some way ahead of her caused her to slow down. A murder of crows rose through the still-bare branches of a massive horse chestnut, their raw, raucous voices raised in a feathered fishwives' brawl.

Something had disturbed them, and Layla was sure it wasn't her: she was still too far off to have created such a stir.

In a slow jog, she approached the spot, thinking she might be lucky enough to spot a deer or a fox. In this part of the estate, the forest path was lined with wild rhododendrons and it was hard to see anything through the dense wall of greenery which was beginning to reveal its spring mantle of blowsy lilac blooms.

A sudden flash off to the left caught her attention. Curious, she stepped off the path, pushing her way through the shrubs and into a clearing. There it was again, glinting through the vegetation growing near the base of the old tree where the crows had been perching.

Her already-racing heart sped up. Was that sunlight bouncing off a glass lens? Was someone spying on her?

In her own body, Layla would have backed away. In Stevie's, however, she strode forward with confidence to confront the unknown. Immediately, there was a rustling noise from the bushes and a large, lumbering figure emerged, a camera slung around his neck.

Murdo!

With a look of sheer panic on his face, the lad turned and ran deeper into the woods, crashing through the undergrowth and raising more outraged caws as he fled.

Layla bent over, hands on her thighs, trying to catch her breath. Fearless though Stevie's physique might be, she, herself, had got a real scare and she needed a moment to recover.

What the hell had he been up to?

Later, sitting at the breakfast bar with Stevie while the professor served them fried-egg rolls, she described her surprise encounter with Murdo.

'... and I think he was just as shocked as I was that I headed straight towards him, but it creeped me out, all the same.' Then she told them about his strange behaviour in the walled garden the previous morning.

'What's a "hoor"?' asked Stevie, regarding her breakfast with little enthusiasm.

'A whore,' said Layla. 'Why on earth did he call me that?'

Stevie rolled her eyes. 'He fancies you: get used to it.'

James pulled up a stool and looked seriously at Layla.

'I know how it must have appeared, out in the forest there, but I'm quite sure I know what the lad was doing.'

144

He poured coffee for them all and explained: 'Murdo is a keen nature photographer; in fact, he's doing a part-time photography course at college. He's forever wandering around the estate taking snaps of anything that moves. I wouldn't read any more into it than that.'

'Okay, sounds plausible, but that doesn't explain his nasty attitude in the garden,' Layla countered, only just remembering not to add milk to her mug; her new taste buds didn't appreciate the "white stuff".

'No, and I'm very sorry to hear about that,' he said. 'I can only say in his defence that he's rather awkward around the opposite sex. He had a wee bit of trouble just before he left school, a couple of years ago. One of his classmates reported him for following her home. But then Jimmy, his grandfather, took him under his wing and since then Murdo has really found his niche in the outdoor life, through both gardening and photography. As far as I know, there have been no more incidents.'

'Until now,' Layla said, but there was little conviction in her tone. She was beginning to regret raising the subject, feeling pity for shy Murdo more than anything else.

'I'll have a firm word with him and tell him to apologise for what he said.'

'Och, no need to go as far as that,' Layla said, biting into her roll and resolving to forget her concerns. As a university lecturer, she understood the awkwardness of youth and the unintentional problems it could lead to. 'We'll be gone from here soon enough and he'll be alone again with his precious foxes and squirrels.'

She demolished her breakfast in seconds. The early-morning exercise had been just what she'd needed to burn off the excess energy that had buzzed through her body for the past couple of days. Gulping down a final mouthful of coffee, she looked up to see her companions staring at her.

Huddled in Layla's soft pink dressing gown, Stevie now appeared tired and resentful. Blunstone looked amused.

'What?' she asked, nervously.

'I see you've inherited Ms Nightingale's ravenous appetite,' he said with a smile.

'And I've been landed with *Doctor Sutherland's* acid reflux,' Stevie said angrily, rubbing her chest and stalking from the room – presumably to fetch the indigestion tablets Layla had given her during their pre-op "handover".

Not for the first time, Layla felt guilty. But she reminded herself that she had tried to forewarn the Australian about the niggling health issues that had become part of everyday life since Calum had left her. Stevie had merely scoffed and insinuated that Layla was a hypochondriac. Well, now she knew better.

Blunstone sighed, but said nothing and sipped at his own coffee.

Layla looked sideways at him and ventured: 'James... I –'

'Last day here, then!' he interrupted with false heartiness. Clearly, he didn't wish to discuss Stevie's moody behaviour.

'Yes, and I think I'm ready, now, to move on to the next phase,' she told him.

'Splendid! You did have me worried for a spell, Layla. I know you have found the post-operative phase very challenging, but you have come through it and I want to commend you for your bravery in the face of extreme mental distress.'

Embarrassed, she smiled at him. 'Thank you; that means a lot.'

'Now,' he went on, 'I understand you and Stevie already have things organised at home for the first couple of weeks, but is there anything you need from me?'

She thought for a moment. 'I don't think so. We've swapped enough clothes, accessories and toiletries for the fortnight, and as we'll be on our own territory, there's not really much else to do. We've told everyone who needs to know that we're going on holiday and that a house-sitter is moving in.'

He nodded and she continued: 'I'm quite looking forward to pretending to be someone else for a while. There's a certain amount of freedom in escaping from your own body and opting out of your life.'

'Yes, I can understand that! But supposing Stevie, by chance, runs into someone who knows you? Or vice versa? You'll both still be living in Aberdeen.'

'We've thought of that. I intend to spend most of the time holed-up in my house. I have a lot of decluttering and cleaning to do before Stevie moves in. I'll do a mega-shop on the way home tomorrow and although I'll no doubt go out jogging from time to time, I'll stay well away from her usual stomping ground.'

'And will she do the same?' he asked, mildly.

'She has promised to. She tells me she wants to get started on her book right away.'

'Good. I'm relieved to hear that she's now speaking about her book, rather than those newspaper features she wanted to write.'

He gave her a meaningful look and refilled their mugs from a large cafetière.

'You will keep in touch, won't you?' he added, almost anxiously. 'Email me your log each week? Meet up with me at the end of the fortnight?'

'Of course, and don't worry: everything is going to be fine.'

He grinned at her. 'That's the spirit! I'm sure it will be. But it's the eight weeks afterwards that will be most challenging for you both. Are you absolutely certain that you want to swap homes, and for that length of time?'

Cocooned inside Stevie's strong, energetic body, Layla had never felt so confident.

'Oh yes; it's an opportunity we can't afford to miss. Bring it on!'

'Bring what on?' asked Stevie, who had showered and dressed and now looked in a better humour. She rejoined them at the counter.

'The next ten weeks,' Layla told her, thinking as she did so that her blue-and-white floral tunic looked quite fetching on her former frame. She hadn't been one hundred per cent sure of it when she'd bought it in the Next sale.

'Oh sure, I can't – oh BUGGER!' Stevie yelled, as the coffee she was pouring sloshed over the new floral top. 'How the hell did I manage that?' she cried in Layla's soft Scottish accent.

Suppressing a sigh, Layla went to fetch a damp cloth. She could hardly blame Stevie for her own physical clumsiness.

After she'd helped the other woman mop up, James Blunstone resumed the conversation, saying briskly to Stevie: 'I was just asking Layla whether she was absolutely sure about swapping homes in two weeks' time. You'll both be putting yourselves under a great deal of pressure.'

'Yeah, yeah – it's not a problem,' she said breezily, helping herself to a croissant. 'After hiding out for a fortnight, I'll be more than ready for a change of scene. It's gonna be great.'

Layla couldn't help noticing that the professor's almost arrogant self-assurance seemed to have waned in the past few days. Did Stevie's brattish behaviour have anything to do with that? And was it her imagination, or was his face etched with more lines than it had been a couple of weeks ago?

She mentally shook herself. Beautiful and restful though it was at Cairnacraig House – for the most part, at least – she needed to get away from this place and move on. Blunstone had done his bit and now it was up to her and Stevie to make this project a success.

Chapter 28
Two Days Later: Aberdeen

Layla's Log – Week 3, Monday

As it might be obvious from previous entries, a book that has haunted me since childhood is *Alice's Adventures in Wonderland*. Its nightmarish, anything-can-happen atmosphere had a profound effect on the seven-year-old me, leaving me unsettled and anxious, frightened by the cold carelessness of its characters and by the relentless, hallucinatory experiences Alice had to undergo. One such was when she ate the "*EAT ME*" cake that made her grow – and grow.

I now understand how she must have felt.

Yesterday, I entered my own house as a stranger. Walking through rooms once comfortably familiar, I felt oversized and awkward. Mirrors were no longer at eye level. The highest kitchen cupboards were now within easy reach. The chair in my study was ridiculously low.

I realised with horror that my home no longer fit me and that I'd lost the haven I'd taken for granted for the past ten years: yet another discovery I hadn't anticipated before the operation.

Body-swapping: the gift that keeps on giving...

Today, despite passing a tormented night in my once-comfy bed, which now puts me in mind of the smallest bear's in *Goldilocks*, I'm feeling marginally better. What kept me from going crazy during those first few hours back home was the thought that this is only temporary, that in ten weeks' time I'll be back in my own body and no doubt wondering, like Alice upon awakening, if my adventures "down the rabbit hole" ever really happened.

I also remembered James Blunstone's advice about not over-thinking things, and I've decided that the only way to survive with my sanity intact is to try to adapt to every new situation as I go along, and also do my best to think like a scientist by objectively observing and recording everything that happens to me while I'm living as Layla/Stevie.

So, the first thing I did today – after going out for an early-morning run to clear my head (I don't know why I ever thought I'd hate Stevie's running regime) – was to arrange things around the house to accommodate my much taller frame. Just a few adjustments have made all the difference and I'm feeling a lot more in control of my surroundings. Tonight, I'll sleep on a mattress on the floor, so that I'm not restricted by the header and footer of my wooden sleigh bed, and tomorrow I'll start on the clean-up and decluttering. I don't want Stevie finding fault with my home, although something tells me she's no housewife!

Chapter 29

Layla's Log – Week 3, Tuesday

I have never felt so alone.

Things were going pretty well today, until my Mum called late this afternoon.

After committing to the operation, I'd spun a story for my family about taking time out from work to travel through Australia for three months in the company of an old university friend from Sydney. They were surprised; but seemed genuinely pleased that I'd decided to treat myself to such a long break.

'Just what the doctor ordered,' Mum told me at the time. 'The next step is deciding to emigrate over here.' I said I'd make one major life change at a time, if it was all the same to her.

The main problem was how to stay in touch during my imaginary travels around Oz. Originally, I had a vague idea that I would try to rope Stevie into staging one or two Skype calls with my parents: she could be me and I could be the Aussie travelling companion. But as I haven't yet got around to broaching the subject with her (probably because I've been too nervous at the thought of putting us both through such a crazy ordeal), I've been emailing my folks from time to time from imaginary 'Internet cafés' and pretending to be in the heart of the Outback, where phone masts and wi-fi connections are patchy. I have no idea whether or not that's really the case!

But today, Mum, being Mum, thought she'd try my mobile, anyway, and I – being scatty old me – absent-mindedly answered her call while working at my computer. The conversation went something like this:

Me: *Hello? Oh, shit!*

Mum: *I beg your pardon! Who is this?*

Me: *Er, who is* this?

Mum: *I'm trying to contact Layla Sutherland. Are you speaking on her phone?*

Me: *Sorry, wrong number!*

And then, panicking, I rang off, shutting down my phone completely.

I felt dreadful. I couldn't even speak to my own mother, because she wouldn't recognise my voice! Then I thought she must have been calling because something bad had happened, and I immediately sent her an email. Of course, I couldn't let on that I knew she'd called.

Her response came instantly: *'Hey, what a coincidence! I've just this minute tried to ring you, but I got a wrong number. Some rude Australian woman answered! All's well here – I just fancied a chat and thought I'd take a chance. How come we can't talk by phone, or Skype, while you're over there, like we do when you're in Aberdeen? Janey, next door, Skypes her Australian grandchildren all the time...'*

I repeated my Outback story and after a bit of to-ing and fro-ing with snippets of news (from Mum) and improvised lies (from me), I signed off with: *'When we reach the nearest town, I'll try to set up a Skype call and also post some photos online; but for now, email will have to do. Love to everyone!'*

Thankfully, this seemed to mollify her, but the whole episode has shaken me up. I feel heartsore at the prospect of losing out on a luxury I've always taken for granted: the simple, comforting pleasure of being myself with those closest to me.

I thought that living without Calum was a solitary existence. It's nothing compared to being a secret imposter in my own life.

Chapter 30
Week 3: Aberdeen

Layla was in the loft when the doorbell rang.

'Och, who's that?' she sighed, setting down the cardboard box of miscellaneous belongings she was trying to find a place for in the confined, dusty space. Grumbling at the inconvenience, but thinking the caller might be the postman, she brushed at her t-shirt and running leggings, shinned back down the ladder, and tramped downstairs to the hall.

It wasn't until she opened the front door and saw Calum's startled face that she remembered she wasn't herself.

'Oh – *hello*, who are *you*?' her husband said, his expression flashing from puzzlement to admiration.

Furious at his intrusion, she almost slammed the door – but then a wicked thought struck her: *I could have fun here.*

'House-sitter,' she said casually, flicking her blonde hair off her face, as she'd seen Stevie do. 'Who are *you*?'

'Er, I'm Layla's husband... soon-to-be ex,' he blustered, clearly awestruck by the golden goddess who'd opened the door. 'Where has she gone? How long will she be away?'

A peculiar concoction of anger, amusement and jealousy churned in Layla's gut as she stared coolly at the man before her. He seemed almost a stranger: it had been a long time since he'd looked at *her* in that way.

'She's gone on holiday for a couple of weeks?' The upward inflection, which she despised, had slipped out before she could stop it. 'She didn't mention you'd be calling.'

'Oh, well, it's actually a spur-of-the-moment visit. We need to sort out a few things and I was passing, so... But it doesn't matter. I'll catch up with her when she gets home.' He took a couple of steps back but appeared in no hurry to leave.

She forced a smile and waited, her head on one side.

'But now I'm here...' he said, a sly expression creeping across his face, 'do you think I might be able to pick up some of my stuff? I haven't properly moved out yet. Layla won't mind; it's all perfectly amicable.'

Outraged, Layla managed to bite back a stinging retort and merely shrugged her shoulders.

'Suit yourself. I guess it's okay. But do you have any ID on you?'

'What? Oh – yes – here's my driving licence.' He delved into his jeans back pocket and fished the document out of his wallet.

Pretending to check the details, she felt herself under scrutiny, and looked up to catch him staring down at her thighs, long and lithe in the black leggings.

Bastard, she thought grimly. But she wanted to see where this would go.

'Okay,' she said shortly, turning on her heel and stalking ahead of him into the kitchen. 'Do you want a tea or coffee?'

She turned in time to catch him appraising her Lycra-clad backside. Oh yes, she could have fun here.

'Well, coffee, please, if it isn't too much trouble.' Calum had regained his composure and leaned against the kitchen doorframe, his hands in the pockets of a new black leather jacket. 'You didn't tell me your name,' he added, as she grabbed the kettle and turned on the tap.

'Stevie.'

'And how do you know Layla, Stevie? I've never heard her mention you.'

'I answered her online ad.'

He whistled. 'Wow, an online ad, eh? That's very un-Layla-like.'

'What do you mean?' She didn't like his tone.

He laughed and shrugged. 'Well, she's a bit of a mouse. And I would never have imagined her leaving our house in the hands of a stranger. But you live and learn.'

She was thankful she had her back to him as she spooned out the coffee, for the fury in her eyes would surely have given her away.

'So, whereabouts in Oz are you from?' he continued.

She knew he was watching her every move. Normally, she'd be self-conscious under such an intense gaze, but in her new guise she felt strangely free. She turned around and slowly leaned back against the counter, waiting for the kettle to boil. She saw that he was trying not to look at her breasts in the tight t-shirt, and suddenly felt a rush of power as she realised she could probably seduce him if she wanted.

Wouldn't *that* be the ultimate revenge on darling Darla?

'Sydney,' she replied. 'How long have you and Layla been separated?'

He seemed taken aback at her question. 'A few months,' he said finally.

She raised an eyebrow. 'And who was to blame?'

His face flushed. *He won't like being grilled like this. Well, tough*, she thought.

'Er, that's not really something I want to go into,' he said, almost apologetically.

Yes, he thinks he's in with a chance here, otherwise he'd be much brusquer. 'No worries; just wondering if you're back on the market yet.'

She almost laughed at his astonishment, but instead turned back to the kitchen counter and poured boiling water into two mugs. 'Here you go. Sorry it's just instant. Milk's in the fridge, if you need it.'

He cleared his throat and hurried over to the fridge.

Oh, how she was loving this. *I'm Stevie on steroids! He doesn't know what's hit him.*

'Well?' she asked, watching his shaking hand pour the milk. '*Are* you back on the market yet?'

He laughed nervously. 'You make me sound like a prize bull!'

She looked suggestively at his crotch. 'Mmm, maybe you are.' *Oh my god – what am I doing?*

Calum ran his hand through his hair and shook his head. 'Are you suggesting what I think you're suggesting?' he asked in amazement. 'You Aussie girls are certainly not backward in coming forward!'

In response, Layla set down her mug and slowly peeled her t-shirt over her head, revealing a black, lacy bra. M&S sensible white was more her thing, but she'd discovered Stevie had a weakness for Victoria's Secret. She glanced down at her cleavage. It really was magnificent.

'Like this, you mean?' she vamped in a husky, porn-star voice.

His jaw had just about hit the floor.

'What are you waiting for?' she teased, leaning back against the counter, her breasts straining against the flimsy fabric.

He moved towards her, pulling off his jacket. His eyes were blazing now with a lust she'd never seen in all her years married to him. Today, she was seeing her husband in an entirely new light – and she didn't like what she saw.

Before he could touch her, she darted sideways and grabbed her discarded t-shirt.

'Look,' she said, coldly, pulling it back over her head. 'I actually don't think this is a good idea? Would you mind leaving?'

She almost laughed at the shock and – yes – hurt in his eyes.

Wh-what...?' he stuttered, looking utterly floored.

'I forgot: I'm expecting someone in ten minutes, so you'll have to go now. You can come back for your stuff when Layla gets home. It's only a couple of weeks.'

With cool detachment, she slipped a kitchen knife from its block and moved towards him, relishing the fact that she was now taller than him.

'Sorry, but you really need to go,' she grinned.

Horrified, he backed away, eyes on the knife, hands held up in submission. 'Okay, okay! What's going on here? You were the one who invited me in! You made the first move, for Christ's sake!'

'And now I'm telling you to *fuck off*.' The last two words, spoken slowly and quietly, were shocking in the silence of the kitchen. She saw real fear in his eyes as she continued to advance upon him.

'Jesus, I'm going!' He ran into the hall and practically fell out of the front door, yelling: 'This is still MY HOUSE, you psycho BITCH!' as she slammed it behind him.

Helpless with laughter, Layla stood with her back to the door and slowly let herself slide down to the wooden floor, where she hugged her knees, deliciously aware of how the tables had turned since she'd last sat there.

'What an absolute arse! Darla is more than welcome to the unfaithful, lecherous creep,' she cried, her voice echoing around the hall.

Unwittingly, Stevie had done her an enormous service: the Calum spell was now well and truly broken.

Chapter 31
Week 3: Cairnacraig House
James

James Blunstone rarely had trouble sleeping. His high-pressure job as a neurosurgeon had had little impact on his natural ability to switch off at night – or to power-nap during the inevitable hours of downtime at the hospital, while harried administrators searched for the surgical beds that would allow his interrupted operating schedule to resume.

But now, in his so-called "retirement", he was lucky if he managed three or four hours in a night.

He knew it was his conscience that kept him lying awake and fretful in the interminable, silent darkness that shrouded Cairnacraig House. A single question haunted him, echoing endlessly inside his head: *What have I done?*

Chapter 32
Week 4, Friday: Aberdeen
Layla

'Come in, come in! Hey, Buller, I've missed you, boy!'

Hugging the big black dog as he washed her face with licks, Layla looked up at James Blunstone, who stood, smiling, on her doorstep. Despite his pleasant expression, his face was haggard and there were dark smudges under his eyes.

She rose from her crouch and felt momentarily awkward. How should she greet him? But he solved her silent dilemma by grasping her hand and kissing her on the cheek.

'My dear Layla, I'm so pleased to see you.'

'Likewise!' She wasn't simply being polite; it was an enormous relief to see someone who knew who she really was.

She led man and dog into the lounge, leaving them to settle themselves while she made coffee. However, seconds later, standing at the kitchen counter, she wasn't surprised to hear the clicking of claws and she turned to give the grinning Lab another cuddle.

'Do you want a drink, lovely boy? I have a treat for you, too.'

She watched with satisfaction as the dog took a long, noisy drink from the bowl of water she'd set down on the floor.

When she and Buller re-entered the lounge, Blunstone was leaning against the sofa back, his eyes closed, hands folded in his lap. He looked like a very old man.

Suddenly, his eyes opened and he sat up straight. 'My goodness, what must you think of me, falling asleep in the middle of the morning!'

160

'No worries! Are you all right, though, James?' Layla asked gently, setting down the coffee tray. 'Did you have a bad night?'

'Afraid so,' he muttered, giving his shoulders a little shake. 'Much as I welcome the joys of spring, the earlier sunrise and dawn chorus tend to play havoc with my sleep patterns.'

He leaned forward and added: 'But never mind me – how are you? I must say, you're looking as fit as a flea.'

She smiled at the less-than-flattering analogy and poured the coffee. Buller lay beside her chair, chomping on the chew bone she'd given him in the kitchen.

'Yes, I'm feeling fantastic,' she said. 'Stevie's body seems to be in the rudest of health, and I'm certainly benefiting from that. Mentally, I feel stronger and more able to cope than I have for a long time.'

He smiled back at her. 'Our physical fitness and hormone levels do, of course, have an enormous influence over our psychological wellbeing.'

'But it's not as cut and dried as that, is it?' she countered, ever the philosopher. 'Remember Patient D's good humour and optimism? As Patient C found out, D had far more pain to contend with than she did, yet the older woman was much happier in herself.'

'And we have to hope Patient C learned from that experience, so that she could make the most of the short time she had left,' Blunstone added solemnly.

Layla nodded. 'I now understand what Patient D meant about it being a privilege to live for a time in someone else's body. It gives you a new perspective on your own life... almost like getting a second chance.'

Blunstone looked at her sharply. 'Really? Are you glad, then, that you signed up for this?'

'I think I'll reserve my answer to that until I'm safely back in my own body,' she said carefully. 'Despite what I said earlier about feeling stronger, there are many aspects that are still hard to deal with.'

'Such as...?'

She looked at him levelly. 'The nightmares, the fear of what lies ahead, guilt about duping my family and friends, and the loneliness of feeling I no longer belong in my own home,' she said. 'It's nothing I haven't already shared with you, but it's all still there in the background.'

He stared down at his hands. 'I'm so sorry you're having to go through all the bad stuff, Layla.'

His despondent tone couldn't have been more of a contrast to the jolly optimism of the weeks before and just after the operation.

'But it's okay,' she blurted, wanting to reassure him. 'I'm getting through it and I'm proud of that. And from a work perspective, I have so many new ideas and experiences to sort through. It's mind-blowing, actually!'

He nodded and raised his mug to drink, his tired grey eyes assessing her over the rim.

Enthusiastically, she continued: 'It's been wonderful this fortnight to have the time to do a proper brain dump. I've written reams of notes so far.'

'You've been holed-up here for most of the time, have you? It seemed that way, from your emails.'

'Apart from the daily runs, I've been an absolute recluse,' she confirmed. She wasn't going to tell him about her encounter with Calum, about which she now felt vaguely guilty.

The professor set down his mug. 'Tell me,' he began hesitantly, 'have you heard from Stevie at all?'

'No, I haven't. We said we'd contact each other only if we needed to. I take it *you* have heard from her, though?'

He shook his head and said quietly: 'No, she hasn't been answering my emails or calls.'

Layla was shocked. It was part of the deal that they kept in touch with Blunstone. What was Stevie playing at?

He saw her expression and sighed. 'Yes, I know. But Ms Nightingale is a law unto herself. I just hope she hasn't got into any trouble.'

'I'll try her right now.' She left the room and returned with her mobile. 'Let's see if she answers *my* call.' A few seconds later, she said into the phone: 'Stevie? Hi, it's Layla. Can you call me back as soon as, please?' She made a face and sat back down. 'Good grief, we're supposed to be swapping houses in a couple of days. We don't need her going AWOL on us!'

Then, seeing how miserable and worried he now looked, she decided to change the subject.

'James, can I ask you a question? When you're talking to me, do you see Stevie or me? I'm really curious to know.'

This made him sit up straighter and, to her relief, a big smile crossed his face. 'You must be a mind-reader!' he said. 'I've just been thinking about that very thing while we've been chatting.'

'... And?' She smiled back at him.

'... And it really is the most curious phenomenon. I see Stevie's face and physical expressions; I hear her voice and Australian accent, but I also see and hear *you*. It's hard to explain, but her hard edges have softened and, helped by the fact that your own facial expressions appear from time to time, I somehow know that it's you "in there" and not Stevie. Does that make sense?'

She considered this for a moment. 'Ye-es, I think so. It's taken a little while, but now, when I look at this face in the mirror, I recognise the essential "me".'

'I believe you're seeing deep into your own soul,' he replied.

'Yes, isn't it amazing?' Layla said. 'Did you know this would happen?'

'No, I had no real idea of what to expect. My other subjects weren't out of their bodies long enough for such a transformation to manifest itself fully. It is quite wonderful – and one of the many, many aspects of this experiment that will feed people's imaginations and discussions in the years to come, I'm sure. In fact –'

He was cut off by the loud ringtone and vibration of Layla's phone and for a startled moment they both stared at the offending object on the coffee table. Then, checking the caller ID, she gave him a nod and answered with: 'Stevie! Thanks for calling back. How are you?'

After listening for a moment, she replied: 'I know, I still can't get used to hearing you speaking in *my* voice... but listen, I have James here with me and he's a little concerned that you haven't been in touch. He's left you several messages.'

She met his anxious eyes and tried to smile reassuringly as a tirade of swearwords hit her eardrum. Embarrassed, she gestured that she'd take the call in private and hurried into the kitchen, closing the door behind her.

'*Stevie*,' she hissed, cutting across the other women's outburst. 'What are you playing at? Why all the hostility towards James?'

'The old fool is *totally* getting on my nerves,' came the tinny reply. 'He's so *clingy*, wanting to know our every move and asking all those intrusive questions. It's creepy! I just needed some time out.'

Layla heaved a sigh. 'I do understand what you mean, but we made a deal with him and it's not fair to break it. A couple of short emails would have kept him happy.'

Hearing Stevie's derisive snort, she continued on a different tack: 'Anyway, I'm glad you're still in the land of the living. What have you been up to these past two weeks? Has everything worked out okay for you? *I've* practically been in hiding.'

'Yes, it's all absolutely fine,' the other woman said breezily. 'Not much to report. Can't wait to swap places with you, though; it'll be infinitely more exciting than being stuck here at home.'

They spoke for a few minutes longer, making arrangements for the imminent house swap, until Stevie said suddenly: 'Got to go – see you Sunday,' and abruptly rang off.

She's such a Secret Squirrel! Layla thought, irritably. However, she was relieved at the brief contact she'd had with her body-swap partner. After James's unsettling revelation about the two-week silence, it made her feel a little more grounded to know Stevie was still on track with the project. But she hated feeling so vulnerable, knowing she had no control over what the other woman was doing with her body. *She must be feeling the same way, though; we are mutually dependent, after all,* she reminded herself for the umpteenth time. Then she plastered on a smile and re-entered the lounge.

'All's well!' she announced, struck once again by the professor's gaunt face.

Hearing her upbeat tone, Buller bounced to his feet, wagging his tail and looking eagerly from his master to his second-best human chum.

'Settle down, boy,' Blunstone murmured, gently patting the dog's head and looking expectantly at Layla.

'She's fine – just a bit prickly about being kept on a leash, as she put it. I'm not making excuses for her; I told her it was thoughtless not to return your messages, but at least she hasn't done a runner on us!'

Relief washed over his face. 'Thank heavens for that. She has no idea what she has put me through these past two weeks. At least, I hope she hasn't,' he added darkly.

'She's not the most sensitive of souls, but surely she wouldn't have been so cruel as to try to deliberately upset you?' Layla said, realising with a sinking heart that the Australian was in fact quite capable of doing such a thing.

'Well, well, no harm done,' Blunstone said briskly, sounding more like his usual self. Then he settled back in his seat and looked at her intently.

'So, Layla, tell me exactly how it felt to return to your home in someone else's body...'

That night, Layla had her most vivid and frightening nightmare yet. Unlike her previous dreams of Dickensian dark places, this one was all the more terrifying for its contemporary ordinariness.

It reeled itself out like an on-screen thriller. She watched herself (in Stevie's body) move around an unfamiliar kitchen, fetching food from the fridge and rustling up a quick meal. What the dream Layla/Stevie didn't realise – but she, the "viewer", did – was that a shadowy shape was watching her through the uncurtained window...

In the next scene, Layla/Stevie was in a bedroom, dressed in her nightwear. She flicked off the overhead light and drew back the curtains just enough to allow spectral fingers of moonlight to stream into the darkened room. As she plumped up her pillow and settled herself for sleep, her back to the window, she was unaware of the sinister, hooded figure staring at her through the gap in the curtains...

The perspective suddenly shifted and the dreaming Layla knew she was now in the "film", in Stevie's body. Her eyes flew open and, in the silvery light, she was horrified to see a man crouching at the foot of her bed. Her heart tripped in fright as the hooded intruder began to crawl slowly and inexorably up the bed towards her, an

166

expression of pure hatred on his face. She found herself utterly unable to move...

She woke, screaming, in the darkness. For a few terrifying seconds, she had no idea who or where she was. Crying now, she flailed out, knocking over the bedside lamp. The clatter brought her back to herself and she reached over and clicked on the switch. As she set the lamp upright again, the familiarity of her own bedroom flooded her senses. She realised that her thin nightshirt was soaked in sweat.

It took several minutes, and the calming tones of the BBC World Service radio presenter, before her normal heartbeat reasserted itself.

'WHY ALL THE NIGHTMARES?' she howled into the room, pounding her fists on the duvet.

Chapter 33
Week 5: Aberdeen

Layla greeted the sound of the doorbell with relief. Stevie was nearly an hour late – but at least she'd turned up.

She set down her coffee mug and went to open the door. Even though she was prepared for it, the sight of *herself* standing on the path came as a profound shock. She saw the same emotion briefly reflected in Stevie's borrowed blue eyes, and then the other woman stepped forward, almost pushing her out of the way.

'Bloody taxi was late,' she muttered, setting down a medium-sized holdall in the hallway.

'Is that all the luggage you've brought for two months?' Layla asked incredulously.

'Yep. I always travel light. Anyway, it was pointless taking my own clothes with me, wasn't it?'

Layla inclined her head, thinking of the large suitcase she had stashed in the master bedroom. It wasn't full of clothes, right enough, but she'd had plenty of other bits and pieces that she'd wanted to take with her, including toiletries, reference books, various electronic devices and their chargers, and her own pillow.

'Coffee?' she asked, heading back to the kitchen.

'Good on ya,' Stevie said, following her. The Aussie-ism sounded strange delivered in a Highland accent, reminding Layla of one of the many questions she wanted to ask her body-swap partner.

She poured Stevie's coffee and refilled her own mug, indicating that they should go next door into the lounge.

'Dinky place,' Stevie said, looking around the room.

'I didn't used to think so until I arrived back here as a giant!' Layla retorted, stung. The house did have rather small rooms, but it had suited her and Calum.

Stevie widened her eyes. 'What's with you, grumpy pants? I'm just saying.'

Layla heaved a silent sigh and motioned for her to sit down.

'Nerves, probably,' she admitted. 'I'm feeling a little apprehensive about doing this swap.'

'Oh, it'll be fine,' Stevie drawled, 'I'm sure we'll soon settle in. I didn't mean to criticise your home, you know. It's a lovely old place, by the looks.'

Layla eyed her with suspicion. She sounded less abrasive today than she'd been during their "confinement" together. What was she up to?

'Yes, well, it's still going to be very strange to start with,' she insisted. Then she remembered what she'd thought about earlier.

'Before I forget to ask, do you sometimes find yourself using words and phrases that you'd never normally use?'

Stevie looked thoughtful, then amused.

'Yeah, now you come to mention it, a few phrases have popped out that I didn't even know I knew. I'm guessing that's your internal influence!'

Layla laughed. 'I've been experiencing the same thing! It's weird, isn't it? I mean, I knew we'd be speaking in each other's voices and accents, but I hadn't realised our vocabulary would be affected, too.'

'It must be the mental equivalent of "muscle memory", or something. A residual part of our own language remaining in our brains?'

'Who knows? It's interesting, though. I must remember to ask James about it.'

Stevie's expression darkened.

'What's with *you* now?' Layla asked. 'You know, I felt quite sorry for him the other day when I heard you'd been blanking him for two weeks. He was genuinely worried about you.'

Stevie tossed her dark curls – now *that* was a Sutherland trait, Layla thought. 'Yeah, I'll just bet he was. Serves the old bugger right if I gave him a scare.'

And despite Layla's quizzing, she would say no more about her antipathy towards James Blunstone. Even more infuriatingly for Layla, she was also reluctant to go into detail about what she'd been up to for the past fortnight.

'Boring stuff, but if you're really interested, you can read all about it in my book,' she grinned.

'Och, you're hopeless,' Layla retorted. She couldn't understand how Stevie – a journalist – could be so reluctant to share information. She, herself, was insatiably curious, not only in a professional sense, but also when it came to other people's lives. And now that the two women were in an entirely unique position, she found the Australian's reticence both frustrating and unfair. She knew, however, that the more she pushed and prodded, the less Stevie would tell her. *It's a power thing for her*, she thought angrily.

Stevie thumped down her empty mug and got to her feet, rubbing her lower back as she did so. 'I'll tell you one thing: your body is not in good shape,' she grimaced. 'I'm giving it a course of vitamins and energy boosters and I've started a serious exercise regime.'

Affronted, Layla snapped at her: 'Well don't be getting it all muscly like your own body. I don't think it's very feminine to be so sculpted.'

The women glared at each other. Stevie backed down first, saying casually: 'So, are you going to give me the tour and show me how everything works? We've still got the same to do back at mine, and I don't have all day.'

Layla sighed. What was the point in getting upset? The woman was quite right about how unfit her body was. But she doubted that some vitamins and few weeks of exercise would make any difference. Then, something

Stevie had said earlier came back to her. 'You mentioned coming by taxi: what's happened to your car?'

'Ah, yes, I was going to get to that.' Stevie looked slightly abashed. 'The car I had when we were staying at the Prof's was a rental. Parking can sometimes be difficult around Footdee, so it's easier to walk or cycle to wherever I want to go. *You* won't need your car while you're living at mine, so can I borrow it while I'm here?'

Layla felt nonplussed. She'd taken it for granted that they'd both use their own cars for the next eight weeks. But what Stevie was saying made sense. In their new and vulnerable position, they'd want to attract as little attention as possible, and sticking to the other's usual mode of transport would fit with that.

'Okay...' she said, reluctantly, 'but I'll miss my Mini, and I want you to be extra careful with it.'

'No worries!' Layla recognised her own relieved smile on the other woman's face and, as she got to her feet to show Stevie around, it dawned on her that she'd given away something very precious. And it wasn't the Mini.

She had trusted a complete stranger with her own *body*.
What the hell *have I got myself into?*

Chapter 34

Layla's Log – Week 5, Monday

Two hours have passed since I walked into your rented house and recognised the rooms from my nightmare.

It gave me such a horrible feeling of déjà vu to see that kitchen that I all but collapsed onto a chair.

You had your back to me at that point, keen to show me how everything worked, so that you could return to my house and begin whatever you have planned for the next phase of the project. For a reason I haven't yet fathomed, I didn't want you to see me upset, so I quickly stood up again and tried to pay attention as you talked me through the controls of the enormous, state-of-the-art range cooker that dominates the room I'm now sitting in.

A few minutes later, you led me into the ground-floor master bedroom – which was dreadfully familiar, right down to the matching duvet cover and curtains. Feeling the four walls closing in on me, I hurried out without saying a word, on the pretext of fetching my suitcase from the hall.

'You should feel right at home here in all this pink fuss,' you grinned when I returned. Sure enough, the dominant colour of the soft furnishings is fuchsia, a shade that would normally delight me, but has been spoiled forever by the memory of a man-monster crawling towards me over the same pink cover I was now staring at.

'Yes, very nice,' I managed to mutter, hovering in the doorway. 'Let's see the rest of the house, then.'

You gave me a curious look (are my eyes always as blue as that in daylight?) but stalked past me without comment and continued "the tour".

While my heart was still thumping with the double fright I'd just had, I couldn't help feeling thrilled by this

172

wonderful old house at the heart of Footdee, or Fittie, as it's known locally.

According to the information pack left by the owner, the three-storey granite building was formerly the home of at least two fisher families during the nineteenth and early twentieth centuries. It has recently been converted into a comfortable three-bedroom holiday let, whose mix of antique and contemporary furniture and fittings has a distinctive maritime theme. Despite my anxiety, I already feel curiously at home here. I have no idea why you've been so desperate to get away from such a characterful place.

Because of its proximity to the sea, the house – like all its neighbours in the fishing village's three squares – faces inwards and has only very small windows at the back. The one exception is the large, north-facing picture window in the top-floor sitting room, which provides a stunning view of the bay, the beach, and the distant dunes of Balmedie Country Park. Way beyond that, along the same coastline, lie Newburgh, Collieston, Cruden Bay and the Bullers of Buchan: James's much-loved stomping ground.

'Marvellous view, eh?' you said, before turning back to practical matters, such as how to light the wood-burning stove upstairs, when to put the bins out, and how the range and central heating work. My head was in such a whirl by the time you left that I had to sit down, and apart from unpacking and setting up my laptop, I've been seated here, at the kitchen table, ever since.

There are probably lots of things I should have asked you about the house and the Fittie community, but I can always email you any questions as they occur to me. I don't know how you feel about this, but I certainly intend keeping in close contact with you, the person who has taken over my house, my car and my body!

All I can think about for the moment, though, is my uncanny precognition of the kitchen and bedroom. I don't for one minute believe it was a supernatural experience; the logical explanation is that I was dreaming one of *your* dreams, whose remnants must be lodged somewhere in this brain of yours. If that's the case, does this mean some part of your subconscious has been left behind? And has the same thing happened in my own brain?

It's a frightening thought, especially as James was so insistent that 'the soul is indivisible' and that ours had been transposed between bodies intact. But how does he really know that? When I think about it, he can only have reached that conclusion based on the brief body-swap experiences of Patients A, B, C and D. *And didn't Patients C and D complain about weird dreams about unfamiliar people and places? Did the professor lie to me when I queried this?*

Am I sharing your dark subconscious, Stevie? Are you sharing mine? And, if so, how will such an unknown experience affect us, both now and in the future?

Chapter 35
Week 5: Fittie

'H-hello?'

The quavering voice was that of a very old man.

'James? It's Layla,' she said tentatively, thinking she might have the wrong number.

'Oh, Layla – hello!' The voice became the professor's. 'Is everything all right?'

She sighed. 'Honestly? Not really. But I might have a solution and it involves you doing me a big favour. Can I borrow Buller for a week or so?'

Silence greeted her hurried words, then Blunstone asked: 'Whatever for? What's happened?'

Yes, what exactly had happened, Layla asked herself. In truth, nothing at all, but she knew she could not spend another night in this house without company, and the big, gentle Labrador was the most comforting presence she could imagine right now.

The previous night, as the darkness had deepened around the self-contained fishing village, old-fashioned street lights winked on, their buttery glow barely illuminating the shady cluster of sheds surrounding the Footdee Mission Hall, which crouched at the centre of the square. Earlier, in the last vestiges of daylight and as the only person out and about, Layla had strolled around the village's three main squares, admiring the proliferation of spring flowers and marvelling at the famous Fittie outhouses whose unique construction and colourful characteristics attracted dozens of visitors each day during the tourist season. The "tarry sheds" were a remnant from the days of the fishing, but several of the originals had been replaced by Scandinavian-style chalets and even a 'Man Shed', as its signpost declared. Each of them belonged to the house or cottage it faced, the two separated by a wide guttering of old granite cobbles, or "cassies", and the paved footpath that ran around the pedestrianised square.

At night, however, the motley collection of outhouses merged in shadow with the Mission Hall to appear as a hunched and sinister entity, and Layla had shivered as she peered out at them before hurriedly drawing the bedroom curtains. But then she'd told herself off for being so fanciful and had kept herself distracted by heating up a ready meal and taking it up to the top-floor sitting room, where she'd become engrossed in a Scandinavian detective drama on TV.

Later still, she had opened her laptop, browsed the net and discovered a website focusing on the history of Fittie. She was fascinated by an excerpt from an article first published in *Penny Magazine*, in 1840, which described the activities and idiosyncrasies of *'the women of Foot-Dee'*, who carried *'great loads of fish to market on market days in creels... sometimes as many as eleven miles before breakfast...*

'... They never walk but in single file, and they have a superstitious dread of being counted, a fear of which the boys of Aberdeen avail themselves to annoy them by crying as they pass – "One, two, three, what a lot of fisher nannies I see".'

The next paragraph was even more bizarre: *'A salutation equally dreaded by them is the cry, "A baud's fit in yer creel" – that is, "the point of a hare's foot is in your creel". This saying derived its meaning from the circumstance that a hare was seen to run through their "fish town" on the evening preceding a day on which a great number of their people were lost at sea.'*

There are wild rabbits aplenty, but I've yet to see a hare running around anywhere in this city, she'd thought with amusement, shutting down the laptop. *And going by this superstition, it's probably just as well.*

She had stayed up late because she dreaded going to bed. Her fear of the master bedroom was illogical, she knew, but that knowledge hadn't helped any, and so she had eventually decided to sleep in the small, single bedroom on the next floor. Except "sleep" was hardly the word to describe the fitful doze that had followed hours of reading while all the time listening out for furtive sounds of invasion. It was only when the first filaments of light started to creep along the polished, pitch-pine floorboards that she felt herself relax into a deeper slumber that lasted until just after eight am.

Now, clutching her mobile in the sunny, south-facing kitchen, she felt slightly foolish about her night-time terrors. But she knew the fear would return with the dying of the day, and she was determined that she wouldn't face another long night alone.

'I'm just a bit nervous about staying in a strange house,' she told Blunstone lamely. 'Buller's such a cheerful chap; I'm sure I'll feel better if he can visit for even a few days?'

'Oh, I see.' He sounded relieved. 'Well, of course you can have the old boy come to stay. He'll love being so close to the beach!'

Thank heavens, she mouthed silently, feeling the tension leaving her body.

'That's fantastic – thank you!' she said, before adding: 'Er, this is a bit awkward. I don't have transport, so would you mind bringing him here, rather than me coming to you?' And she told him about Stevie borrowing her Mini and leaving her carless.

'Yes, yes – I'll come to you,' he said cheerfully. 'Shall we say around one o'clock today? We could take a walk along the promenade and have lunch at one of the cafés.'

177

'That sounds perfect,' she replied, and before ringing off, she thanked him again.

What an absolute sweetie, she thought with a smile.

Chapter 36

'This bluster is certainly blowing away a few cobwebs!' cried the professor, as they battled their way along the Esplanade in the face of a chilly north-east wind, both he and Layla muffled up in beanie hats and warm jackets. A few yards ahead, Buller turned at the sound of his master's voice and waited for them, a wide panting grin on his face.

'You're right there!' Layla shouted back, realising that the bracing walk was exactly what she needed.

By the time man and dog had arrived at her door, Blunstone armed with a large squashy dog bed and a carrier bag of Buller's food and toys, the early sunshine had been obliterated by heavy clouds and a strong wind was whipping up white horses on the slate-coloured sea. She'd felt like a half-shut knife due to her disturbed night, but she'd greeted them both with a tired smile and a hug, welcoming them to her temporary new home.

'I didn't sleep well,' was her answer to his questioning glance. 'I'll tell you why over lunch.'

They were standing in the hall and, as she pulled on her jacket, she'd added: 'Shall we go, now, and I can show you around the place when we get back?'

'I'm no stranger to Fittie,' the professor had told her, as they set off through the squares, Buller straining at the lead. 'I've wandered around here many a time. It's a fascinating village.'

'I know, don't you just love all this?' Layla replied, pointing out a blue lion's-head standpipe, a tiny front garden populated by gnomes and meerkats, and a shed plastered with nautical memorabilia.

'A photographer's dream,' he smiled. 'Which reminds me, you'll never guess who I bumped into on my way from the car.'

Seeing her puzzled look, he said: 'Murdo. He's out and about at the beach today taking pictures for his coursework. I didn't tell him why I was here, though,' he added hastily. 'I somehow didn't think you'd welcome an impromptu visit!'

'You're right there!' She'd forgotten all about Murdo and his creepy appearances. 'How does he get to and from the village and town? Does he drive?'

'He has an old, beat-up Land Rover his grandfather gave him,' James explained. 'Ah, now: I never get tired of that view.'

Walking south through the village, they'd ended up on one of the harbour quaysides, whose main features were a contemporary glass-fronted control tower, a quaint old harbour master's office, and an upmarket seafood restaurant. Across the choppy water, above the rocky shoreline, rose the grassy hill housing the Torry Battery, its former military function long muffled by nature. Today, it was a popular dolphin-spotting site, people coming for miles in the hope of glimpsing the gleeful mammals soaring and splashing in and around the bay.

As the three of them paused for a moment to watch a massive offshore supply vessel being piloted into the harbour, Layla wondered how many visitors knew that the Battery was reputed to be haunted – perhaps by poor souls forever searching the horizon for those who never returned. It struck her then that she would need to reconsider her ideas about ghosts and spirits. She'd never believed in them previously, but the body-swap project had opened new avenues for exploration in that direction.

I can't face thinking about that just now. I'm spooked enough as it is.

Then she'd almost laughed at the irony of her all-too-human reaction. Here she was, a philosopher dedicated to discovering truths about reality, ignoring the unprecedented opportunity to explore the project's earth-shattering spiritual implications for fear of the ghosts in her own head.

'Layla? You're miles away and this lad is nearly tugging me off my feet,' James had said gently. 'Shall we go?'

'Sorry; yes, let's move on,' she'd replied, leading them left, away from the quayside and on to a footpath. They'd skirted a colourful children's play area and made their way down a set of wooden steps leading to a small sandy cove: the southernmost part of the beach. This was bordered by the quayside and by a curved berm of broken pink-and-grey granite blocks, which protected the low backs of those Fittie houses parallel with the sea front.

'I can't imagine what it must be like here during a really bad storm,' Layla had cried, pulling on her beanie as the wind hit her with full force.

'It must be extremely scary,' the professor replied. 'The waves can be enormous at this point. Luckily, the Fittie folk have their hatches very well battened down.'

They'd watched indulgently as Buller had a blast on the beach, splashing into the churning sea to retrieve his ball and throwing it down triumphantly at their feet. Eventually, even he grew bored with the activity and after he'd shaken the sand and water off his fur, they'd set off on their northbound walk, the cold air stinging their cheeks. Seeing that the tide was already fully in further ahead, they'd climbed the steep stone steps from the sands to the pedestrianised Esplanade, which ran below and parallel with the main Promenade, and headed towards the distant façade of shops, cafés, funfair and amusement arcade fronting the large leisure complex of Aberdeen Beach.

Now, James chatted happily – albeit at a shout – as they walked. 'Did you know, Layla, that there were once plans to construct a magnificent nine-hundred-foot, cast-iron pleasure pier here in the bay?'

She looked at him in surprise. 'No, I didn't! When was that?'

'Oh, late-Victorian times. A harbour engineer, William Smith, designed it. It would have had a pavilion and a bathing station, and there would have been a small harbour at the end to allow pleasure craft to deposit holidaymakers directly on to the pier.'

'Never heard of it! How do you know this?' she cried, walking slightly ahead and turning her back on the wind to face him.

'I told you I enjoyed researching local history,' he smiled. 'Such a pity the plans never came to anything: the councils of the time and thereafter decided to concentrate on local on-land developments instead. But Aberdonians could have had their own version of Brighton's Palace Pier. Imagine that.'

Turning back and looking out over the blustery bay, Layla *could* imagine it: a grand, cantilevered construction extending from the Esplanade, bustling with excited Victorian families decked-out in holiday garb and straw hats with streamers.

She gave a rueful smile and they ploughed on, up a shallow incline which led to the Promenade pavement, and across the quiet road to the row of small seaside cafés. Over the shrieks of seagulls swooping and soaring overhead, she shouted: 'I don't think dogs are allowed inside any of these places. We'll need to eat outside!'

'Not to worry,' he replied, 'there's a sheltered spot that I see is free, just beside that doorway. We should be all right there.'

Sure enough, a small table and two chairs sat snugly between a green-painted café's bay window and entrance, and, taking a seat, Layla realised they were completely sheltered from the wind. As Buller settled down at their feet, a smiling young waiter appeared and they ordered two vegetarian all-day breakfasts and accompanying pots of tea. Blunstone took some bone-shaped biscuits from his pocket and slipped them to the grateful dog.

'Now,' he said, turning to Layla. 'Tell me what's made you so nervous in your new digs.'

And so she told him about her "prophetic" dream – and watched as his face drained of colour.

'It's true, isn't it?' she asked sharply, alarmed at his response. 'Some part of Stevie's subconscious is still here, in her head? It's the only logical explanation for why I dreamt about real-life rooms I'd never seen before.'

He sighed deeply and ran his gloved hand over his face. Then he looked at her and she saw a hint of fear in his tired, grey eyes.

'Yes, that does seem to be the case,' he said finally, his tone flat.

Anger flared in her. 'But you led us to believe that our consciousness would be delivered into the host brain intact! Obviously, this hasn't happened. At least part of Stevie's subconscious has been left behind and I can only assume that something similar has happened to mine. So, what the *hell* does that mean for us?'

He hushed her, as the waiter appeared with their meal. There was a chilly silence as the lad transferred everything from tray to table and cheerily invited them to 'tuck in and enjoy!'

'I seem to have lost my appetite,' Layla said dully, staring down at her laden plate.

183

But the professor, who appeared to have recovered himself, said: 'Nonsense; get some food down you. You'll feel much better for it.'

He picked up his cutlery and started to eat. Slowly, she followed suit, but this was Stevie's physical reaction, not hers.

'Now, I realise how alarming this development must be,' he began, as he poured milk and tea for them both. 'But I really don't think we should over-react.'

She stared at him. 'And what gives you the confidence to say that? You're as much in the dark as we are! You know, I should have questioned you more deeply about those nightmares Patients C and D spoke about. You said neither of them recognised what the other had been dreaming about, but that wasn't true, was it? They *were* dreaming each other's dreams – and you lied to us!'

He winced at her hostility. 'I *was* a little circumspect with the truth, Layla,' he said softly, but his eyes now carried a glint of steel. 'You must understand that from a single experiment it was impossible to deduce that the same phenomenon would occur again. I took the decision not to share it with you because I felt it would complicate matters unnecessarily at a very delicate stage in our discussions.'

She was outraged. 'Because you thought it would put us off – and it probably would have! How could you have been so calculating?'

His expression went hard and Layla felt a chill that had nothing to do with the bracing sea air. She realised she had crossed a line and would now have to tread very carefully.

I can't afford to alienate this man. He holds my future in his hands.

She forced herself to calm down. 'I just want your reassurance that this is not going to compromise my mental health, or Stevie's,' she said in a more conciliatory tone. 'If you think it will have any negative effects on us, you will tell us, won't you? So that we can swap back sooner, before too much harm is done?'

He seemed to freeze at that, but then his expression softened and he continued mopping up the remains of his fried egg with the last morsel of toast, which he popped into his mouth, chewed and swallowed.

'Layla,' he said firmly, 'we are all working in the dark at the moment; this is unexplored territory. If the nature of consciousness is mysterious to even the best minds on the planet, the nature of its subconscious element is even more so. But, as I say, I don't think we should over-react. My tests following the operation showed that neither you nor Stevie had lost any of the memories or mental abilities you shared with me prior to the op. And there is every indication that each of you is still, essentially, "you". Haven't you said so yourself?'

Reluctantly, she nodded and he continued rather forcefully: 'Well, then. I have no doubt whatsoever that this will still be the case when your me-glands are returned to their rightful place. All right, so there are some vestiges of your subconscious that remain behind; but is that any worse than those host-body muscle memories you have both been experiencing? Or the fact that each of you appears to have brought along for the ride some of your own attributes, which manifest themselves in facial expressions and physical gestures?'

This time he didn't wait for a reply. 'No, of course it's not! I have every faith that your consciousness will reassert itself fully when you swap back – and so there will be no reason to cut the experiment short. Now, does that reassure you?'

And he dabbed his lips with his napkin and sat back, sighing contentedly: 'Well, I must say, that was a most delicious breakfast!'

She sat there, speechless.

Have I just been steamrollered?

Chapter 37

Layla's Log – Week 5, Tuesday evening

It was a surreal and unsettling walk back along the Esplanade. James chattered on as if everything was fine; Buller trotted ahead, greeting every dog he encountered as a long-lost friend, and I tried to act as if all my fears and doubts had been blasted away by the wind buffeting our backs.

But they hadn't been.

Today, I had my first real glimpse of the steely side of James Blunstone. His strong reaction to my tentative suggestion about curtailing the experiment revealed that his benign exterior masks the same self-serving ruthlessness that you, Stevie, are careless enough to wear on your sleeve. And something has become very clear: there is no way our kindly old professor intends to cut short his precious project.

So where does that leave us?

Well, obviously I need to contact you to find out if you're experiencing the effects of *my* subconscious, whether in the form of nightmares or otherwise. You insisted, following the operation, that you didn't remember any of your dreams. Is that still the case? Tomorrow, I intend to find out. You and I need to talk this through and decide whether we feel threatened by what's happening in our heads. Surely, if we both insist we want to swap back, James will have no option but to bring the "restoration" operation forward?

Meanwhile, if I am to have any chance of sleeping tonight, I must try to calm down and at least consider what he said to me today. *Am* I over-reacting? Is sharing some residual part of your subconscious such a dangerous thing? Shouldn't I just accept and observe what's happening, in the interests of furthering the understanding of human consciousness?

Talk about being on the horns of a dilemma.

As I write this, sitting at the kitchen table, Buller is dozing in his bed beside the still-warm range. He appears wiped out by his exertions today, but has one eye on me and is no doubt waiting for his bedtime walk. It's such a comfort to have his doggy presence in the house. I have no fear of sleeping in the master bedroom tonight.

James seemed happy to leave him with me this afternoon, after I'd (grudgingly – but he didn't seem to notice) given him a quick tour of your place and he'd admired the top-floor view. With Buller now on his holidays for a couple of weeks, he has decided to head down to Edinburgh again to visit his friends for a few days. 'I'll be contactable at all times, of course,' he told me, just before he left. Big deal! He clearly has no intention of acting on the concerns I shared today, so what would be the use in contacting him about any others?

If I sound bitter, Stevie, that's because I am. I no longer believe he has our best interests at heart and I'm deeply disappointed in him.

Oh well, no point in going there again. Time for a last quick walk around the squares and then it's off to bed.

Layla's Log – Later the same evening

Thought I'd add a quick postscript: I've made a friend in Fittie!

Well, it's all Buller's doing, really. We were on our way back to the house after our walk when suddenly someone stepped from the shadows, crying out (in what I thought was an Aussie accent!): 'Hello, handsome! And what's *your* name?'

I got such a scare that my heart almost stopped. In front of me stood a small, curvy woman with a bag of rubbish in her hand – one of the neighbours on her way to the wheelie bin. Fright over, I then began to panic, wondering if she was someone you knew well, Stevie. This was my first opportunity to 'fly by the seat of my pants', as you'd put it, and I was completely unprepared.

'How's it going?' I said tentatively, smiling down at the woman, who was now crouching beside the dog and making a huge fuss of him. 'This is Buller; I'm looking after him for a friend for a couple of weeks?'

'He's lovely! Aren't you, gorgeous boy?' she said in that indulgent tone reserved only for pets.

I still wasn't sure if we were supposed to know each other, so I waited for her cue. Eventually, she straightened up and peered at me in the gloom. 'Do you live in Footdee?' she asked. 'I just moved in at the weekend, so I don't know anyone around here.'

What a relief that was! She told me her name was Victoria and that she was delighted to have secured a lease on a Fittie cottage after having had to share a poky flat in the city centre for the past year. 'I can't believe that the first neighbour I've met is a fellow Antipodean,' she said, laughing. 'You're from Sydney, right? I'm from Wellington.'

I went cold at the thought of the gaffe I'd nearly made. A native Australian would certainly have recognised a New Zealand accent – but I hadn't. Quickly, I said that I'd thought so, from her accent, and she told me she was a petroleum engineer: 'over here to seek my fortune in the North Sea oil and gas industry'. I said I was a journalist, in Aberdeen on sabbatical to write a book, and we chatted for a while about what a 'nifty' place Fittie was.

She must be about ten years younger than us, Stevie. She has dramatic looks: black, wavy hair in a widow's peak; dark brown eyes that seem to bore into you; a long nose, and a wide, full-lipped mouth. Despite her intensity, she was very friendly and said she hoped she'd see me around again soon.

It was so lovely to exchange a few words with a stranger who knew nothing about my true situation. A really upbeat end to the day!

That night, as Layla lay deep in the healing sleep she'd hoped for, the sound of someone passing the bedroom window made Buller prick up his ears. The dog sat up, listening intently.

At first, he could hear only the dull pounding of surf on the beach. Then the letterbox flapped and he gave a low growl in response.

Across the room, his new housemate slept on.

Chapter 38

Next morning, as soon as Layla opened the bedroom door, Buller made a beeline for the large white envelope lying on the doormat. He sniffed at it, then looked up at her expectantly.

'What's this, boy?' She had just been congratulating herself on a great night's sleep: knowing the Labrador was watching over her in the darkness had indeed proved an effective soporific. Still smiling, she bent to pick up the envelope, which she noticed was blank. Only mildly puzzled, she let the dog out to urinate on the cobbles opposite the front door and when they both entered the kitchen, she laid the thin packet on the pine table and busied herself brewing coffee, refreshing Buller's water bowl and digging out some biscuits for his first snack of the day. Finally, she sat down with her coffee and opened the envelope.

The contents made her gasp.

Printed in colour, on plain white paper, was a photograph of her and James Blunstone battling along the Esplanade. Scrawled underneath in black marker pen was the legend: *'One of your conquests, Bitch? Bit old for you, isn't he??'*

Horrified, she could only stare at the picture. Who the hell could have sent her such a thing?

Then it struck her: *Calum.*

'The vindictive bastard!' she cried, surprising Buller out of his post-breakfast slumber.

Then reason prevailed. How would Calum have known where "Stevie" had moved to following her house-sit? Surely he couldn't have been spying on her over the past few days? It just wasn't his style; he was far too lazy to go to all this trouble, even allowing for the deep humiliation he must have felt at being led on, then rejected, by the weird Australian woman living in his estranged wife's home.

But who else could it be?

Murdo? Surely not! Yet, an uneasy feeling overtook her as she considered the possibility that the strange young man had been watching her, unobserved, since she left Cairnacraig House just over a fortnight ago. There had been no sign of him in her own neighbourhood. But James had met him in Fittie yesterday morning – and he had been carrying a camera.

Taking a gulp of her rapidly-cooling coffee, Layla was horrified to think that either man could act in such a poisonous manner, regardless of what they thought of her. Perhaps it was someone else: someone Stevie had encountered since moving to Aberdeen.

Impulsively, she picked up her mobile and rang Stevie's number. It went straight to voicemail.

She cursed softly and waited for the beep. 'Stevie! I've just received the most horrible message through your letterbox.' The words tumbled out of her and she tried to take a deep, calming breath.

'Someone is stalking me – or you – and I need to find out if you know who it is. I have a suspicion, but I might be wrong. Will you please call me back as soon as, Stevie? We have to talk about this.'

A couple of hours and several unanswered calls later, Layla came to the conclusion that Stevie was avoiding her.

Well, she wasn't going to get off with it.

'Enjoying your city walk, Buller?' It was another cool and blustery morning, but the sun was out and the mica in the old granite buildings flashed and sparkled as woman and dog passed by at a brisk pace.

Layla was certainly enjoying the exercise, her long stride eating up the pavement at a rate she could only have dreamed of achieving in her own, diminutive body. Buller looked up at her briefly and it was evident from his expression that any kind of walk suited him just fine.

They had left Fittie and the seafront via the Beach Boulevard, by-passing the city centre and its historic, mile-long Union Street and taking the shorter, less scenic route west, through the concrete subway bisecting the sprawling Mounthooly Roundabout and past Brutalist Seventies high-rises.

As always, she found walking helped to soothe her nerves, which had been sent into overdrive by the shock of seeing the photograph. Unable to eat more than a few mouthfuls of toast – and those only because she knew she'd need the energy – she had called Stevie's mobile yet again, only to hear the familiar abrupt voicemail response. She'd left her own equally terse message: 'Stevie, it's Layla – again. I need to see you today. I'm coming over to the house, so please be there at noon. It's urgent.'

There had been no return call and now she and Buller were powering up Hutcheon Street, about halfway through their journey across town. She slowed and paused momentarily to admire an ornate fitment – one of a pair in the street – which resembled a colourful, bulbous lamppost. She remembered reading in the local community magazine that the elegant nineteenth-century structures were originally built to vent noxious gases from the sewers below.

'Only the Victorians could make such a pretty silk purse out of a sow's ear,' she told the solemn dog at her feet.

They picked up pace again and soon reached two more grand legacies from the eighteen hundreds: the ornamental Victoria Park and the functional Westburn Park, laid out on either side of a busy main road. Although she loved to see the spring multicolours of the former, with its flower-bordered fountain and garden of rhododendrons, Layla chose to cut through the Westburn Park, which allowed dogs off the lead. She and Buller ran around for a while, chasing his favourite ball among the mature, newly-greened trees that added old-world grandeur to the wide grassy space.

After the panting dog had drunk from the stream that gave the park its name, they continued their trek up Westburn Road, pausing only to watch a small, yet deafeningly-noisy rescue helicopter lowering itself to land in the hospital grounds opposite. From the occupants' lack of urgency in leaving the aircraft, Layla was relieved to assume that it was a training flight, rather than a medical emergency. She walked on, guiding Buller to make a left turn when they reached the end of her own street.

She had been away for only two nights, but it felt as if weeks had passed since she'd allowed Stevie to drive her from her home. *Literally – but hopefully not metaphorically*, she thought grimly, opening the wrought-iron gate and leading the way up the garden path.

It felt strange to be standing on her own doorstep, waiting for someone to answer the bell. However, no one did, despite several rings.

Layla sighed in frustration. 'We've come all this way and she's not here,' she grumped at Buller, who was sniffing at the door.

There was nothing for it but to turn and retrace their steps. But before they were halfway down the path, someone called over the fence.

'Are you looking for Layla?'

It was her neighbour, Bob. He stood in his doorway, arms folded across his substantial stomach in the traditional way of the perennial gossip. She sighed again, this time inwardly.

'Er, yeah – do you know where she is?'

'Australian, are you?' her nosy neighbour asked. Very little got past Bob Martin.

'Yeah, but Layla...?'

'Oh, she left this morning with a couple of suitcases. I was putting the bin out and asked her where she was off to. Said she was going away for a last-minute break. That's all I can tell you, I'm afraid.' The balding man looked genuinely regretful. 'Nice girl, if a little shy,' he added. 'Is she a friend of yours?'

'A former colleague,' Layla said automatically, her mind in a spin at the news. Where the hell had Stevie gone? She saw the man looking at her expectantly and muttered: 'Thought I'd look her up while I'm in the neighbourhood, but it doesn't matter – I'll email her.'

'I take it you didn't bring *him* over from Oz,' Bob said, pointing at Buller, who had sat down patiently while they talked.

'Eh? Oh yeah, you're right,' Layla said with false heartiness, but she didn't go into any explanations and began to make a move towards the gate.

'Do you want to leave a message with me, for when she gets back?' It was her neighbour's last-ditch attempt to keep her chatting. *Little wonder the postie does his deliveries at a trot in this street*, she thought. *Bob's nearly as bad as the Ancient Mariner when he gets his claws in you.*

'No, ta; as I said, I'll email her. Thanks, anyway...' She reached the gate, Buller hard on her heels.

'Bob's the name – and you're welcome. Any time,' he called after their retreating backs.

195

Oh my god, Oh my god. The words reeled like a mantra around her panicked brain as she strode back down the road on autopilot.

Stevie had gone AWOL and she had no way of knowing where.

Chapter 39

After a brief pit-stop for a late lunch at the beachfront café they'd visited the previous day, Layla and Buller arrived back in North Square, footsore and – in Layla's case – fearful of the implications of Stevie's disappearance.

As she'd sat outside the café, sipping at her second large coffee of the day, she'd rebuked herself for not using her own door key and entering the house, where she might have found some clue as to where the other woman could have gone. She was sure it would have occurred to her before she'd reached the end of the street, but for Bob's interruption, which had confused her and prompted a cover story that made it impossible to gain access to her home at the time. Cursing Stevie for commandeering her beloved Mini, she'd vowed to return by taxi under cover of darkness.

Now, as she fumbled with the still-unfamiliar key to the Fittie front door, another neighbour intercepted her – but this was a far more welcome interruption.

'You two look pooped. You must have walked for miles! I saw you leave this morning,' said Victoria, smiling broadly across at them from her doorway.

'We are,' Layla laughed, cheered by the sight of a friendly face.

'Look, I won't hold you up now, but would you and Buller like to come over for something to eat this evening? Pizza for one is just too sad.' Victoria mock-pouted her scarlet lips and put her head on one side like a little girl.

It took only a few seconds for Layla to decide to postpone her return visit home to the following evening. She felt emotionally drained and the normality and diversion of a girls' night in were too tempting to resist.

'Go on, then: you've persuaded me. Shall I bring some wine?'

'Fantastic! Let's say seven o'clock.'

The new friends grinned at each other and turned to enter their respective houses.

She hadn't laughed so much for months.

Victoria was hilarious, wickedly mimicking her boss's broad Ulster accent and red-faced bluster, and detailing some of the foibles of her workmates, who included a particularly pompous subsea engineer who had just joined the company and to whom she had taken an instant dislike. 'He seems to think his new female colleague has a lot to learn from him,' she explained, pushing her empty plate to the centre of the table. 'But I've already put him straight on that.'

Layla didn't doubt that she had. Eyes flashing beneath lowered brows and mouth momentarily downturned, Victoria looked as if she'd make a formidable enemy, despite her size. But an instant later, she was smiling again and telling a story about another colleague's pet 'cot' ('don't you just love the local accent?') that had followed her all the way to work and had to be carried home, mewling and scratching.

'The boss nearly exploded when she told him why she was so late,' she giggled. 'He's a man on a very short fuse.'

'Sounds a laugh a minute,' smiled Layla, reaching for her near-empty wine glass. 'So that's what I'm missing out on, working from home?'

'Yeah, right. Just be glad you don't have office politics to deal with. Victoria slid off her breakfast bar stool and opened a kitchen cupboard. 'More red?'

Layla nodded, although she knew she had probably drunk enough. Now that the laughter had stopped, she felt her mood dipping and her mind returning to the terrifying thought that Stevie had gone missing – with her body.

She looked up from her glass and caught Victoria staring at her. 'You okay, Stevie?' the younger woman said, unscrewing the top of a bottle of Merlot. 'I know we've only just met, but I get the impression something's weighing on your mind. You seem distracted.'

If only you knew, my friend.

But in the cosy atmosphere of her new pal's kitchen, Buller snoozing contentedly beside the glowing wood-burning stove, Layla felt an overwhelming need to unburden herself of the least outrageous of her worries.

'Well, I suppose I am,' she said slowly. 'This morning, I received what can only be described as a poison-pen letter. It was delivered overnight.'

Victoria's eyebrows shot up. 'No! You're kidding. What did it say?' She climbed back on to the opposite stool and, dark eyes boring into Layla's, poured wine for them both.

'It's more of a picture, actually; I'll go and fetch it.' And before she could reconsider, Layla hurried from the house and retrieved the sheet of paper from her own kitchen table. She was back in under a minute.

'My god, that's horrible,' Victoria said, after she'd examined it carefully. 'Do you know who sent it?'

'No.' Layla took a large swallow of her drink. 'I did think it might be my ex, but it's not at all his style.'

'Your ex in Sydney?' The other woman looked puzzled.

She realised her mistake. 'Er, no – not him. A fella I hooked up with over here for a while. He was very controlling, so I dumped him.' She prayed that Victoria – who was clearly sharp as a tack when it came to reading people – couldn't detect the lie.

199

'Why wouldn't it be him, then? He sounds a prime candidate.' She was still staring at her curiously but didn't seem to suspect anything.

'Oh, he's too busy controlling his new girlfriend now: a quiet little mouse who thinks he's wonderful.'

Victoria nodded thoughtfully and looked back down at the photograph.

'So, who *is* the old guy? Not your latest boyfriend, I take it?'

Layla laughed nervously. 'God, no! James is Buller's owner. He's an old family friend I looked up when I first came over. Nice man... I'm happy to dog-sit for him while he's on holiday.'

Her new acquaintance nodded again. 'Is it the first time you've received something like this? I'm not surprised you're feeling unsettled. It's pretty nasty, if you ask me.'

Layla answered honestly this time. 'Yes, it's completely out of the blue.'

Victoria gave her a long, concerned look. 'Are you sure? It doesn't read as if it's the first one. You can tell me, you know. I won't blab.'

She felt a little uncomfortable under the intense gaze. 'I'm sure,' she said firmly. Whether or not the sender had previously delivered similar messages to Stevie was something she intended trying to find out. But she couldn't share that with Victoria. She was beginning to regret mentioning the letter and decided it was time to close down the conversation.

Looking at her watch and standing up, she said: 'I'm sorry to spoil the mood with my problems, Victoria. This evening has been a real tonic, but I should be going. It's been a long day, hasn't it, Bully-boy? And I'm sure you'll be looking for a bedtime walk?'

The Labrador cocked his ears and sprang to his feet.

'Oh, that's a shame.' Victoria looked put out for a moment, but quickly flashed a smile. 'We must get together again soon. You've told me hardly anything about your own life.'

Layla grinned. 'That's because I couldn't get a word in edgeways.' In fact, she'd been happy to be Victoria's audience for the past couple of hours, asking lots of questions to ensure her vivacious new friend stayed in the spotlight.

'That's not fair! You're too good a listener.'

'I'm a nosy journo, remember? It comes with the territory.'

As Layla left the small Fittie house, Buller at her side, she was surprised and touched when her neighbour reached up and hugged her.

'Will you be all right walking in the dark?' Victoria asked her, her expression serious. 'You should go to the police about that picture, you know. Stalking is no joke.'

'There are still lots of dog-walkers around at this time of night and I'll stay on the main road,' Layla assured her, setting off across the square.

The police? Huh – if only, she thought bitterly.

No law-enforcement agency on earth could help her right now.

Chapter 40

Layla's Log – Week 5, Wednesday evening

Despite you going AWOL and that creepy stalker frightening the life out of me today, Stevie, I found our evening stroll surprisingly calming. With so many other dog-walkers on the go and the fact that the sun doesn't set until around nine-thirty at this time of year, I felt quite safe walking Buller along the Esplanade and back.

It gave me time to think.

What on earth am I doing getting friendly with one of your neighbours? And why did I tell Victoria about the letter?

The answer is, of course, that I'm lonely. I had no idea how much I would miss the daily routine of work and the accompanying chat and companionship. I miss Morven – she, too, thinks I'm in Australia – and I would so love to be able to pick up the phone to say hi to my family. I know there's a time limit to this loneliness, but it's still very hard to bear.

Back to Victoria: although I know we could be great friends, I can't encourage it. It's not fair on her. What's going to happen when the operation is reversed and Victoria encounters the real Stevie? I have the feeling the two of you wouldn't get on at all. And meantime, now she knows about the letter, it's likely she's going to keep pestering me to contact the police. I should never have accepted her invitation tonight. But I did so enjoy the distraction...

No, I need to keep my distance from now on. My priority is to find out where you are and if you know who this stalker could be. I also want to persuade you and James that we should reverse the operation as soon as possible. We've both had long enough to experience what it's like to live literally as someone else, and I've learned that I'm not cut out to be a pioneer. Only when I'm back in my own body will I feel safe – and sane – enough to get down to the serious work that's going to make the rest of my life worth living.

Chapter 41

Layla's Log – Week 5, Thursday morning

I've just awakened from the most fantastic dream.

I don't know whether it was the opportunity to relax and laugh with Victoria or the refreshing ozone from my seaside walk with Buller – perhaps it was a combination of both – but last night I fell asleep at once and dreamed I was surfing in what could only be Australia.

I've never surfed in my life – hell, I've never even been to Australia – but the experience was so real that I could taste the salt spray and feel the strain in my leg muscles as I fought wind and tide to stay upright on my board. It was the most exhilarating sensation: nothing else mattered except riding that forever wave and feeling at one with the powerful, pounding ocean. Then the dream morphed into a beach scene, where I woke from a nap to find myself stretched out on a towel on sun-spangled white sand, being expertly lathered with cocoa butter by a blond stranger in Bermudas... a *very* hands-on surf dude!!

Hmmm, anyway, it wouldn't take a psychologist to tell me that this was either a memory, a fantasy, or a dream of yours, Stevie, reinforcing my belief that your brain has retained some residual elements of your subconscious. The intensity of the experience has given me an idea of how I can pass some time today until I can return home under cover of darkness. While I still inhabit your brain, I'm going to record how I perceive the world through your five senses and how this differs from how I do so when in my own body.

First, though, I need to reassure an impatient dog about some breakfast and yet another walk...

To her relief, Layla, peeping out of her kitchen window, saw Victoria leaving her cottage at around half-past eight. The other woman had told her the previous evening that she would be returning to work that morning after having had a few days' leave to get settled into her new home. Her absence from the square meant Layla wouldn't have to keep trying to avoid her as she came and went from the house.

Her plan was to fill the day with activity until early evening, when she'd sneak out with Buller to find somewhere dog-friendly to eat. Then, after dark, she would take the bus to her own house in Midstocket to do some detective work without fear of being seen by Bob, her nosy neighbour.

She had to find some clue as to Stevie's whereabouts. The alternative didn't bear thinking about.

Layla's Log – Week 5, Thursday late afternoon

Okay, I'm back at the kitchen table, ready to record some of my sensory impressions.

I've noticed over the past few weeks that you have a very keen nose, Stevie. And standing on the beach at Fittie this morning, I could strongly detect a melange of smells, ranging from seaweed, to fish, to diesel fuel from the boats, as well as a whiff of wood smoke from one of the nearby cottages. My own sense of smell is not nearly as acute, so I'm making the most of yours.

With taste being linked to our sense of smell, it's no surprise that food has much more flavour just now. Previously wishy-washy coconut ice cream has never tasted so good...

Before the body-swap, you told me you had twenty-twenty vision, and you weren't lying. From the beach, the horizon appears as sharp as if I'd been looking through binoculars. And I would certainly have needed binoculars to have seen the horizon with my own eyes, even with my contact lenses in. I wonder how you're coping with my short-sightedness.

But I'm glad to say that there's one thing, Ms Perfection, that you're missing out on, and that's excellent hearing: something I've always taken for granted in my own body. So, make the most of my ears, mate!

As far as the sense of touch goes, I can't say I've noticed much of a difference. Is this because we share a similar number of nerve endings in our skin??

Touch and feeling (physical sensation) are two sides of the same coin, but feeling, in your body, is different. Judging by its stamina during physical activity, your body definitely has a higher pain tolerance than mine, as I know my own muscles and lungs would seize up long before yours do. Also, wonderfully, this body is entirely free of the aches and pains that have plagued mine over the past few months. I wonder how you're coping with that, too.

Pain is a strange beast. Philosophers have argued over its nature for centuries. Even taking the "common sense" point of view, there's an anomaly: on the one hand, we perceive pain as objective – we most often describe it as having a physical location, in time and space, in our bodies; but on the other, it's entirely *sub*jective, as only we can experience our own pain. Can something be both objective and subjective at the same time? And does pain require the presence of consciousness – a perceiver – in order to exist? Again, common sense says 'yes' – we don't feel pain when we're unconscious during an operation – but that by no means implies it's all in the mind. It can't be, because if that were the case, surely I would feel the same level of physical pain (when running, for example) in your body as I would experience in my own? And I don't. The logical conclusion is that I haven't brought my personal pain tolerance along for the ride because it's related to my own physical body and is not part of my consciousness. So, does that mean pain tolerance is objective? Groan...

One thing I do know for sure, and it backs up the testimonies of Patients A, B, C and D, is that even as a "visiting consciousness", I have no control over whether or not I experience your body's physical pain. I *do* experience it and I do so as directly as if it were affecting my own body. I could no more deliberately cut your wrist than I could my own, because I know I would feel pain. Maybe not as keenly as if I were in my own body, it could be argued, but I certainly do feel it. So, my consciousness is not merely an observer in this new body; it is inextricably linked with it.

Although your body's tolerance of physical pain is different from mine, when it comes to *non-physical*, or emotional pain, such as stress, worry, anguish, fear, etc, I find I am experiencing these feelings in exactly the same way as I would in my own body. That's no surprise, of course, as they originate in my own consciousness. But what's interesting to me is that your body reacts to these emotions in exactly the same way as my own body does, with the same spikes of adrenaline, sleep disruption, loss of appetite, etc. This is when "mind over matter" really does seem to apply. I wonder if some of these physical disturbances, caused by my own emotional stress, are actually new (perhaps even harmful??) to your body, Stevie. You are so confident and you don't seem the type to lie awake worrying at night. I'll probably never find out if you do stress out in such a way, because I can't imagine you ever admitting to it.

Just a thought: if my consciousness is able to cause physical changes in your body, *can your body, in turn, influence my consciousness?* Am I thinking differently because of how I now feel, physically?

I'll need to think about that!

Whew, well, that's my whistle-stop tour of your senses. It's by no means academic and it will require proper scientific analysis when the experiment eventually goes public. But at least, for a while, it's done the trick of keeping my mind off tonight and what I might find out about you – and our stalker.

Chapter 42

She felt like a thief in the night.

After creeping around the side of the house, Layla and Buller entered the back door. Not wanting to attract any neighbourly attention, she quickly pulled down the kitchen blind and switched on the large rubber torch she'd retrieved from a cupboard. The room appeared to be just as she'd left it and a quick check revealed an empty fridge.

This didn't bode well.

She motioned to Buller and they moved into the hall, shadows leaping and retreating as if sporting with them in the light's wobbly progress towards the lounge. The dog, too, treated it as a game, yipping for attention and jumping around in play, but he soon quietened when Layla produced a rawhide bone from her shoulder bag, and he settled by the sofa happily enough while she drew the lounge curtains and continued with the bizarre scenario of searching her own home.

It would help if I knew what I was looking for, she thought edgily, amazed at how such familiar surroundings could appear so sinister by torchlight. Beside every piece of furniture, a dark doppelganger lurked, elongating and shrinking as she moved around the room. *Get a grip*, she told herself. *One click of the overhead light and everything returns to normal, so forget the spooks and just get on with it.*

The lounge also appeared undisturbed by Stevie's short stay: nothing had been moved nor any surface cluttered by the woman's possessions. Exasperated, she sighed and strode back into the hall. As she reached her bedroom door, her heart leapt with fright as something bumped against her legs.

'Buller! What a scare you gave me,' she cried. But of course the dog hadn't wanted to be left alone in the dark. He looked up at her, bone in mouth, as if to say 'What now?'

She couldn't help laughing. 'This is like a scene from *Scooby Doo*! Okay, fearless mutt, let's see what's what in here.'

The bedroom appeared as unoccupied as the other rooms. Opening the wardrobe and chest of drawers, she noticed that quite a lot of her clothes and underwear were missing. She remembered Bob's words about the two suitcases Stevie had been carrying. *She'd better not have stolen my stuff*, she thought, then laughed mirthlessly as she realised losing her clothes would be the least of her worries if Stevie really had run off.

She moved over to the bed. It was neatly made and the small tables on either side held nothing more than the familiar lamps and radio alarm clock. She was about to turn on her heel when the downcast torchlight illuminated a dark shape sticking out from under the valance. Kneeling, she retrieved Stevie's iPad, its deep green cover unmistakeable.

'Well, lookee here, Scoob: we may have hit the jackpot!'

The dog glanced up momentarily from his gnawing as if to say 'Huh?' and she laughed again.

'What a team, eh?'

She guessed that the device must have slipped, unnoticed, to the floor when Stevie was packing to leave. The journalist obviously hadn't missed it yet, most likely because she also had a phone and a laptop.

She was about to take it into the kitchen when a thought struck her and she entered her small study instead. She went straight to her desk and opened the top left-hand drawer.

'I don't believe this! The bitch has stolen my passport!'

After a fruitless search through both the left- and right-hand drawers, Layla checked that the missing passport hadn't fallen down the back of the desk. No such luck. Horrified, she had to conclude that Stevie was seriously on the run.

She sat down with a thump in her office chair and laid the iPad on the desktop. Her only hope was that the device held a clue to the woman's plans and whereabouts. But first she had to find a way in. She opened the cover and Stevie's home page picture – a beaming selfie – appeared. She clicked through to the passcode keypad and shone the torch on the shiny glass surface. Her faint hope of finding a pattern of four distinct fingerprints above the relevant numbers was soon dashed at the sight of the greasy smear which dulled the entire screen. Evidently Stevie shared her own bad habit of failing to clean it regularly.

She knew she could sit here tapping on digits until doomsday and still be no nearer guessing the correct sequence. And, anyway, she'd be locked out after only a few tries. She slammed the cover shut, dropped the torch on the table and sat for a while, head bowed. At her feet, Buller continued to chew happily, oblivious to her despair.

Then she had an idea. She reopened the case, clicked to the keypad again and, before she could think about it, tapped out '4868'. A desktop full of app icons appeared.

She was in.

'Yes!' she yelled, startling the dog. Muscle memory – or was it some residue of Stevie's subconscious? – had kicked in. All she'd had to do was clear her mind, unfocus her gaze and let her fingers do the rest. She felt exhilarated, but knew time was short. The Australian, on discovering the loss, might shut down the iPad remotely to prevent anyone else accessing it.

'Right,' Layla said firmly. 'Let's take a dive into Stevie's secret life.' And she tapped the 'Mail' icon.

Chapter 43

Layla felt no guilt at opening Stevie's inbox. She was beyond that. As far as she was concerned, her body-swap partner had forfeited all rights to privacy when she disappeared from the scene after stealing her passport.

She quickly scanned the folder's short list of emails, but to her great disappointment they all seemed to be junk. Then she checked the 'Favourites' section, which contained only the one folder.

Its title, *'Threats'*, made her catch her breath.

The list of messages, all from the same innocuous hotmail address comprising only numbers and letters, dated back several months, to the preceding August. Layla read through them and was shocked to uncover a litany of abuse, each new paragraph making her feel more and more disgusted as the unknown writer described in graphic detail how much they hated Stevie and what they would do to her when they decided to remove her from her 'cosy life'. One or two emails even carried jpeg attachments depicting candid street shots of the blonde Australian, who seemed oblivious to the photographer's attention. But it was the messages from recent weeks that were the most terrifying. The sender's tone grew incandescent with rage, as he or she realised Stevie had disappeared from her life in Sydney. Then the latest email, dated only the previous week, indicated that the torment would continue: *'You will never escape me, Bitch from Hell.'*

She sat back, repulsed by all she'd read, her mind reeling. Stevie had indeed had a stalker in Australia, and whoever it was, was quite clearly insane.

Had he finally tracked her down and followed her over to Scotland? Or did the creep who'd sent Layla the poison-pen message live and work a little closer to home?

She went back to the screen. It quickly became obvious that the iPad contained no clue as to its owner's current whereabouts. The internet search history had been wiped; the desktop's generic apps provided nothing useful: there were no travel documents in the 'Wallet' app; and she was surprised by a complete absence of text documents in 'File Explorer', this leading her to conclude that Stevie must do all her work on her laptop.

Layla cried out in exasperation. All hope of finding her body-swap buddy had dissolved, leaving her faint with panic.

'This can NOT be happening! Where *is* she?'

Chapter 44
Stevie

In fact, Stevie wasn't all that far away.

Sitting in the quiet lounge of a granite-built heritage hotel only a few streets from Layla's home, she sipped from a bottle of local craft beer and stared moodily out at the rainy darkness beyond the building's spotlit strip of garden.

By now, she should have been back in Sydney leading a carefree existence. She'd easily found Layla's passport and, right up until the previous day, her exit plan had been well under way.

But instead, here she was: still hanging around Aberdeen, hiding out and apparently still vulnerable to the mysterious stalker who'd destroyed her old life.

After listening to Layla's first distressed voicemail message, she'd begun to worry that the sick bastard had somehow managed to follow her all the way to Scotland. She'd needed time to think things through, away from all the fuss and complications presented by the professor and his project. So, she'd quickly packed a couple of cases with the clothes and possessions she'd need to tide her over should she manage to leave the country, as previously planned. Then she decamped to the nearest hotel, where she believed Layla and the professor would never think of looking for her.

She took another sip of beer and pondered further. If her stalker was here and believed she was living in Fittie, could that "night-attack" nightmare which had haunted her in the weeks before the operation become a dangerous reality? If so, Layla was the one at risk – but it was her own, discarded body that would come to harm. The body which, infuriatingly, she now needed back!

Her ire rose again at the thought of how Layla's substandard physical frame had ruined everything. *Of all the bodies in the world to swap with, hers had to be a dud*, she thought resentfully.

Plagued by aches and pains and sudden bouts of weakness ever since the operation, Stevie was damned if she was going to spend the rest of her life in such a state, even if the new identity did provide her with a passport home to Australia and the ability to hide in plain sight from the stranger who wanted her dead.

No, they would have to swap back now, and it would all have been for nothing, at least as far as she was concerned. Contrary to what she'd claimed to Layla and the professor, she had no real interest in writing a book. But before she could reclaim her body, she'd have to find out for sure if the weirdo who'd scared Layla was indeed her own stalker from Sydney.

And if he was, she'd have to deal with him for once and for all. It was the only way she could safely return to her old life.

What a bloody mess!

Still scowling, she turned from the hotel window in time to see a man and woman making their way across the room towards her. They were smiling and the woman gave her a little wave.

'Oh-oh – time to go,' she muttered, slamming down the beer bottle. She rose stiffly to her feet and, mouthing 'Sorry, must dash' to the surprised-looking couple, hurried through the door, up the spiral staircase and along the corridor towards the sanctuary of her room.

Being recognised was one of the hazards of staying in Layla's neighbourhood, but it didn't worry her too much. She had almost enjoyed brazening it out with anyone who tried to chat to her, doing exactly as she'd done in the hotel lounge: pretending to be in a tearing hurry and unable to give them the time of day. And she'd fairly shut down that nosy Bob yesterday morning, cheeky bugger.

As she opened the door and spotted her laptop on the neatly-made bed, the scene reminded her of something. She wracked her brain and then realised what it was. She had placed her iPad on Layla's bed while she was packing and she didn't remember taking it with her. A quick search of her possessions confirmed her fears.

'Shit... I must have left it in the house!'

Furious with herself, she grabbed a jacket and her car keys, banged the door behind her and tore back downstairs, pushing her way through surprised patrons in the busy lounge and bar, until she reached the back entrance.

The Mini was waiting in the hotel car park, a private space bordered by high walls and tall trees, where she had been pretty sure the car wouldn't be spotted when Layla inevitably returned to her own neighbourhood to look for her.

Stevie slammed the vehicle into gear and hurtled from the exit, determined to retrieve her iPad without delay.

She couldn't let it fall into Layla's hands.

Chapter 45
Layla

An onlooker would have found it hard to tell who was angrier.

With enormous relief, Layla had heard her car pulling into the drive and had steeled herself for the confrontation. Stevie, on the other hand, got the shock of her life when, as she inserted her key, the front door was wrenched open and nearly sent her flying.

Now the two women stood glaring at each other.

'Where the *hell* have you been, Stevie?' Layla hissed, pulling the diminutive journalist into the hall and shutting the door after her. She switched on the light, deciding there was no longer any need for subterfuge.

'None of your business!' Stevie retorted, her face twisted with rage and frustration at finding Layla back home. From the kitchen doorway, Buller growled low in his throat and she turned her furious gaze upon him.

'Keep that brute away from me.'

The dog started snarling at her and all she could see were black lips mashed back to reveal the wolf-toothed leer of childhood nightmares.

'I mean it, Layla – I have a phobia. Make him stop!' she screamed, her blue eyes now wide with terror.

Astonished at her extreme reaction, Layla hushed Buller and shut him in the kitchen. They could hear him whining behind the door.

'Why didn't you tell me about this before?' she asked. Stevie, recovering herself, didn't reply, but the answer was obvious. *She wouldn't want to admit to what she sees as a weakness*.

'Look,' she said more gently. 'Let's go into the lounge. We really need to talk.'

'No, we really don't,' Stevie said defiantly and pushed past her, on her way to the bedroom.

'It's not there,' Layla called after her. 'I already found it. And I've read your emails.'

Stevie whirled around, her face once more a mask of fury. 'You hacked in? How did you do that? How *dare* you do that!'

'Come through here and sit down for a minute,' Layla urged again. 'I know someone has been stalking you and since I *am* you for the time being, I think you owe me an explanation.'

For a scary split-second, Stevie looked as if she might attack her. Then she seemed to reconsider, took a deep breath and trudged into the lounge ahead of her. She sat rigidly in an armchair, while Layla took the sofa and leaned forward.

'Look, maybe I can help you? Please will you tell me what you know about this psycho? Is it a man or a woman? Am I in danger? Don't you think I have a right to know the full story?'

Stevie scowled at her, but finally said: 'I haven't a clue who it is, but I'm guessing from all the sexual references that it's a man.'

'Okay, has he followed you over from Australia?'

'I don't know!' the other woman shouted. 'Maybe.' She slumped back in her seat, arms folded.

'Why is this man fixated on you?' Layla wanted to know.

'I have no earthly idea. I'm an investigative journo, so I rub a lot of folks up the wrong way. I wasn't exactly going to hang around to ask him who he was and why he was so pissed off at me.'

'And is this stalker the reason you were so keen to take part in the project and to hurry it along?' Layla's voice was now dangerously quiet.

'Wouldn't you have done the same thing?' Stevie challenged.

'No, I bloody well wouldn't!' Layla exploded. 'I would have gone to the police and nipped it in the bud as soon as possible. I wouldn't have travelled across the world, swapped bodies with an innocent stranger and put her directly in the line of fire. I can't believe what a callous bitch you are, Stevie. You horrify me!'

'Stop being such a self-righteous wuss,' the other woman said derisively. 'You have no idea what I've been through. I did go to the police, but they were no help at all. They told me the messages were untraceable and that there was very little they could do until the person made himself known. Well, I wasn't waiting around for that! I needed to get away fast and the project was the perfect solution.'

She leaned forward. 'And for your information, I didn't deliberately put you "in the line of fire". I didn't expect the bastard to follow me over here!'

Layla shook her head. 'This is unbelievable.'

Then something else struck her. 'But why are you still here? The stalker surely doesn't know you've swapped bodies, so why haven't you already done a runner – with *my* passport and *my* body?'

Stevie sneered at her. 'Oh, yes: *your* body. The body that feels some days as if it belongs to a seventy-year-old. Well, I don't want to run away with *your* body anymore. I want my own fit one back – but not until I know that that crazy fucker has been locked up and can't threaten me anymore.'

Layla could only stare at her. This had to be the most pathologically selfish person she'd ever encountered. She even put Calum in the shade.

But she had a point about her body.

They sat glaring at each other. Then Stevie said: 'Anyway, we don't even know if it *is* my Australian stalker who sent you that letter. What did it say?'

In a monotone, Layla described the image and its message.

Stevie looked grim, then her expression cleared. 'But you said in your voicemail that you might have an idea who sent it to you? Who are you thinking of?'

Layla didn't reply. The full scale of Stevie's deception had finally sunk in and she felt a surge of hatred towards the woman who had planned to steal her life. She couldn't spend another minute in her company.

'Right now, I don't care who's after who,' she said suddenly, getting up and moving towards the lounge door. Buller followed her.

'Where are you going?' Stevie cried, jumping to her feet. 'We have to get to the bottom of this!'

'I'm taking my car and going back to your house to fetch my things and come back here. *You* can go back to wherever you've been hiding,' Layla said loudly from the doorway.

'But we can't leave things like this!'

'Oh yes we can.' Her voice was low and dangerous now. 'Give me my car and house keys and *get out of my home.*'

Fury crossed Stevie's face and she seemed about to retaliate. But seeing the much taller, fitter woman advancing menacingly towards her, she backed down and pulled the keys from her jacket pocket.

'Take them, you stupid cow!' she spat, throwing them at Layla. 'But running away from me will do you no good. We need each other and you know it. Call me when you're feeling more rational.'

And with that, she pushed past her and left the room. Layla heard the front door slam and felt her anger morphing into despair. She looked down at the dog.

'Oh Buller, what an absolute disaster. Where do we go from here?'

Half an hour later, Layla steered the Mini off the Prom on to North Pier Road, which ran behind Fittie's pedestrianised squares. She squeezed into the last parking space and she and Buller got out and slowly walked the short distance to Stevie's house.

She felt exhausted and completely disillusioned. But she also knew she couldn't afford to wallow in self-pity for long. Her need to get away from Stevie was entirely natural, but the circumstances were anything but. The two of them were inextricably connected and she would have to contact the Australian soon to discuss their mutual escape from the ruins of Blunstone's ill-fated project.

Anger once again surged in her at the thought of how such an earth-shattering experiment had been desecrated by the personal problems of a supremely selfish woman.

'And never mind what she was planning to do to me!' she said aloud, on Stevie's doorstep. 'We humans really are our own worst enemies; we don't deserve to learn the secrets of the universe.'

With a sigh, she removed the keyring from her pocket, unlocked the heavy front door and pushed it open.

A swishing sound put her on high alert. Something was lying on the doormat.

Switching on the hall light, she saw that another large white envelope had been delivered. This time, however, it appeared to carry more than a sheet of paper. Full of dread, she bent to pick up the bulky envelope and saw that it was addressed to '*Prize Bitch*'. She gave a shiver and carried it through to the kitchen, where the slow ticking of the old maritime wall clock sounded unnaturally loud.

She sat down at the table, ripped open the package and peered in.

'What the hell?'

She gasped and dropped it reflexively. A small plastic Ziploc bag fell out onto the worn pine surface. Layla could see that the bag was opaque with what looked like fresh blood.

Although she recoiled in horror, some brave part of her – or Stevie – had to know what lay inside. Slowly, she reached out and unzipped the top of the bag, revealing what looked like the bloody severed paw of a wild rabbit.

Her ears began to ring and she felt faint. Looking into the envelope, she withdrew a single sheet of paper. On it was printed: **'A baud's fit for yer creel. Lucky you: you're next. See you <u>very</u> soon :-)'**

Layla's skin crawled as she recognised the twisted reference to the old Fittie superstition she'd read online on her first evening in the house.

With shaking hands, she retrieved her phone from her bag and tapped out a number. When her own voice answered on the second ring, she cried out: 'Something horrible has happened. Call a cab and get down to Fittie right now!'

Within twenty minutes, Stevie was sitting opposite her at the kitchen table. Her initial hostility on arrival had been replaced by shock and disgust when Layla showed her the grisly contents of the package and explained the context.

'Well, he's certainly done his homework,' the Australian said at last, dropping the sheet of paper and sitting back in her seat.

223

'The information is easily accessible online,' said Layla dully. 'Anyone with an interest in Fittie would have hit on it more or less right away.'

Stevie rubbed her eyes. She looked as exhausted as Layla felt.

'Okay, let's think this through,' she said in a businesslike tone. 'Who's the other guy you mentioned as a possible suspect?'

'Murdo,' was Layla's simple reply.

'Who? You mean Blunstone's gardener's lad?'

'Grandson.'

'Whatever. What makes you suspect *him*?'

Layla reminded her of her two unsettling encounters with Murdo at Cairnacraig House and added that James had met him in Fittie the previous morning.

'He was carrying his camera,' she said. Then a thought struck her. '*And* he'd have no problem catching and killing a rabbit from the estate. Both he and Jimmy have a shotgun licence. I remember James telling us that during the first weekend we met.'

'Oh my god,' breathed Stevie. 'Do you really think it could be him?'

'I have no idea, but one thing I do know is that we must persuade the professor to reverse the operation as soon as possible. The stalker, for whatever reason, is after *you* and you're the one who should be dealing with it.'

Seeing the woman's shrug, Layla felt her anger resurfacing.

'You know, you really are despicable, Stevie! After we swap back, I want nothing more to do with you.'

But the Australian only smiled coldly at her and said: 'Believe me, I want nothing more to do with *you*, or your pathetic body. But I told you already: I won't be swapping back until we find out who the stalker is.'

'You selfish, bloody coward!' cried Layla. 'I can't believe –'

The sudden shrill ring of the doorbell had them both leaping to their feet. Buller started barking and ran out into the hall. Layla's heart tripped in her chest as she glanced at her watch and saw that it was eleven-thirty pm.

Throwing off her anger with Stevie, she cautiously followed the dog to the front door and peered through the peephole. To her utter relief, she saw a fish-eye distortion of Victoria's concerned face. She flung open the door and her new friend bustled in.

'Are you okay, Stevie? Sorry to bother you so late, but I was just coming back from a night out and saw from the lights that you're home again. There's something you need to know right away!'

The younger woman seemed breathless with excitement. Before Layla could reply, she added dramatically: 'I saw him!'

'Saw who?' Stevie was standing in the kitchen doorway, arms folded.

'Victoria, this is my friend, Ste- er, Layla,' Layla stuttered. 'Layla, Victoria's my new neighbour.'

'Victoria from New Zealand, eh?' said Stevie without warmth.

'Wow, well done,' the black-haired woman replied with a faint smile. 'Most people over here think I'm Australian.'

Then her expression turned serious again and she looked at Layla. 'I think it was the stalker? It was dark and rainy, but around teatime, I saw someone shoving what looked like a large envelope through your door. *Was* it him?'

'It was,' Layla confirmed, ushering Victoria past Stevie into the kitchen and ignoring the Australian's 'WTF?'

expression. 'Let me put some coffee on and you can tell us exactly what happened.'

Victoria briefly made a fuss of Buller and then joined Stevie at the table. The pair eyed each other with what looked to Layla like suspicion.

'So, what did you see?' she prompted, filling the kettle at the sink.

Victoria launched into her tale. 'Well, it was about six o'clock and I was just about to draw the kitchen blind, when I noticed someone walking through the Square. A tall, burly bloke wearing a black hoodie and jeans? As I said, it was dark and rainy and I couldn't see his face properly, but he stopped at your door and shoved an envelope through. Then he ran back the way he came.'

She waved her arms around dramatically as she spoke, clearly relishing the attention.

'So, I rushed over and rang your bell, but there was no reply. I didn't know what to do – whether to call the police, or wait until you came home? Then I thought "Without you around, what would calling the police achieve?" And I didn't know what time you'd be back, so I went out as I'd planned and I've only just got back.'

Her gaze kept returning to the large envelope on the table.

'What did his message say this time?'

Stevie glared first at Victoria and then at Layla.

'You didn't tell me you'd told anyone else about the stalker,' she said coldly.

'You didn't ask,' Layla retorted, turning back to the work surface. She poured hot water into a cafetière and took three stoneware mugs from a rack. The silence behind her was unnerving and she could feel two sets of eyes boring into her back. She transferred the coffee and mugs to the table.

'Here,' she said to Victoria, pushing the envelope towards her. 'But I warn you, it's not pretty.' She retrieved a carton of milk from the fridge and sat down opposite Stevie, who was still looking daggers at her.

Victoria peered gingerly into the envelope and gave a little scream. 'What is it?' she shrieked, dropping it on the table and looking at Layla with horrified eyes.

'It's a gruesome reference to an old Fittie superstition about hares,' Layla explained, picking up the envelope and drawing out the message. 'Apparently, hares are rare around here, so we think it must be a rabbit's foot – but it serves the purpose.' And she started to repeat the story she'd told Stevie earlier.

However, Victoria interrupted her. 'Yes, I know this tale! I remember reading it online when I was researching the area. The stalker probably did exactly the same and took a punt on you knowing what he was referring to!'

'Yes, thank you, Sherlock,' Stevie said sarcastically, putting down her mug. 'But we've already worked that out for ourselves. And we'll be able to take it from here on our own.'

Victoria's face flushed and her dark eyes narrowed. 'What's *your* problem?' Her voice was anything but friendly now. 'I'm just trying to help out a mate.'

Before Stevie could reply, Layla butted in. 'Okay, ladies, I think we're all feeling the stress here. Let's not fight, though, eh?'

She turned to Victoria. 'Thanks so much for looking out for me. I'm going to report this to the police first thing in the morning and meantime I have Stevie – I mean Layla! – here to keep me company overnight. Along with our trusty guard dog, of course.' Her laugh sounded unconvincing even to her.

Still staring hard at Stevie, but rising to her feet, Victoria said to Layla: 'Okay, Stevie, if you're sure. But I'll give you my business card in case the police want a word while I'm at work.'

'Great. I'll pop over now to fetch it.'

'And take him with you!' shouted Stevie, pointing a shaking finger at Buller.

Layla sighed, but clipped on the dog's lead and the three of them trooped out and across the square to Victoria's cottage.

'Seriously, what is her problem?' Victoria said angrily, unlocking her door. 'How are you even friends with someone like that?'

'She's actually my cousin and having family here was one of the reasons I chose Aberdeen for my sabbatical,' Layla improvised wildly. 'And yes, sorry, she can be a little over-possessive and confrontational. Her mother – my Mum's late sister – was exactly the same, apparently.'

'Shame you can't choose your rellies,' the smaller woman muttered, delving into the pocket of a jacket which hung in the small vestibule. 'Anyway, here's my card. Give me a call at work tomorrow to let me know what the police are saying. We don't want this guy getting any closer.'

'Too right!' Layla said with false heartiness. 'Well, goodnight, and thanks again, Victoria. I really appreciate your concern.'

This was greeted by a tight smile and then the door was closed firmly in her face.

'We're surrounded by over-assertive Antipodeans,' she grumbled to Buller as they retraced their steps.

But she knew that Stevie and Victoria locking horns was the very least of her worries.

Chapter 46

'Jesus Christ, Layla – what were you thinking, telling that *Kiwi* about the stalker?'

They were hardly through the front door when Stevie, hands on hips in the kitchen doorway, started in on her.

She held up her own large hand, as if to fend off the woman's anger, and pushed past her with the dog, taking a tiny amount of pleasure from the way Stevie jumped out of his path. Buller headed for his bed, where he fussed around, ruffling his blanket and thumping down with a sigh that expressed his disgust at the short length of the walk he'd waited for all evening.

Layla took a seat at the table and refilled her mug from the cafetière.

'Well?' cried Stevie.

'She's a new friend, she was there, I was lonely and scared – you had done a runner, for god's sake – and I needed a sympathetic ear. Anyway, what's the harm? She's done us a favour tonight by giving us a description that we can take to the police. If she hadn't known about the stalker, she wouldn't have paid any attention to a random guy delivering something through your door.'

'She's a nosy cow and she's loving every minute of this!' said Stevie. 'And now she's more or less forcing us to go to the cops before we're ready.'

'What do you mean, "before we're ready"? I'm ready now!' Layla retorted. Her indignance almost choked her at the thought of Stevie's earlier refusal to cooperate. 'If you insist on holding my body to ransom until we find the stalker, I want the police on board right now.'

'They won't take us seriously,' Stevie scoffed at her.

'I don't agree – with that *thing* as evidence,' Layla indicated the white package, 'they'll have to take us seriously.'

Stevie plunked herself down opposite her. 'Oh, they'll *say* they're taking it seriously,' she sneered. 'But I've had experience of this, remember, and all they'll do is tell you to keep a record of every nasty little incident so that they have more evidence to build up a case. They're not exactly going to post someone outside the door, Layla.'

She leaned aggressively across the table and continued: 'And anyway, I don't *want* the police involved.'

Layla felt her cheeks flush. 'Why not?' she cried. 'We can't handle this on our own! Whoever he is, the guy is clearly insane and who knows what he'll do next? And as it's me who's the one in danger, I say we go to the police.'

'We both have an equal stake in this,' Stevie hissed. 'It's *my* body he'd be messing with, don't forget.'

God, my face looks ugly when I'm angry, Layla thought distractedly. Then, realising that confrontation was no way to handle the other woman, she changed tack.

'Okay, let's try to calm down a bit. What bright idea are you proposing instead?'

Stevie poured herself more coffee and took a sip.

'We need to catch him in the act. From *her* description, it could quite easily be Murdo. He's just an overgrown kid and I'm not afraid of *him*. With the element of surprise, we could surely overpower him. Then we could deliver him into the hands of the police.'

Seeing Layla's doubtful look, she added: 'Believe me, I want this over with just as much as you do; but going to the cops right now would only drag things out; it could be ages before they actually do anything proactive to catch the bastard.'

Layla was about to say something, but Stevie wasn't finished.

'And, anyway, have you thought about all the questions they'd ask you about your life and background in Australia? Unless you're a supercool liar (*like you*, Layla

230

thought), you'd make a mistake and they'd know there was something fishy going on. They'd probably dismiss you as a flake.'

'I wouldn't make a mistake,' Layla said wearily.

'Yeah, right. You already called me by my real name in front of the Kiwi. You'd crack in a police interview, I just know it.'

Layla considered this. Much as she hated it, Stevie was right. She wasn't entirely confident she could handle all the questions a detective would throw at her. What's more, if the Australian was determined not to have the operation reversed until the stalker was safely locked up, a police investigation based solely on threatening messages from an unknown – or suspected – source, could take weeks or months, and neither of them wanted that.

'This whole situation is abhorrent,' she announced coldly. 'I really can't express how disgusted I am with you and what you've done. I wish you were a million miles away.'

'But...?' Stevie taunted, apparently unaffected by Layla's contempt.

'But... we're stuck with each other for now. Let's just get this over with so that we can reclaim our old lives and I never have to see you again.'

Grinning triumphantly, Stevie thumped both hands on the table. 'Excellent! Welcome back to reality. Now, we need to hatch a plan.'

Chapter 47
Week 5, Friday Morning: Edinburgh
James

Professor James Blunstone cursed himself as the tiny ball landed in the rough. His golfing buddy made a 'hard luck' face at him and he was just about to stomp off in pursuit of the damned thing when his mobile rang in his pocket. Seeing the caller was Layla, he answered with more cheer than he felt.

'Hello! I'm busy hacking up turf down here before heading home this afternoon. How are things with you?' He turned away and began walking briskly down the green.

'Oh, just grand.' Her voice dripped with sarcasm and he felt the ever-present knot in his stomach tighten.

'Has something happened?' he asked quietly, hoping his friend was now out of earshot.

He heard her sigh. 'Yes, you could say that,' she said. 'Look, I won't go into it now, but I wanted to give you a heads up from both Stevie and me. We need you to bring forward the reversal operation.'

He felt a flash of anger, but kept his voice calm. 'Whatever for? What's going on up there, Layla?'

'This is non-negotiable, James?' Layla's borrowed Australian accent was more pronounced than ever. 'You can forget about our three-month deal; we both want our bodies back as soon as possible, and we need you and your team to be ready.'

'Layla! This isn't like you. Please tell me what's happened. Is Stevie forcing your hand?' *Nothing would surprise me about Stevie's actions*, he thought. *The woman is toxic.*

'Drop in past Fittie on your way home and I'll explain everything,' was all she would say before cutting him off.

Now fear clutched at Blunstone's innards and he tramped back towards his friend, who was about to tee off.

'Sorry and all that, but I have to get back home right away,' he said as breezily as he could, clapping the surprised man on the shoulder and heading towards the clubhouse before any awkward questions could be asked.

He walked on leaden legs, a feeling of dread descending on him.

What fresh hell awaited him in Aberdeen?

Chapter 48
Fittie

Layla's Log – Week 5, Friday

I hate you, Stevie, for what you've done to me. You were going to steal my body until you decided that it wasn't good enough for you. And now you've roped me into being a decoy for a lunatic stalker!

You laughed when I told you James didn't sound at all happy when I called him earlier this morning.

'That's too bad,' you said. 'He'll have to come on side when you tell him we're going to report him unless he complies with our wishes.'

'When *we* tell him,' I corrected you. And then you told me you weren't going to stick around for that. You had to check out of the hotel, you said. You'd be back later, you said, to kick off stage two of 'the plan'.

Well, thanks very much, *you utterly selfish bitch*. At this moment, if there was any way I could let the stalker know who the real Stevie is, I would tell him in an instant. Yes, my own body would suffer for it – perhaps even die. But would that really be such a bad thing?

That's how low you've brought me.

Chapter 49

When the doorbell rang, around noon, Layla thought it was the professor.

Heart thumping wildly, and with Buller barking excitedly at her feet, she opened the door to find Victoria standing there, a frown creasing her pale brow.

'Oh!' she said in surprise. 'I thought you'd be at work.'

'I was,' Victoria said, shortly. 'But I took the afternoon off because I was worried. I was waiting for you to call me. Why didn't you call?'

Layla tutted in exasperation. She really didn't need this right now.

'You'd better come in,' she said, and Victoria followed her through to the kitchen.

'Coffee?' she asked, half-heartedly, indicating that the New Zealander should take a seat.

'No thanks,' she said, remaining on her feet. 'Well, did you go to the police?'

Layla reminded herself of the story she and Stevie had agreed on.

'Yes, we went this morning. A constable took an initial statement from me and said a detective would be back in touch as soon as possible. I'm just waiting for the call.'

Victoria ran a hand through her curly dark hair. 'Well, why didn't you let me know?' she said angrily. 'I was going crazy! I thought maybe he'd returned and attacked you. And it's not just you I'm thinking of. Any of us in the Square could be in danger with someone like that hanging around!'

Layla was taken aback by her outburst. Clearly, the whole mess had upset her young friend more than she'd realised. Her anger with Stevie ratcheted up another gear.

'Oh, Victoria, I'm so sorry that I worried you. I kept expecting someone to call and my head's all over the place just now. I promise I'll let you know as soon as I have something to tell you. And I'm sure the detective will want to speak with you, too, since you're a witness?'

Victoria seemed mollified. 'Well, okay... Do you think –'

Her words were interrupted by Layla's mobile ringing in the lounge. 'Oh! That might be them now,' she said, excitedly. 'Go and answer that and I'll hang around just in case.'

Layla smiled weakly and left the room, Buller trotting at her heels.

Alone in the kitchen, Victoria spotted Layla's laptop sitting, open, on the table. She crept over to the door and listened. She couldn't hear what Layla was saying, but it was obvious she was arguing with someone. 'Not the detective, then,' she whispered to herself, gliding over to the table and sitting down in Layla's chair.

Acting swiftly, she awoke the device, scanned the work history and saw that the most recently-read document was labelled *'Layla's Log'*. *Layla?* she thought with surprise. What was Layla's log doing on Stevie's desktop? Now, that was interesting. Straining her ears to make sure the other woman was still on the phone, she opened it and began to speed-read the contents.

'Blackbirds sing me awake, their fluty song as familiar as a nursery-rhyme...'

As she read, her eyes widened in astonishment at the incredible tale spinning out before her.

When Layla returned to the kitchen several minutes later, Victoria was sitting in the seat opposite her own, reading something on her phone. She looked up. Her face was white; her eyes black holes, devoid of expression.

'Everything okay?' Layla asked, concerned.

'What? Oh, yeah; just crappy work stuff. I leave my desk for half an hour and twenty demanding emails pile in.' She closed the cover with a snap and tucked the phone back into her bag.

'What about you? Was it the detective?' she asked, but she seemed distracted.

'No, it was my darling cousin.' Layla gave a little laugh. 'We had a bit of a disagreement.'

'Uh-huh,' said Victoria, getting to her feet. 'Well, I must be going. It looks as if my half-day off will now be spent working from home.'

Layla accompanied her to the front door. 'I'll be in touch, then, when there's anything to report?'

'Yeah, fine – see you, Layla.'

Layla frowned as she shut the door. There was something very odd about Victoria's manner. She had expected her to say more about the police and the stalker, but she'd seemed desperate to leave.

It wasn't until she was back in the kitchen that the thought struck her.

Layla. She called me 'Layla'!

Chapter 50

The doorbell rang again, startling her from her despair.

Having quickly checked the time stamp of '*Layla's Log*' on her laptop, she now had confirmation that Victoria had read all or part of the document while she was out of the room.

Everything was spiralling out of control.

And now she had James Blunstone to deal with.

Buller was already at the front door, his tail wagging madly. He knew who was standing behind the stout wooden structure. Sure enough, when Layla opened it, his beloved master stepped into the hall and immediately hunkered down to greet him. The dog was lavish with his affection.

When Blunstone straightened up, he saw that Layla had left the hall. Buller led him into the kitchen, where she was sitting, solemn-faced, at the table. She motioned for him to take the chair opposite.

'Where's Stevie?' were his first words, as he sat down wearily.

'Not around, as usual,' Layla said. 'But at least I now know where she is.'

He rubbed his face and placed both palms flat on the table. 'Layla,' he said quietly. 'I've had a very stressful journey, worrying myself sick about what's been happening up here. Why don't you start at the beginning and tell me all about it?'

He looked haggard. Dark shadows had gathered under his eyes and his usual "golfer's tan" had been replaced by an unhealthy greyness. Despite her wariness of how he was going to react to what she had to say, Layla couldn't help feeling sorry for the man.

She recalled Stevie's bossy instructions to tell him nothing, but to remain resolute in their joint demand for him to be ready to reverse the operation sooner than planned. The Australian had even called her earlier to reiterate the message, and that was the reason Layla had been arguing with her over the phone. She silently cursed Stevie for giving Victoria that window to spy on her, but she pushed away the thought and decided to handle this her own way.

She believed she owed the professor a full explanation of what the past couple of days had brought to light and why she and Stevie needed him to be on standby. She hoped he would feel compelled to do the right thing. The threat of public exposure would be her very last resort.

Stevie would be furious at her approach, but that was too bad. Stevie wasn't here.

'I've made some sandwiches,' she said, rising to her feet. 'Let me set out lunch and I'll fill you in.'

If the professor had appeared drawn before she told him the story, he was now looking positively ill. He had barely touched his lunch, sitting in shocked silence as Layla described the unfortunate chain of events: the first sinister message she had received; Stevie's disappearance; her own discovery of the stalker's emails; her subsequent confrontation with Stevie and the realisation that she had planned to escape back home in Layla's body, and finally, the horror of finding the bloody package left on the doormat.

'...and we don't even know who this maniac is,' she concluded.

'Surely it's the person who was threatening her in Sydney?' he said faintly.

'It could be – but it could equally be someone else.' And she told him her suspicions about Murdo.

'Never!' James cried. 'I know he's a strange lad, but he's harmless. I've known him since he was a baby!'

'I understand your reluctance to suspect him, but as a woman, I find him creepy and disturbing,' Layla insisted. 'You saw him hanging around here with his camera the very day I received the first message. And he could quite easily get his hands on a rabbit.'

'Oh no, this is a nightmare,' he said, running his hands through his hair.

'And I'm afraid there's something else, James.'

Nervously, she told him about Victoria's peripheral involvement and the disturbing news that the New Zealander had, that morning, read her personal log.

At that, he burst out with: 'Oh, for god's sake, Layla! How careless can you get?'

She had no defence. 'I know how stupid it was to leave the laptop unattended. I didn't think, and even if I had, I would have trusted her not to spy on me like that. She seemed a really nice person.'

'Trusting someone you've known only five minutes? How unbelievably naïve!' Now he was shouting, his expression livid, and Layla caught a glimpse of the latent surgeon's temper that had surely kept his staff in line during his hospital career. Buller, who had been sitting under the table waiting for scraps that never came, shot into his bed, ears flat against his head. She wished she could join him.

Her lower lip was trembling, but she was determined not to break down. She had told him the worst and now she had to focus on persuading him that the only course of action left to them was to follow Stevie's plan. Before she could speak, however, he raised his hand.

'Wait – give me a moment to digest all this.' Then he said angrily: 'It's absolutely preposterous that a project of such global importance should be *hijacked* in this way by something as – as *grubby* as a stalking scenario.'

Layla inclined her head. 'My sentiments, exactly. But surely you can't be that surprised, James? Because you've known all along that Stevie was trouble, haven't you?'

He glowered at her. Undaunted, she continued: 'So why don't you tell me *your* side of the story and then we can talk about how we're going to sort this out?'

His expression remained fierce for a moment longer, then his shoulders sagged and he sighed. 'Yes, yes, you're right. I haven't been completely forthcoming with you.'

'She's been blackmailing you, hasn't she?'

He looked surprised. 'How did you know?'

It was Layla's turn to sigh. 'From what I've discovered about the extent of Stevie's ruthlessness, it wasn't very hard to deduce.'

He poked at his sandwich and looked up. 'You know, Layla, I was delighted when you came forward as a research subject. Your interest and motivation were genuinely professional and I very much admire the bravery you have shown in the face of your own fears and anxieties since the operation.'

She felt a faint twinge of guilt at the mention of motivation, but quickly shrugged it off and nodded at him.

'Go on.'

'Stevie, on the other hand, was a mistake from the outset. I knew as soon as we met that she was motivated entirely by selfishness. Don't get me wrong; I had no idea that stalking was at the root of this, but I could see that money was her main driver.'

'So why did you let her participate? Wait, let me guess. She wouldn't take no for an answer?'

'Right again. After that initial meeting, I sent her a polite email of rejection and she let me know in no uncertain terms that she wouldn't accept it. And so I had to include her. She would have "outed" me, otherwise, and I couldn't let that happen.'

He looked at her almost pleadingly. 'You can understand that, can't you? This project is the pinnacle of my life's work. I couldn't let her destroy it at such a crucial stage.'

Layla regarded him coldly, but a tiny inner voice reminded her that each of them was guilty of selfishness in one form or another, and so she simply said: 'Yes, I can understand. But I'm still horrified that you brought such a dangerous person on board.'

'I thought I could control her! I made it clear that I wasn't going to give her a penny until the project was complete. Her greed kept her quiet, although it didn't stop her threatening me from time to time. She wanted far more money than the generous sum I offered you both.'

She remembered the angry whispers she'd interrupted during that first visit to his house; the raised voices at Slains Castle; Stevie's increasing hostility and lack of respect towards the professor. It all made sense now.

There was something else she needed to know. 'Did you have any suspicions beforehand that she planned to run away with my body? To start a new life back in Sydney?'

'Certainly not!' His indignation seemed genuine. 'I'm as shocked as you must have been to find out she'd intended doing that.

'I will say, though, that when she refused to answer my phone and email messages during weeks three and four, my imagination ran riot and I did begin to fear that she might have gone into hiding – temporarily, or otherwise.'

He paused to think for a moment. 'But what I don't understand is: what changed her mind? Why *didn't* she run back home at the first opportunity? She could just as easily have blackmailed me from Australia to ensure she got her money... Ah, but she would have needed your passport.'

Layla hesitated, then said: 'She has my passport. I'm embarrassed to say that I left it in my study. Yes, I know it was stupid,' she added, seeing his look of incredulity, 'but it didn't enter my mind that she would steal it!'

'So, what has kept her here?' he demanded.

'She's discovered that my body isn't as fit as hers and she wants her own one back,' she explained in a rush, her colour rising.

He didn't seem to notice her discomfort. 'Luckily for you,' he said grimly, adding in a low voice: 'The woman is an absolute monster!'

'I won't disagree with you there. The problem is, she's *our* absolute monster and we're absolutely stuck with her until all this is over!'

He shook his head, exasperated. 'I really can't tell you how angry I am at what has happened.'

She raised her eyebrows. 'I think I can guess.'

Ignoring her wry tone, he continued: '*And* how very sorry I am that your life has been put at risk due to what boils down to my own hubris.'

Relief flooded her, as she realised that she had him on side.

He slapped both of his palms on the table, apparently reaching a conclusion. 'There's only one way to put it right, of course: I'll reverse the operation tomorrow, pay Stevie off, and hopefully neither of us will ever see or hear from her again.'

'Er, it's not quite as simple as that,' Layla replied.

Chapter 51
Victoria

Victoria sat at her kitchen table, deep in thought.

The enormity of her discovery had not hit her at first. On her hasty exit from her neighbour's house, she'd thrown the 'See you, Layla' comment over her shoulder as a sly joke, which she'd instantly regretted, as it gave away the fact that she'd had a sneaky read of *'Layla's Log'*. She could only hope that the slip-up hadn't registered with the woman she'd still believed was Stevie.

While scanning through the log, she had reached the conclusion that the document held a draft of the novel Stevie had told her she was writing. But it had been so disturbing that she'd needed to get away to think about what she'd read.

Stevie's characters were exact replicas of real people: Stevie, her cousin, Layla (why on earth had she written it from Layla's perspective, with herself cast as the "baddie"?), and the family friend, James Blunstone. Hell, even she, Victoria, had made guest appearances and the scenarios in which she featured were exactly as had happened over the past couple of days. What's more, the whole stalker thing was part of the story, which described events as they were unfolding in real life!

She had been sitting, vexed, for several minutes, trying to figure out what it all could mean. Now she had an idea.

She searched for Layla's name online and the engine brought up a list of items, mainly relating to Layla's work at the university. Frustratingly, she didn't have a Facebook page, but she did have a presence on a business network site, which gave very little away, other than her professional qualifications, job status, and the information that she was currently on sabbatical for three months. But it was enough to set Victoria's heart racing, *as it was all just as described in the log.*

Next, she searched for information relating to James Blunstone. From the wealth of data that appeared on the screen, she gleaned that he was a retired, highly-respected neurosurgeon, etc, etc – again, just as described in the log.

'This is bloody incredible,' she breathed. She was about to close down the browser when an item further down the page caught her eye. It was from a philosophy forum website and read: *'Research subjects required for "body-swap" study... Professor James Blunstone...'*

'What the hell?' Quickly, she clicked on the link and read on.

'Retired neurosurgeon Professor James Blunstone seeks two adult females to assist in his groundbreaking research into the transposition of human consciousness. The successful applicants – preferably living and working in the North-east of Scotland – will receive substantial remuneration for their participation. Interested parties should apply by email to the address below, briefly stating why they would like to be considered for the project.'

Her shriek echoed around the kitchen.

'OH MY GOD. This is REAL!'

Chapter 52
Layla

'You can't be serious.' James Blunstone uttered a laugh that carried no mirth.

'That's what she wants to do,' said Layla. 'Can you think of a better solution?'

They were now sitting in the top-floor lounge, a subdued Buller licking his paws at his master's feet. On this blustery spring day, the view north was spectacular: the sun illuminating the far-off golden sands of Balmedie Beach; the sky a vast, pale blue arc striated by long wisps of wind-combed cloud.

But neither of them was looking out of the window.

'How on earth are we going to capture a stalker who is clearly deranged and dangerous?'

Under his scornful scrutiny, she felt like a schoolgirl who had said something ridiculous in class.

'*You* don't have to do anything; no one is asking you to get involved,' she said pointedly. 'And I repeat, can you think of a better solution? You must understand why we can't go to the police about this?'

He raised his eyes to the ceiling and heaved a sigh. 'Of course I understand that we – and I mean *we*, as it's as much my concern as yours – can't tell the police the full story, or even part of it. But if we can get them to take our story at face value, that is, that your life is being threatened and that Stevie and I are concerned family friends of yours who have persuaded you to report the stalking – I'm *sure* they will treat it very seriously and will act quickly to try to catch the perpetrator.'

'*We're* not so sure, and I've told you why,' said Layla firmly.

'Yes, but don't you see? There won't be any need to go into your "back story" from Australia. You can pretend that the stalking started when you arrived over here. That way, you won't risk faltering or making mistakes when you're interviewed.'

She considered this, then said: 'That could work... but it would leave us with only two pieces of evidence to take to the police, and from what Stevie has said, that won't be nearly enough to get them to take action.'

'I don't agree! By Jove, I'll make sure they take action!'

Sitting bolt upright in his seat, eyes blazing, the surgeon left Layla in no doubt that he could create merry hell if he wanted to. Suddenly, she felt utterly exhausted. Perhaps they could give it a try, at least. She was about to say as much to him, when, two floors below, the front door banged open and a voice yelled: 'Heeeere's Johnny!!'

In a flash, she saw her own fright reflected in Blunstone's eyes; then fear turned to relief as she recognised the voice. Buller looked up, growled, and then resumed his grooming session.

'It's just Stevie, doing a Jack Nicolson,' Layla said, rolling her eyes. 'She's back here to stay until all this is over... We're upstairs, in the lounge!' she called.

'Her *The Shining* reference is very apt,' said the professor drily. 'This dreadful scenario has all the makings of a horror film, with Stevie standing in for the evil spirit.'

She smiled faintly, but her expression grew serious as the Australian entered the room. Her gut told her that a difficult scene was about to be enacted.

Stevie took one look at Blunstone's stony expression and turned to face Layla.

'You've told him, haven't you? You stupid –'

'Enough!' he interrupted imperiously. 'Of course she told me. Layla is loyal and has integrity, unlike *you*.'

Stevie whirled on her heel and was about to leave the room when Layla said wearily: 'Where are you going now,

Stevie? There's nowhere else to run. We need to face and overcome this together.'

The woman turned and put her hands on her hips. 'Oh, how very cosy the two of you are,' she taunted. Once again, Layla baulked at the sight of such ugly rage on her own face.

'We have had enough of your childish nonsense,' Blunstone said sharply. 'Come and sit down.'

Layla could only guess what fury boiled beneath his seemingly calm exterior. She hoped he would manage to keep it under control.

Stevie stomped across the room, giving the professor and his dog a wide berth, and plunked herself down in a small armchair, next to the unlit wood-burning stove. From her own seat opposite, Layla could see how much it had cost the Australian to do as she was told. She was trembling with suppressed anger.

James leaned towards her and said in an arctic tone: 'Ms Nightingale, your actions are beyond contempt. Not only have you tried to blackmail me into paying you an extortionate amount of money for your silence regarding the project, but, like the worst possible coward, you have also put Layla's life in danger by lumbering her with your despicable baggage in the form of an out-of-control stalker. Whom she found out about only by accident!'

Stevie rolled her eyes and tapped her fingers on the arm of the chair. She looked like a sulky teenager.

'DO YOU HEAR ME?' After the quiet, controlled words, his roar was shocking. Buller leapt to his feet and ran from the room, tail tucked under his body. Layla could hear the dog clattering downstairs and guessed he would once again be making for the safety of his bed.

Stevie looked over at the angry man, her face an emotionless mask.

'Yeah, and so? I'm trying to help her out of it, aren't I?'

248

'Hah! From what I hear, that's only to serve your own self-interest.' He practically spat the words. 'Had you been satisfied with your new body, you would quite happily have disappeared in the aftermath of the operation, leaving Layla stranded in your body, forever isolated from her family, friends and all that constitutes her world. It is utterly monstrous behaviour!'

It's a complete waste of time trying to shame her, thought Layla. *He's talking to a sociopath.*

True to form, Stevie merely laughed and shook her head. 'It's called *survival*, mister. She would have been getting a good deal, wouldn't she? And, correct me if I'm wrong, but you're hardly the paragon of virtue yourself. What you've done in this project goes way beyond the bounds of morality.' Still glaring at him, she pointed her index finger at Layla. 'And *she* is just as bad for getting involved, knowing the whole deal is unethical. So let's just drop the sanctimonious crap, shall we?'

Blunstone glowered back at her but said nothing.

Layla decided it was time to intervene. 'Look,' she said, 'I'm just as angry with her as you are, James, but things are desperate and we need to get beyond this.'

She turned to Stevie. 'For the record, I don't believe for one minute that we're as immoral and unscrupulous as you are, but you're right about one thing: we *are* far from blameless.'

The other woman arched her eyebrows impudently.

She ploughed on, addressing them both: 'The most important thing right now is to extricate ourselves from this hideous situation as soon as we can. Can we agree on that, at least?'

After a frosty silence, the professor gave a curt nod and Stevie said: 'I think you'll find that that that's what I've been saying all along.'

Looking at her smug face, Layla remembered that Stevie didn't know about the latest fiasco. She decided it wouldn't be prudent to divulge that Victoria had evidently read her log. The Australian would go ballistic.

'Okay,' she said, 'so, I've outlined your plan to James...'

'Who thinks it's utterly preposterous,' he intercepted.

'... and I've told him he needn't get involved,' she finished.

'Yeah, we don't need *you* interfering,' Stevie said venomously. 'So why don't you go back home, muster your little team of acolytes, and let us get on with it?'

Ignoring her, he turned to Layla, who shrugged her shoulders, trying not to see the pleading in his eyes. Then all at once, the energy seemed to go out of him and he sat back in his seat, defeated.

'Clearly, I'm outnumbered,' he said quietly.

Layla felt anything but triumphant.

'However,' he continued in a stronger voice, 'I am not going anywhere. If you two insist on implementing this ludicrous plan, you'll need all the help you can get. And if, god forbid, the stalker really is Murdo, I may well be able to exert some degree of influence over him.'

Chapter 53

Before either of the women could respond, the doorbell sounded, prompting a flurry of barking from a now ebullient Buller.

The three of them looked at each other.

'Ignore it,' ordered Stevie. 'We don't want any interruptions.'

After a few seconds, the bell rang again. Then a muffled voice called through the letterbox:

'Stevie, Stevie! Can you hear me? Are you okay?'

'It's Victoria,' said Layla, giving James a warning look. 'She knows I wouldn't leave Buller home alone. I'll need to go and get rid of her.'

As she hurried down the stairs, she hoped he'd understood her signal not to refer to Victoria's spying episode earlier. Then she thought: *Who am I kidding? Those two are hardly going to be having a cosy chat up there.*

She opened the door and before she could stop her, Victoria barrelled into the hall.

'Thank goodness! I was beginning to worry. Have you heard from the detective yet?' she asked breathlessly.

Taken aback, Layla said the first thing that entered her head. 'No, I did call again, but apparently there's been some sort of serious incident and it's all hands on deck. They told me someone would definitely get back to me tomorrow.'

Was it her imagination or was that scepticism in Victoria's dark eyes? She soon found out.

'You didn't report it, did you?' The outrage in the New Zealander's voice was unmistakeable.

This was the last straw. Dropping the charade, Layla went on the attack. 'And did you find that out from reading my private document?'

Victoria's manner changed in an instant.

'Oh, you did guess... I'm so sorry,' she said, looking up her imploringly. 'The laptop was right there and it was too tempting? I didn't mean any harm... I just wanted to have a sneaky peek at your novel-in-progress?'

She smiled nervously and babbled on: 'I think it's a stroke of genius having it mirror real life. Well, at least in some parts. All that gothic body-swap stuff is amazing. What an imagination you have!'

Layla's relief at her assumption was short-lived.

'What the hell is going on? *What* did she read on your laptop?'

Stevie was standing at the top of the stairs.

Layla's heart sank at the thought of further confrontation.

Victoria, however, was unabashed. 'I know what you two are planning and I'm here to help,' she announced, beaming at each of them in turn.

Layla sighed deeply and gestured towards the staircase.

'Then I guess you'd better come up and join us.'

Chapter 54
Victoria

Victoria followed Layla up the stairs towards the woman she now knew was Stevie, enjoying the look of incredulity on the Australian's borrowed face.

At the top, she heard Layla hiss: 'Just hear me out, *cousin*,' and then she was ushered into the lounge, where a surprised-looking James Blunstone – the so-called 'family friend' – half-rose as Layla started to introduce her.

'James, this is Victoria, the new neighbour I was telling you about?'

'Oh, er, yes; pleased to meet you,' he said, coming forward to shake her hand.

So this was the world-renowned neurosurgeon who had stepped off the straight and narrow to pursue his own dark obsession.

'Likewise,' Victoria said, switching on her most charming smile. 'Stevie tells me you're an old friend of her parents.'

'What? Oh, indeed,' the professor bumbled. Clearly, improvisation was not one of his finer skills.

'This is lovely, Stevie,' she now said to Layla, gazing around the room. 'And you definitely have the best view at this side of the Square.'

But Layla was distracted and seemed in a hurry to explain herself to James and to the real Stevie, who was standing, arms folded, in the doorway.

'As you're both aware, Victoria knows about our stalking issue and has, in fact, seen the man himself posting the latest package through the door.'

Returning to his seat, James nodded, while Stevie said nothing.

'She has also sneaked a read of *'Layla's Log'*, my *draft novel*,' she added, emphasising the last two words, 'and so she knows about our plan to confront the stalker before going to the police.'

'*For fuck's sake*,' spat out Stevie, looking at Layla with contempt. 'Why don't you announce it on Facebook, you idiot?'

Yes, this was definitely the spiteful spitfire Victoria had read about. She experienced a tiny thrill at the thought of the secret knowledge she now possessed.

The Australian's Scottish voice rose as something seemed to occur to her: 'So does this mean she also knows about –'

'She has apologised for what she did,' Layla cut in sharply, 'and she's been very complimentary about my novel, saying I must have a good imagination. You both know it's about body-swapping and that I've used the pair of you and myself as my main characters, right?'

From the bewildered look on his face, this was apparently news to James, but he nodded again, while Stevie merely glared from the doorway.

'Oh, I think it's wonderful,' Victoria gushed, her eyes bright with excitement. 'But fusing the fictional sci-fi elements with real-life events, *as they're actually happening*... well, it must be really complicated to write.'

'I'm sorry, I thought we were talking about stalking, not holding a book club meeting,' snapped Stevie, moving into the room to stand beside the window.

Victoria flushed, but chose to ignore the jibe and addressed Layla.

'I did think that the bit about you wanting to catch the stalker yourselves might have been made up, but when the police didn't call me today...'

'We have good reason not to contact the police at this stage,' Layla said firmly.

'But not because of body-swapping, I take it?' Victoria's mischievous glance took in all three of them. Blunstone looked alarmed.

'Of course not!' Stevie said swiftly. 'And our *real-life* reason is none of your business.'

'Suffice it to say that it has to do with a problem I had in Sydney – one that I don't want the police here knowing about?' Layla continued in her inherited Australian drawl. 'We need to be able to prove that I'm genuinely under attack, so that they'll take action immediately and get the mad bastard off the streets. The best way of doing that is to catch him in the act.'

'Wow, you really do mean to do it yourselves, then?' said Victoria, her eyes wide. 'This is just as good as any novel.'

'And as *you're* not one of the main characters, we can do it without you,' Stevie said.

She really was becoming annoying. However, it was not in Victoria's interests to antagonise her further and so she said mildly: 'So, can I sit down and tell you how I think I can help? Then you can all make up your minds?'

She noted the helpless look Layla shot at the others. Blunstone still appeared completely bemused but shrugged his shoulders. Stevie sighed and threw herself into an armchair.

Layla indicated that Victoria should take a seat in the other armchair, while she went to sit on the sofa, next to the professor. Buller did a circuit of the room, tail wagging, and then settled himself at Layla's feet. She stroked his big head gently, seeming to take comfort from his closeness.

Victoria began: 'Now, I don't know the full details, but I gather that one or more of you are planning to keep watch on this house overnight, to see if the stalker returns. Am I right?'

255

Layla nodded, her lips pursed.

'Okay, well, there's some pretty awful weather forecast for this evening and overnight, so how about whoever plans to keep watch doing so from my house, out of the rain and wind? If the stalker appears, you'll still be close enough to be on the scene in a matter of seconds.'

Interest suddenly sparked in the real Stevie's eyes, confirming Victoria's guess that she planned to be the watcher.

'Well... I had intended to hide out in Stevie's tarry shed, but I suppose your house will be a little warmer,' she said in a marginally friendlier tone.

Cheeky cow, thought Victoria.

'Ladies, I have to say that I still have very grave doubts about trying to do this ourselves,' James Blunstone said forcefully. 'How do you think we will manage to restrain him, for a start?'

'I was just coming to that,' smiled Victoria. 'If you haven't already decided on a method, I have just the thing in my own tarry shed?'

'Oh yeah?' snorted Stevie, resorting to type.

'Yeah,' she replied. 'It's an old fisherman's net. That would do the trick.'

Layla laughed in surprise and Blunstone stroked his chin. 'Well, it certainly sounds safer than a rugby tackle,' he mused. Then he turned to Stevie, who was also looking pensive. 'What do *you* think?' he asked coldly.

She didn't answer right away, but finally said abruptly: 'Sounds okay. We do this tonight.'

Victoria felt victorious.

Chapter 55
The Stalker

Hunched in a crow-black hoodie, the stalker sat on a large granite block, staring out to sea.

A spring storm was brewing.

Driven on by the roaring easterly wind, dark and colossal cloud formations bulged and barrelled their way towards the coastline, bringing the sky ever-nearer to its gunmetal reflection, now fractured and fragmented by the vengeful North Sea.

A slate-grey swell slammed the nearby pier, sending spray soaring upwards to soak the ragged wings of wind-flung gulls. Furious waves pounded Fittie Beach, their frenzied energy ever-so-reluctantly dissipating into a foaming filigree whose lace-clad fingertips reached closer and closer to claw at the berm on which the stalker was perching.

In the dying afternoon's premature gloom, the wind skirled and shrieked, bullying and buffeting the shadowy figure, which nevertheless refused to budge.

The stalker was listening to a different, but no less discordant melody: an insidious earworm which writhed and twisted with Neil Young's plaintive promise:

'Tonight's the night...
Tonight's the night...'

Chapter 56
Layla

'Will you two stop bickering – you're doing my head in!'

Layla glared at Stevie and the professor, who had been at loggerheads when she'd slipped out to take Buller for a blustery walk, and were still arguing on her return, twenty minutes later.

'I am not doing this with him in tow,' said Stevie, pacing around the upstairs lounge, where the wind howled in the flue of the stove as if imprisoned behind the smoky glass door.

'I can't let her do it on her own,' James said, looking to Layla for support.

'I won't be on my own; the Kiwi will be with me.'

'Stop calling her that,' cried Layla. 'She's been good enough to offer to help us and the least we can do is show her some courtesy.'

'She's a nosy cow who has read your diary, forced her way into this situation and now expects us to be grateful,' corrected Stevie. 'I should think she'd *better* be prepared to help us catch the loony.'

'Why her and not me?' Blunstone demanded.

Layla could see he was distressed and frustrated. Before the other woman could retort, she said: 'James, I'm feeling nervous about all this and would be very glad of your company this evening. You, me and Buller can hole up in the kitchen and we'll be right on hand to help with the capture if the stalker does turn up – and there's no guarantee of that, of course.'

'He'll turn up, all right,' said Stevie grimly, as she finally sat down in an armchair. 'He's escalating and he'll feel compelled to keep the momentum going, whether it's delivering another grisly package, or trying to break in.'

'Now the woman is a psychologist,' the professor said sarcastically, getting to his feet and removing his phone from his trouser pocket. 'I've had enough of all this speculation.'

'What are you doing?' Layla asked.

'Calling Murdo's house,' he snapped, leaving the room.

Layla and Stevie could only stare at each other.

A couple of minutes later, he returned upstairs, his face paler than ever.

'Well?' Stevie challenged him sarcastically. 'Did he admit to being our stalker?'

'He's not at home,' he said slowly. 'His mother says he's staying in town for a few nights. One of his college friends is celebrating his twenty-first birthday this week and he's putting Murdo up in his flat.'

Stevie raised her eyebrows. 'I don't know whether to be worried in case he *is* the stalker, or shocked that he has any friends.'

'Oh, shut up, Stevie!' cried Layla. 'This is serious. We now know Murdo is in town. He could very well be the stalker. James, are you still convinced he's not?'

The older man sat down with a sigh. 'I don't know what to think any more. His mother gave me his mobile number and I've just tried to ring him, but it went straight to voicemail.'

Layla looked at them both. 'Regardless of whether we think it's Murdo, we need to continue with our plan. James, there's another good reason for you not going with Stevie to Victoria's place. Whoever the stalker is, he could be watching this house right now, and he'll know who all is here. Stevie popping over to Victoria's later won't arouse much suspicion, but the two of you trooping over there and leaving me here with the dog will look a little strange, don't you think?'

'She's right,' said Stevie. 'For all we know, the guy could already be lurking anywhere around here: in or behind one of the sheds, in the Mission Hall, or even walking along the beach.'

Layla shivered at the thought that some malevolent stranger could have been watching her hurry Buller along the Esplanade only minutes before. It had felt safe enough, being remarkably crowded with bundled-up walkers despite – or perhaps because of – the burgeoning storm.

The professor looked thoughtful. 'But if he knows I'm here he may not make a move.'

'He will,' said Stevie impatiently. 'You're an old man and if he does intend an attack, he's arrogant enough to think you're no match for him. I'm sure he'll just be glad that there's no sign of any police.'

Now he looked outraged.

'You have a wonderful way with words, Stevie,' Layla said wryly. 'But James, surely you can see that it's best if you stay here with me?'

Blunstone breathed heavily and then threw up his hands in defeat.

'Oh, all *right*. Once again, I find I'm overruled. But we will be watching and listening, Stevie, and we'll be out like a shot at the first hint of trouble.'

'Just wait for me and Victoria to net him first,' Stevie replied, a glint of excitement in her eyes. 'Remember, she'll set off her personal alarm and that's the signal to jump.' She got up and headed for the door. 'And now that that's sorted, I'm going to grab something to eat before it all kicks off.'

After she had left the room, Blunstone's eyes followed Layla as she drew the curtains on the storm-driven darkness that pressed ominously against the picture window. 'I do believe that in a perverse way she's enjoying this,' he said.

'She's certainly pumped with adrenaline,' she replied, resuming her seat. 'I suppose it's the culmination of months of worry, when try as she might, she hasn't been able to shake off her persecutor. And tonight, at last, she has the chance to take action.' Layla laughed at herself. 'Now who's the pop psychologist?'

He didn't smile. 'I understand all that, but her "bring it on" attitude doesn't alter the fact that this is a highly-volatile situation. I'm still not convinced it's Murdo and if it's Stevie's Australian stalker, the man could very well be carrying a knife or other weapon. Someone could be gravely injured, or even killed.'

'I know it's a huge risk, but we're in a desperate position and I really can't think of anything else to do...

'Besides, remember it came out in our pre-op conversations that Stevie is a karate black belt? Although she's now restricted by my small body, her consciousness will have retained all her martial arts knowledge and skills. And I can help, too, because this body will have retained the muscle-memory to make any necessary moves. That's bound to stand us in good stead.'

Layla wondered if she was trying more to convince herself than the professor.

'We can only hope you are right,' he said gravely.

Chapter 57
Victoria

If Stevie was excited at the prospect of the evening's adventure, Victoria was ecstatic. Life in Fittie was turning out to be even more interesting than she'd expected.

As the wind-harried rain strafed the old skylights in the sea-facing roof of her cottage, the chirpy New Zealander sang tunelessly to herself in the hallway.

She was laying out on the floor what she believed to be the necessary tools of capture: a personal alarm; the patched-up remnant of an ancient fishing net that still trapped the faintly-fetid reek of countless catches; a set of white plastic zip-ties, fresh from their cellophane wrapper; a fetishistic red ball gag, left over from a rather intense previous relationship, and a serrated-edge kitchen knife.

'Perrrfect,' she purred softly in her version of a Scottish accent. Then, as the door chime announced the arrival of her guest, she gave a low chuckle.

'Oh, Stevie – what larks we're going to have tonight!'

Chapter 58
Layla

It was shaping up to be one of the strangest evenings of Layla's life. Here she was, trying her best to behave as normally as possible in someone else's body, while preparing to snare a predator. Her insides were chewed up with nerves.

She and James had decided to postpone their meal — a microwave vegetable lasagne and thrown-together salad — until Stevie had left for Victoria's. Now they were sitting at opposite ends of the kitchen table, in full view of anyone peering in from outside, trying to find their appetites and at the same time straining their ears for the screech of a personal alarm. Buller, as usual, was within range of any stray scraps that might possibly find their way to the floor. For the second time that day he was out of luck.

Layla finally gave up picking at her food and threw down her fork. 'This is utter madness!' she cried. 'Supposing he doesn't show up? Do we go through this same farce every evening until he does? I feel like a sitting duck!' She knew her voice was bordering on hysteria, but could do nothing to control it.

Blunstone's face was grim. 'I feel as helpless as you do. Let's hope that it all comes to a satisfactory conclusion tonight.'

There was silence for a moment and then Layla, staring at the colourful mess on her plate, said in a more measured tone: 'You know, ever since the operation I've felt detached from reality, as if this is a weird dream I can't waken from. And now it's morphed into the worst kind of nightmare.'

She looked up at him. 'I just want to go back to the way things were.'

He shifted uncomfortably in his seat. 'And you will, Layla, I promise. Life will return to normal, as soon as the operation is reversed.'

'It will never return to normal,' she said dully. 'That we can be sure of.'

But he wasn't listening, going off at a tangent of his own. 'I still find it absolutely infuriating that this project should go so horribly wrong, not through any bad practice, but as a result of base human greed.'

Eyes blazing, he continued bitterly: 'Isn't it just typical that a revolution in humanity's understanding of the nature of reality should be reduced to – to *rubble* by blackmail, viciousness and violence? We just can't ever drag ourselves out of the mud, can we?'

'It seems not,' she replied. 'But it hasn't all been for nothing, has it? I mean, we've learned such a lot in these past five weeks. I know it's all coming to an abrupt end, but surely we can salvage something from the rubble?'

He smiled thinly. 'Oh, undoubtedly. But I had much more in mind for this project. After your time in the field I had intended to record some more video interviews with you both. Something similar to what I did with the previous four patients, but in much more detail.'

He leaned forward. 'For one thing, video would have captured and demonstrated the amazing way in which your individual consciousnesses have imposed themselves on the physiognomy of your temporary bodies... in other words, the way in which I see Stevie's face before me right now, but know that *you* are in control of it. When compared with the video interviews we recorded pre-op, these changes would be quite obvious to any viewer. That kind of evidence can't be faked.'

Layla considered this and said: 'I suppose you could film me briefly just now, using your phone? At least that would give you partial video evidence. I wouldn't count on Stevie being quite as amenable, though.'

'Believe me, I won't,' he said, but his expression had brightened. 'You are quite amazing, Layla. In the midst of all the stress and chaos, you are still willing to carry things through.'

'Of course,' she replied, shrugging her shoulders. 'Like you, I'm a professional. I want to make this project a success despite all the crap that's conspired to cut it short.'

'Well, then, I'll go and fetch my phone!' he smiled, getting to his feet. 'At least we'll be doing something positive to distract ourselves.'

But she raised her hand to halt him. 'Before you do that, can we talk about what you plan to do once you've reversed the operation? Are you going to go public, or are you going to try to set up another long-term project... one that isn't – contaminated?'

He laughed heartily and Buller slid out from under the table to look up at him curiously.

'Hah! I will certainly *not* be going down this path again,' he said resolutely, sitting back down. 'No, despite the derailment, I think I've gathered the minimal amount of evidence to support a public announcement, especially if I can interview you just now. But we will have to think very carefully about how we go about presenting the project. We don't want either the blackmailing or the stalking business to get out, do we?'

'No, we don't,' agreed Layla. 'It would muddy the waters and divert attention away from the all-important scientific and philosophical elements. And there's no way Stevie would want it all to come out, in any case. It wouldn't exactly show her in a good light.'

She thought for a moment and then added: 'But you do realise we won't be able to control what happens once

265

the stalker is caught? The court case will be based on a crime whose timeline will become a matter of public record. When you announce your breakthrough to the world and Stevie and I are presented as your latest research subjects, someone is bound to do some online digging and find out about her involvement in the stalking episode and that the whole thing escalated while the project was ongoing.'

The professor stroked his chin and sighed. 'Yes, you're right. Perhaps that part of the story will come out, after all. But let's not be the people to tell it.'

'No one will hear about it from me,' she said firmly.

The momentary silence between them was punctuated by the low moan of the wind and the fierce batter of raindrops against the kitchen window. Layla shivered, at once hoping and dreading to hear their shrieking call to action.

'Oh, the sooner we get that poisonous woman out of our lives, the better!' James suddenly exclaimed.

She nodded slowly. 'Yes, but look on the bright side: Stevie can no longer blackmail you. The project will very soon go public, plus we now know her sordid little secrets, so she's lost her leverage over you.'

'Yes, there is that consolation, I suppose.'

He looked so wistful that for the second time that day, Layla felt sorry for him. But she pressed on earnestly: 'Just one more thing I want us to be clear on, James: we need to do the reverse body-swap as soon as the stalker is safely behind bars. The stalking business is Stevie's problem and she has to be back in her own body right away in order to deal with the police investigation.'

'Of course,' he said soothingly. 'If we catch him tonight, I'll muster my colleagues first thing in the morning. I've actually had them on standby since the operation, in case of emergency.'

He got up and fetched his surrphone from the work surface where it had been charging. As he resumed his seat, he said, with more of his old confidence: 'At least we can be assured that Stevie *will* deal with the aftermath without running away, otherwise there will be no case and the stalker – whoever he is – will be free to continue his persecution of her.'

But on this surreal, storm-lashed evening, Layla felt assured of nothing.

Chapter 59
One Hour Earlier
Stevie

The Kiwi greeted her with a stupid grin.

'Hey, Layla! Welcome to my humble abode,' she said, giggling, as she stepped aside to let her in.

'What are you on?' Stevie said rudely, stomping into the hallway out of the downpour. 'Don't you get how serious- my god, what *is* all this?' She stared down at the paraphernalia arranged on the wooden floor.

'Oh, just a little catch-a-creepo kit I rustled up,' laughed Victoria, who seemed oblivious to Stevie's brusque manner. 'I've left it here for easy access.'

'A knife? Seriously?' She prodded the offending object with the toe of her boot.

'Just a safety precaution, in case he's carrying one, too. I'm not suggesting we use it!'

Stevie sighed. She hated Kiwis. Her sole encounter with one in Sydney had ended in disaster.

'So, where do we wait?' she asked, indicating the doors to the immediate left and right of the hall. 'This place has a different layout from mine – er, I mean, Stevie's.'

Victoria, who was toeing the knife back into line with the other objects on the floor, didn't seem to notice the slip. 'I suggest we sit in the kitchen? You get a great view along the path to the front of Stevie's house. The lounge here looks out on to my tarry shed, so it's not much use.' And she showed her guest through to the room on her left.

'Cosy,' the Australian said, remembering that she'd promised herself to be at least civil to the nosy cow.

'Yes, it's much smaller than Stevie's, but it does me fine.' Victoria clambered up on one of the two stools and leaned her elbows on the tiny breakfast bar, which held a bottle of red wine and two glasses. 'Drink?' she offered.

Stevie hesitated. 'Well... okay, just the one.' She didn't want to lose her edge now that the crucial moment might finally be approaching.

'Why don't you hang up your jacket – there's a peg over the hall radiator,' Victoria suggested, looking her up and down. 'There's no point sitting here dripping. This could be a long haul, for all we know.'

Stevie realised that Layla's anorak was drenched from the short journey between the two houses. She took it off and re-entered the hall, where she hung it up to dry. As she did so, she eyed the motley collection of items on the floor, feeling uncharacteristically anxious.

Walking back into the kitchen, she hauled herself up on the stool opposite Victoria's and said, more confidently than she felt: 'So, we'll need to work out a plan of capture. Who does what and when. We'll probably have to improvise, of course, but it's better to be prepared.'

The other woman, who had been gazing out of the window, turned her head to face her. 'Yeah, yeah, but have a drink first,' she said, indicating the full glass she'd poured for Stevie.

'This isn't a social call,' Stevie reminded her, but took a large swallow of the rich ruby liquid, which tasted surprisingly sophisticated.

'Good, eh?' said Victoria, her eyes twinkling. 'It's a Martinborough Pinot Noir: from New Zealand, of course. Far superior to your Aussie vinegar.'

She was a piece of work, this one. 'And why should I care?' she retorted.

'Well, you're the one with the rellies from Oz – thought you might be biased.'

'Not a bit. It all goes down the same way, doesn't it?'

'Spoken like a true connoisseur. Cheers!'

Victoria raised her glass in a mocking toast which Stevie ignored. She was looking out at the darkness beyond the small-paned window. A faux-gas lamp standing sentinel on the path cast a narrow pool of light upon the slick granite paving stones lining the Square's northernmost edge. It was just wide enough to illuminate her own front doorstep. She saw the warm yellow glow emanating from her kitchen window and an irrational feeling of homesickness washed over her. She found herself wishing she was sitting at the old wooden table with Layla and the professor. *What the hell's the matter with me tonight?* she thought. *I couldn't care less about those two!*

'Look, we haven't exactly got off on the right foot, have we?' Victoria said suddenly, bringing her back to herself. 'I really like your cousin, and she and I could be good friends. I don't know what your beef is with me, but can't we at least make an effort to get on, for her sake?' Her mouth was smiling tentatively, but her black eyes bored into Stevie's in cold interrogation.

This was too tedious, but as Stevie needed to stay put for a while, she gave a small shrug and said: 'Whatever.' She took another large glug of wine. '*Now* can we get to the plan?'

Victoria laughed, as if in disbelief. 'Okay... since I guess that's all I'm going to get, let's talk stalker.' She sat up straighter and folded her arms across her ample chest. 'Why is Stevie being stalked?'

'That's none of your business,' Stevie said crossly.

'So she does know why, then? She told me it had started just the other day.'

'No comment,' Stevie replied, draining the contents of her glass and immediately regretting it. The premium wine already seemed to be taking effect, making her feel a little woozy.

'Oh, come on. I'm helping you to catch him! It'll all come out once the police get involved, so why not tell me now?'

Victoria's face had started to look a little fuzzy round the edges. Stevie shook her head, trying to clear her vision. It dawned on her that Layla's body's tolerance for alcohol was very different from that of her own.

'She *doesn't* know why – and she doesn't know who. There's a local lad who's been hanging around her and there was a creep who stalked her in Sydney. Or it could be any other lunatic out there, for all we know. Take your pick.' She was surprised at herself for giving so much away. *In vino veritas*, she thought. *No more booze for me.*

'You mean to tell me, she really has no idea why someone wants to kill her?' The New Zealander's incredulity sounded as if it was coming from a long way off.

'Yes, she has no idea! Maybe the crazy bashtard doesn't know, himshelf,' Stevie slurred. God, she really was pissed already. She felt herself sway a little on the stool.

'Oh yeah? And what makes you think *he's* a he?' Victoria challenged, her eyes as intelligent and watchful as a crow's.

'Stands to... reason... the kinds... of threats ...' She felt as if she were speaking in slow motion.

'So you can't imagine a female making threats like those? How delightfully, demurely, old-fashioned,' laughed the other woman, leaning aggressively towards Stevie, whose eyelids now felt like shutters of stone much too heavy to support.

The room receded and darkness began to devour the edges of her vision.

'STEVIE! Stay awake!' The sharp command brought her back to herself and she forced her eyes open.
Inexplicably, her swimming head was now resting on the

hard Formica surface of the breakfast bar. She couldn't move any part of her body.

Panic set her heart tripping. Something was very wrong here.

'Not... Shtevie...' she managed to whisper through lips of lead.

Suddenly, Victoria's face was inches from hers. 'Oh, yes you *are*,' she spat, her features ugly with hatred. 'And *you're* the bitch from hell who killed my brother.'

Chapter 60
Layla

'Still nothing,' Blunstone sighed, as he switched off his phone and peered out of the window.

The rancorous storm seemed intent on tearing apart the tiny fisher town, sending massive breakers crashing over the beachside berm and unleashing invisible wraiths that howled and careened along the deserted narrow paths criss-crossing the battened-down community.

'I don't even know if we'll hear anything above that awful wind,' Layla replied, pushing back her chair and heading for the kettle.

She had spent the last half-hour chatting to James while he videoed her with his phone. The impromptu interview had been surprisingly therapeutic, giving her the space to speak candidly about her "visiting consciousness" experiences – good and bad – in a host body. Despite the stressful circumstances, she felt lighter and happier than she had in a long time and she was now psychologically primed to tackle the final obstacle on what she knew would be a bittersweet journey back home to her own small frame.

The professor, too, was delighted with the conversation he had captured on film. Talking from the heart, Layla had allowed her true self to shine through, stamping her own personality on Stevie's features as surely as if the Australian's model-perfect face had been made of wax. The video was incontrovertible proof of the success of his experiment and he had carefully emailed the precious file to his own address, to ensure a copy was readily available should anything happen to his phone.

As Layla brewed tea for them both, he now felt the urge to be equally open with her.

'My dear Layla, I can't help feeling I've let the genie out of the bottle with this project,' he began.

She raised her eyebrows. 'Really? I hadn't noticed.'

He laughed nervously. 'I know, I know; it's something I should have considered in greater depth long before I ventured down this path. But I was so excited, so passionate, about my discovery that no amount of reasoning could have held me back.'

'You and countless other scientists following in the footsteps of Dr Frankenstein,' she said quietly.

Seeing his wounded expression, she quickly added: 'I don't blame you, James. I can understand that irresistible temptation to cross the line and do the unthinkable in the name of furthering our understanding of reality. I've been a willing participant, after all. But what really worries me, as I see it does you, is: what's going to happen next? What is the world going to do with this new knowledge? In all the excitement, and all puffed up with our various petty reasons for forging ahead, we really haven't thought this through, have we?'

'I may have created a monster,' he said miserably.

'Well, you've certainly coined a cliché,' she laughed, trying to cheer him up.

His reply was intercepted by a banshee shriek that ripped through the night and reverberated relentlessly around the terraced granite buildings of the Square.

They looked at each other in horror.

'It's happening!' Layla cried, above Buller's frantic barking. 'We're on!'

Chapter 61

In a burst of adrenaline, Layla sprinted for the front door, Buller just beating her to it. The professor was hot on their heels.

She fumbled with the key and threw the door open, allowing a blast of wind and rain into the hallway. Fighting against it, she followed the excited dog over the threshold and stopped dead.

There was no one out there.

Buller raced up and down the deserted path, driven wild by the siren-screech of the personal alarm. The small black device sat on a paving stone immediately beyond the doorstep. Beside it lay the remains of a hoary old fishing net as sodden as if it had just been hauled out of the brine.

'Where have they gone?' shouted Blunstone above the din, looking around in astonishment.

Layla didn't reply, but grabbed Stevie's anorak from the hall and took off towards the west side of the Square, shrugging on the waterproof as she ran. James paused only to push the ripcord pin back into the alarm, which brought blessed silence; then he whistled Buller to heel, hauled his own raincoat off its peg, and, after slamming the door shut, rushed along the southbound path towards the outer edge of Fittie. A few faces peered out from parted curtains as curious residents tried to see what had caused the cacophony, but no one opened their doors.

After a fruitless scan of the storm-pounded playground, beach and pier, he battled his way back to North Square and almost crashed into Layla, who ran into his path just as he reached the shadowy bulk of the Mission Hall.

'I've been round the whole place, inside the squares and out, and there's no sign of them,' she cried. 'I must see if they're up on the Esplanade or Prom. Go and check if anyone is at Victoria's!' And she raced off again, leaving both man and dog dazed in her wake.

The professor got his breath back and pulled up his collar against the storm. 'Come on, boy,' he said, turning back in the direction of the cottage. 'Let's go and see if there's a rational explanation to all this pandemonium.'

Minutes later, Layla returned to Stevie's house, soaked through and shivering. She found Blunstone sitting in the kitchen, his hair plastered to his head; his face as pale as bleached bone. A rain-spotted plastic folder lay on the table in front of him.

'What's happened?' she cried, all thoughts of her failure to find the women and stalker forgotten.

'This was pinned to her door,' he said dully, pushing the transparent folder towards her. Seeing that it contained a handwritten note, she sat down to read it.

'Dear Layla and Professor Blunstone,
Stevie and I are taking a short road trip. We'll see you back at "Ground Zero", where your little adventure began.
Don't even think about calling the police. If I see any cars approaching other than your Mini, Layla, I will kill her.
Come quickly. I have a proposition for you both which I can't wait to share.
Love,
Your well-wishing stalker,
Vx
PS: I took the liberty of borrowing your car and house keys, Professor. It was a little careless leaving them in your coat pocket, don't you think? ;–)'

Layla put a trembling hand to her throat. She felt as if she were suffocating.

'*Victoria* is the stalker?'

He nodded, miserably. 'So it would appear. And she knows everything.'

She shook her head in disbelief. 'I can't take this in. *Why* is she doing this? She's off her head! What does she want?'

Another thought struck her. 'My god, she found out about the body-swap only this morning. She could have attacked or kidnapped *me* – thinking I was the real Stevie – at any time over the past few days! Why didn't she?'

'I HAVE NO BLOODY IDEA!' His angry shout was as unexpected as it was shocking. His face was now red with fury. 'She has stolen my car and is about to invade my house! I can't take much more of this, I really can't!'

To her horror, he put his head in his hands and his shoulders heaved with noisy sobs. Buller, who sat quietly at his feet, put a paw on his master's knee and whined.

Layla hauled herself back from the verge of hysteria, knowing that one of them had to be strong. Forcing her spinning thoughts into some sort of order, she said, grimly: '*And* she has taken my body.'

He looked up at her helplessly. The great surgeon, reduced to a broken man.

'What are we going to do, Layla?'

She regarded him, pityingly.

'We have no choice, James. We have to go to Cairnacraig House to find out what she wants. And we have to go alone.'

Chapter 62
Victoria

It was all she could do not to laugh out loud. She knew the sound would be swallowed by the rapacious wind, but she wasn't taking any chances.

Hunkered down in the murky shadows of her tarry shed, a gleeful Victoria could almost sense the steadily-mounting panic that must by now be sending Layla and the professor into a maelstrom of confusion. Her own heart was still racing as a result of her frenzied movements immediately following the release of the personal alarm pin.

After dropping the screeching device and fishing net outside Stevie's door, she'd dashed the short distance to North Pier Road, thrown herself into Blunstone's magnificent cream Aston Martin and powered it around the outside of South Square to the small, dark car park facing the pier. There she'd sat, deep in shadow, watching in delight as Layla appeared, looked wildly around and then hurried off again to continue her search. Seconds later, James Blunstone arrived and did exactly the same thing. It was almost comic.

She'd waited several minutes before skulking back to North Square, where she saw with satisfaction that the plastic-coated message had been removed from her front door. Then she'd crept back into the musty, crypt-like confines of the tarry shed, glad to be out of the storm.

Now she pulled the phone from the pocket of her still-wet waxed jacket and checked the time. Ten-thirty; twenty minutes since she'd set off the alarm. Surely they must have left by now?

She stood up and regarded the hulking black shape that shared the cramped, dusty space. There was no sound from within. Carefully, she opened the creaky shed door, pulled up her hood, and edged her way along the front façade. She peeked around the corner – and quickly withdrew her head at the sight of Layla, Blunstone and Buller hurrying towards North Pier Road, where Stevie had parked the Mini earlier that day.

'Close shave,' she giggled quietly, thrilled that this afternoon's hastily-improvised plan was so far spooling out beautifully.

But there was no time for self-congratulation. She re-entered the shed and grasped the handle of the large, black wheelie bin, hauling it over the threshold. Manoeuvring it around in front of her, she trundled it full-tilt through the Fittie Squares, its chunky wheels rolling easily along rain-slick paving stones worn smooth by more than two centuries of footfall.

Reaching the car park, she quickly scanned the area to make sure there was no one around. Then she wrestled the heavy bin on to its side and dragged out its deadweight cargo. An unconscious Stevie – hands and feet bound with cable ties; ball gag in her mouth – flopped on to the wet tarmac.

'Good job you're not in your own big, bastarding body,' Victoria told her conversationally, as she heaved and hauled her on to the Aston's leather-clad back seat. 'I'd really have struggled with that.'

After returning the wheelie bin to the shed, she raced back to the car and slid behind the wheel.

'Woo-hoo!' she all but screamed, as the six-cylinder engine roared into life.

'Cairnacraig House, here we come!'

Ten minutes later, weighed-down by dread and distracted by the darkness and driving rain that even the Mini's high-powered windscreen-wipers had difficulty keeping at bay, neither Layla nor Blunstone recognised the car that roared past them at reckless speed on the northbound dual carriageway.

Its fast-receding tail lights were quickly blotted out by the blinding curtain of spray thrown up in its wake.

'Maniac,' muttered Layla under her breath.

Chapter 63

She really hadn't *had* to do it like this. But she was such a lover of drama.

Quietly absconding with Stevie, in her own car, to Cairnacraig House, would have been the sensible thing to do — but it would have been far less fun. No, the personal alarm, the empty net, the deserted square, the stealing of Blunstone's car, the teasing note... it all appealed to her overblown sense of mystery and theatre. And now she was on her way to set the scene for the final act in a melodrama that had stolen her soul many months ago and brought her raging and cursing across oceans and continents, to seek the ultimate revenge.

Thrillingly, that revenge had now changed guises in a way she never could have foreseen.

Victoria had left Stevie's house on a high that late afternoon, after pocketing the professor's car and house keys on her way out — a bonus she hadn't bargained on. Then she went into overdrive: sourcing the materials for her "catch-a-creepo kit"; removing the satnav from her rental car; researching online the whereabouts of Blunstone's rural mansion, and all the while fine-tuning the outrageous plan currently under way.

Now, having reached the heart of the wind-blasted Buchan coastal countryside and knowing the others were far behind her, she slowed the car, carefully following the satnav instructions along treacherously-wet, winding lanes littered with unnerving amounts of tree debris. A fathomless black mass to her right was all that could be seen of the rampant North Sea, but she could well imagine enormous waves smashing manically at the serrated rocks of the ancient, rugged shoreline.

A quick glance in the rear-view mirror revealed that Stevie had awakened from her dose of Rohypnol. The

Australian was lying, eyes wide with terror, flat on her back and still unable to move her paralysed limbs.

'Welcome back, Bitch!' she called to her, cheerfully. 'Boy, do we have some serious fun in store.'

Chapter 64

The heavy oak door creaked open on the dark and chilly interior of Cairnacraig House.

Victoria held her breath in anticipation of an alarm, but there was only silence.

'Silly old fool,' she muttered, but she was grateful for the professor's security lapse. She knew from previous experience that she was capable of disabling a house alarm, but it would have been a time-consuming nuisance.

She fumbled for and found the light switch, illuminating the stark slate-and-granite hall of the grand old mansion which had taken her breath away when she'd caught first glimpse of it on her approach. The gothic atmosphere of the house and its secluded grounds couldn't be more appropriate for her purpose.

Shivering with both cold and excitement, she strode boldly from room to room, switching on lights and marvelling at the mix of stately and contemporary décor that greeted her on the ground floor. Climbing the staircase, she thrilled at the long, low lament of the wind as it soughed through the rooftop crenellations. On discovering the "hospital wing", she couldn't help but laugh out loud. She danced with delight through the pristine whiteness of the two-bed ward, and peered through the small glass aperture of the locked operating-theatre door.

'Unbelievable!' she cried, at the sight of all the plastic-shrouded surgical equipment.

But there was no more time to lose. She hurried back downstairs and out to the car.

She needed to be ready to greet her guests.

Chapter 65
Cairnacraig House
Layla

With a scrunch of gravel, they skidded to a halt behind the professor's luxury car, which was parked haphazardly just outside the front entrance.

Every light in the house was blazing, creating a brilliant beacon that surely could be seen from miles out at sea.

Layla glanced over at James Blunstone, who was staring up at his home – his fortress – which had been so insolently breached. His face was a mask of steely resolution.

'Ready?' she asked, her stomach flipping over with fear.

He nodded, his lips compressed into a thin line. 'I forgot to set the bloody alarm,' he hissed.

'It probably wouldn't have stopped her getting in,' she said placatingly, but he was already opening the car door and getting out.

She followed suit, pausing to release Buller from the back seat and grab his lead as he leapt out.

Seeing that the front door was ajar, she wanted to approach cautiously, but James charged forward, flung it wide and marched into the hall. Layla and the Labrador followed him.

'WHERE ARE YOU?' he shouted into the echoing space. 'SHOW YOURSELF, DAMN IT!'

'In here, my dears!' The cheerful voice hailed them from the back of the house.

'She's in the kitchen,' whispered Layla.

Blunstone scowled and strode forward, but she caught his sleeve and said, in a low voice: 'James, be very careful. We need to stay calm and listen to what she wants. Losing your temper will only escalate the situation.'

He shook her off but nodded curtly. 'Don't worry. I'm well aware of the danger here.'

He was no longer the broken man she'd comforted in Stevie's kitchen. She was relieved that now, on his own turf, he had regained his authoritative manner.

The three of them advanced past the grand staircase and stepped down into the sunken kitchen, where they were confronted by a horrifying sight.

In the centre of the room, Stevie was seated on one of the antique carver chairs from the dining-room, her wrists and ankles bound to its arms and legs with white plastic zip-ties. Her mouth was stretched painfully over a ball gag; her eyes projected sheer terror. By her side stood Victoria, a large serrated knife held casually in her right hand, which hung at her hip. Just behind her was a brown leather footstool, which she'd removed from the lounge.

The small woman's beady eyes glittered venomously in the overhead spotlights. Her mouth was a sneering red slash.

Layla, seeing her own body restrained in such a cruel manner, felt a rush of nausea, which she forced away with difficulty.

'*So* glad you could make it,' the New Zealander said, the disdain on her face contrasting weirdly with the pleasantness of her tone. 'Why don't you sit down?' She indicated the rocking-chair and another seat from the dining-room set, which she'd placed a few yards in front of her terrifying tableau.

Layla and Blunstone looked at each other and took their places. Layla, perching awkwardly on the edge of the rocking-chair, kept Buller firmly at her side, but the dog showed no resistance, seeming to understand that his new friend was now an enemy not to be approached.

The professor spoke first. 'What is all this about?' His tone was colder than the granite blocks from which his house was built.

'Can't you at least take the gag out of her mouth?' cried Layla.

Victoria regarded each of them in turn, her gaze lingering on Layla's borrowed body in an uncomfortably lascivious fashion.

'No; she needs to be silent for now,' she replied. Then she turned to answer Blunstone.

'I have a story to tell you, so I hope you two, at least, are sitting comfortably?'

They nodded mutely, knowing they were completely at her mercy.

'Good,' she said, settling herself on the footstool, her knife hand now resting on Stevie's left thigh.

'Then I'll begin.'

Chapter 66

'Once upon a time,' began Victoria, making big eyes at her audience as if they were children, 'there was a beautiful boy and his vivacious little sister.'

Her strange, singsong voice unnerved Layla even more than the knife did, as the young woman seemed not to be fully present in the cold kitchen that stormy night.

'They lived in a wonderful land called New Zealand, where they enjoyed an idyllic childhood until the terrible day when their parents were killed in a car crash.'

Layla risked a glance at James, who was staring at Victoria with an inscrutable expression.

'The siblings were devastated,' she went on, 'but handled their grief in very different ways. The boy was heartbroken, but bravely looked out for his little sister at the Washington children's home they'd been dumped in: a horrid, nasty place, full of bullies and worse. The girl, on the other hand, was twisted with rage, and soon became one of the bullies herself. But that part you don't need to know.'

She settled herself more comfortably on the footstool. 'What you do need to know is that the girl's name was Victoria and the boy's was Simon.'

At that, Stevie made a strangled sound in her throat and began straining against her bonds.

'Recognise the name, do you, Bitch?' Victoria hissed, without looking at her captive. Then she continued. 'Simon survived the ordeal of the home with great dignity and as soon as he was old enough, he got a job as a junior reporter with the local newspaper. He rented a small apartment and single-mindedly worked his way up to his dream role of crime correspondent.

'Meanwhile, Victoria had run away countless times and, at the age of fifteen, ended up on the streets, dependent on hard drugs. Simon tracked her down, got her clean in rehab, and took her to live with him while she completed her school studies. Thanks to him, she went to university and ended up with a great engineering job, a passion for amateur dramatics, and her own network of close friends.

'Everything seemed to have worked out well for our two "Babes in the Wood",' she continued, punctuating her last words with air quotes. 'Then Simon landed a job as an investigative journalist in Sydney.'

Stevie squealed again, her eyes begging Victoria to let her speak. She was wasting her time.

'My beautiful brother was in two minds about going. He was excited about the work but didn't want to leave me behind. I told him it was too fantastic an opportunity to miss and I promised I'd visit him as often as I could. And so he went.'

She stared at the floor.

'I never saw him again.'

Despite the coercive circumstances, Layla felt some sympathy for the woman and wanted to hear more. She nodded at her encouragingly.

'I missed Simon dearly, but he kept in close contact with me, sending emails and messaging endless pictures. Much as he'd loved Washington, he said Sydney was a wonderful place to live and work, and he quickly made friends with folk on the paper and at the sports club he'd joined. He was a real outdoorsy fella: he loved biking, hiking, volleyball, surfing – you name it.'

She smiled wistfully.

'I was glad for him, but I was also worried about what he was working on. He told me he'd started investigating a local drugs cartel. He was very anti-drugs after seeing what I went through. It sounded dangerous, but... SHUT UP with the racket, or I'll cut you,' she snarled at Stevie, who immediately fell silent and closed her eyes in defeat.

'He assured me it was all perfectly safe. He'd teamed up with a freelance – an older woman – and the two of them had worked out a plan for gathering information while staying under the radar. He wouldn't go into details, except to say that he'd already fallen hard for his colleague. He described her as "funny, sexy and drop-dead gorgeous" and said he knew she was a keeper, if only he could persuade her to take him seriously. She had him wound around her little finger. Didn't you, Bitch? DIDN'T YOU?'

As she spoke, Victoria's voice became increasingly vicious and she kept nudging Stevie hard with her elbow. The Australian resumed her high-pitched puling but didn't open her eyes.

James Blunstone spoke up. 'Please, tell us the rest, but leave her be. You've achieved your aim in terrifying her out of her wits.'

'You think so?' scoffed Victoria, tossing back her black curls. 'Oh, you don't know the half of it yet.'

She carried on with her story.

'This all happened last July. I decided to visit him to find out just what he was involved in and to meet this superwoman he couldn't stop talking about. I tried to call him to make arrangements, but his phone was switched off. When I couldn't reach him for several days, I contacted the newspaper and his editor told me very angrily that Simon had gone missing and that he believed he was working undercover – entirely unsanctioned – on the drugs cartel story. He couldn't get through to him, either.

'Well, I knew something was badly wrong. My brother wouldn't have scared me by deliberately going silent. I was frantic and booked a flight to Australia. But before I could leave for the airport, the local police came to my door with the worst possible news.'

Her red mouth turned down in a sad-clown expression as she forced out the next words.

'Simon's body had been found in Sydney, dumped in an alleyway. He'd been badly beaten and tortured with a knife, before his throat was finally slashed.

'My poor, darling brother didn't stand a chance against the bastards he was investigating. And it was all HER fault!' She prodded the tip of the knife into Stevie's thigh, prompting a thin scream from behind the ball gag.

'How was it Stevie's fault, Victoria?' Layla asked quickly, hoping to distract her from her cat-and-mouse cruelty.

It worked. The New Zealander turned to her, eyes streaming, and howled: 'She made him do it alone! She was supposed to buddy-up with him so that they had each other's back, but she chickened out and started working on some other story, for a national newspaper. But Simon went ahead, anyway, against his editor's orders. In his last email to me, he'd said he was scared he might be losing her, and so he must have thought that this was how he could prove himself worthy of her. He was so besotted! But she treated – him – like – shit.'

More thigh-prodding with the knife, this time deep enough to bring a dark red stain to the surface of Stevie's jeans.

Stevie keened pitifully and the professor and Layla both leaned forward, hands outstretched.

'Please don't do that!' Layla cried.

But Victoria wasn't listening. 'SHE DIDN'T EVEN ATTEND HIS FUNERAL!' she screamed, frightening Buller to his feet. '*That's* how little he meant to her.'

'Victoria, look at me – look at me,' demanded Blunstone, who also had stood up. She turned her eyes to him, her pale face pinched into the very essence of misery.

'We are so, so sorry to hear what happened to Simon,' he said in a gentler voice. 'I can't begin to imagine the pain you are carrying with you. But don't you think you should give Stevie the chance to tell us her side of the story?'

With astonishing speed, her wretchedness transformed into delight. 'Yes, of course,' she laughed. 'That's one of the reasons we're all here.

'I want to hear from the Bitch's mouth how she justifies living her life between then and now as if *nothing* had happened.'

Chapter 67

Layla watched as, with one hand, Victoria roughly removed the gag from Stevie's mouth. She exchanged glances with the professor, but they both knew there was no chance of overpowering the younger woman, who kept her eye on them and had the knife trained on her prisoner's mid-section.

Layla was still trembling, partly from fear of seeing Stevie stabbed, but also from the flashback she'd experienced when the name 'Simon' was mentioned. Stevie hadn't been the only one to get a surprise on that score.

As Victoria had carried on talking, she had clearly seen in her mind's eye the face of the surfing dude she'd dreamed about a couple of nights previously: the beautiful man conjured up by the scrap of Stevie's subconscious that had not transferred across with her into Layla's brain. She knew intuitively that this man must be Simon and her borrowed heart felt sore with a sadness and a shame that should not have been hers to feel.

As soon as she was free to speak, Stevie let out a howl which, to Layla's amazement, contained more rage than terror.

'You can't do this! YOU CAN'T DO THIS TO ME!' she screamed at Victoria, who also seemed taken aback by the woman's aggressive reaction. But she quickly recovered herself and said menacingly: 'This knife here says I can.'

'Calm down, Stevie – for your own sake,' ordered Blunstone sternly. 'This is your chance to give your side of the story and if I were you, I'd use it wisely.'

The Australian's blue eyes bored into his, full of burning hate.

'Go to hell!' she yelled. 'I don't have to explain myself to any of you.'

Spoken like a true sociopath, thought Layla, marvelling at the woman's bravado.

'Then we'll all be sitting here until kingdom come,' said Victoria.

In the ensuing lull, Layla could hear the storm still in full spate, the relentless wind hurling rain against the curtain-glass wall and rattling loose slates on the kitchen roof.

When – and how – will this dreadful night end? she wondered fearfully.

Buller broke the spell with a loud and protesting yawn, which spoke of his yearning for food, water and a warm bed.

Patting his dog's head reassuringly, the professor tried again. 'Stevie, you must understand that you are in no position to refuse to cooperate. We need to find out what Victoria wants from us...' He eyed Victoria warily and added: '... and we can't do that until you explain yourself.'

Layla said sharply: 'How could you have behaved in such a callous way, Stevie? You threw the poor guy to the wolves!'

Her move to antagonise the Australian succeeded. Stevie turned her blazing gaze upon her and spat: '*I didn't ask him to do it!* Both Stan, the editor, and I decided that the undercover work was too dangerous, but the drongo went ahead, anyway. *It wasn't my fault.*'

'Don't you *dare* call my brother a drongo, you arrogant bitch,' Victoria hissed. 'He was the most sensible person I ever met. He only wanted you to admire him, to love him back. He would never have taken such a risk if he hadn't been obsessed with you.'

293

'The guy was a loser,' taunted Stevie, prompting another wave of fear in Layla's breast. The woman was being reckless with *her* body, her future, the life she needed so badly to return to.

'Oh, he was a good enough reporter,' Stevie continued, before an incensed Victoria could respond, 'but he didn't have the balls for undercover work. Stan and I realised it would end in disaster – and, as it turned out, it did.'

'But you had your fun with him first, didn't you?' Victoria cried. 'You strung him along, knowing he worshipped you. Then you chewed him up and spat him out!'

'Simon was cute... but for me, it was just sex,' admitted Stevie casually. 'I hate it when men get all boring about love and settling down. It's so not my style.'

Victoria looked as if she were about to explode. She raised the knife threateningly towards the defiant woman's throat.

Once again, Layla intervened. 'Victoria! Tell us what happened after you got the news about your brother? What did you do?'

The younger woman lowered the knife and slumped back down on the footstool. 'I flew to Sydney,' she said dully. 'I decided to have him cremated there, since he loved the place so much. I scattered his ashes on Bondi Beach.'

Tears flooded her eyes. 'And *she* didn't have the courtesy to attend the funeral. Christ, she never even sent me a sympathy card!

'Why didn't you pay your respects?' she cried at Stevie. 'I could have confronted you then, told you what I thought of you, instead of letting it fester inside me and ruin my life. I've lost my brother, my job, my friends, all because of *you*!'

Stevie was looking at her incredulously. 'Is that what all this is about? All those months of stalking and sending hate mail, and then following me thousands of miles across the world... all that, *just because I didn't go to the funeral and you didn't get the chance to rip me a new one?*'

Victoria's look was pure poison. 'Yes, that's exactly what it's about,' she replied in a low growl. 'You treated my brother, my darling Simon, as if he was dirt on your shoe. *Nobody* does that to my blood and gets away with it.'

There was another heavy silence, broken by James clearing his throat. 'So what do you intend doing, Victoria? Why have you brought us here? If you had wanted to kill Stevie, surely you would have done so already?'

'I could have killed her – or at least the person I thought was her – at any time over the past few days,' she retorted, looking pointedly at Layla. 'But that wouldn't have been nearly as much fun as I've had tormenting her. Sustained psychological torture is a wonderful form of revenge; what a pity it's not enough.'

'Does that mean you intend killing her now?' Layla asked bravely, prompting a furious look from Stevie.

Victoria laughed dramatically. 'Oh, no, no. My original plan *was* to kill her slowly and painfully, just as Simon died. But now I have a far worse punishment in mind.'

The three of them looked at her in puzzlement.

'What could possibly be worse than death?' Blunstone asked.

She smiled sweetly at him and replied: 'That's easy: a lifetime condemned to living in the body of the person who hates you most in the world.'

Chapter 68

As the full horror of Victoria's words sank in, Layla finally realised that the woman was utterly deranged.

Until now, she could almost understand how someone with a chaotic background such as Victoria's could be driven by grief and rage to seek revenge in the sadistic manner she had employed over the past few months.

Until now, she hadn't believed that the vulnerable young woman would go so far as to murder Stevie in cold blood – particularly in front of an audience.

But that single sentence changed everything, revealing the true extent of the New Zealander's madness.

'You can't be serious!' James sounded as horrified as she felt.

'Oh, believe me, I am,' Victoria replied triumphantly, clearly delighted at having delivered her denouement to maximum effect.

'You want me to transpose Stevie's consciousness into your body?'

She nodded.

'And where do you propose your own consciousness should go?'

'Why, isn't it obvious? Into Stevie's body, of course,' she replied scornfully, adding: 'Cannibalistic warriors wreak their revenge by eating the flesh of their enemies. For the same reason, I want to take over the body of mine. There's no getting away from the fact that it's a fabulous one,' she added, her gaze resting hungrily on Layla.

Both Blunstone and Layla were lost for words. Stevie had no such problem.

'You crazy cow!' she yelled, frantically bucking up and down in her chair. 'I'll *kill* Layla rather than let *you* get hold of my body!'

More than ever, Layla felt as if she were trapped in one of her most malevolent nightmares.

She was sharing a room with two psychopaths.

She looked over at James. His head was down and his shoulders were shaking. At first she thought he was crying again, then she realised he was helpless with laughter.

'Ha-ha-ha! I've heard it all now,' he shrieked hysterically.

Fearful that he was about to fall apart completely, Layla reached out and put her hand on one of his. It was freezing.

Then, seeing that Stevie's furious struggles had almost capsized her chair and momentarily distracted Victoria, she leaned over and whispered: 'Be strong, James. She's off her head, but we need to play along for now until we can think of a way out of this mess.'

Chapter 69

'So, what's the plan?' Layla was amazed at how calm she sounded. Really, she felt faint with fear.

Victoria was busy retying Stevie's gag. The Australian's protests became muffled squeaks; then she fell silent and sat still, clearly wanting to listen to the conversation.

'Well, you'll be happy to know that *you'll* be all right, Layla,' Victoria said pleasantly, returning to her sentry position on the footstool. 'I like you – you're one of the good guys – and you deserve to have your consciousness reunited with your body.'

Despite her revulsion for the woman, Layla felt a rush of relief and gratitude. However, she merely nodded.

'I like you, too, Professor,' Victoria continued, turning to James and grinning broadly. 'Who, in your shoes, wouldn't do what you've done? Your breakthrough is truly mind-blowing. I fully intend to participate when you announce the project's success to the world. I'll pretend I'm Stevie and nobody will be any the wiser. And no one will listen if *she* starts bleating. They'll think she's just some kook who's trying to cash in on all the publicity you'll be attracting.'

Stevie's eyes flashed pure hatred at her.

Taking his cue from Layla, Blunstone nodded mildly, as if Victoria were merely remarking on the weather. Then he said: 'That's all very well, but how do you propose that we manage the operation itself? What guarantee do you have that I won't put you under and then alert the authorities... or worse?'

Layla inhaled sharply, fearing that he had antagonised the woman with his veiled hint at violence. But Victoria kept the grin on her face and said: 'Oh, you won't do that. Not if you want to get out of this alive.'

'What do you mean?' he asked uncertainly.

'I *mean* that I have a foolproof method of getting what I want from you.'

She leaned towards them both, her eyes dancing with excitement.

'I'm going to rig up a bomb.'

Chapter 70

There was another shocked silence. Once again, Victoria appeared elated by the impact on her captive audience.

Just when we think things can't possibly get weirder, she drops another bombshell,' Layla thought, feeling a bubble of inappropriate laughter rising in her chest as the unintentional pun hit home. But she managed to control herself and instead blurted out: 'A *bomb*?'

'Yes. It's a very elegant plan, if I say so myself,' smirked the New Zealander. 'As a civil engineer – yes, I lied about my oil and gas job – I've always been fascinated by incendiary devices, and I've used more than a few in various projects. Rigging up a home-made bomb is a cinch. It'll be armed and ready to blow should James or either of his colleagues try to escape the operating theatre while we three ladies are under anaesthetic. Then, when I come around and see that my instructions have been carried out, I will disarm the bomb and no harm will have been done.'

'No *harm*?' repeated James incredulously, as Stevie rolled her eyes. 'What if something goes wrong with either the bomb or the operation?'

'Nothing will go wrong with my bomb,' Victoria replied. 'And nothing *better* go wrong with the operation.'

Seeing the professor's look of sheer hopelessness and fearing for his already-fragile psyche, Layla stepped in.

'But have you thought through all the practical details?' she asked. 'James will have to call his colleagues up from Edinburgh; none of them has ever performed the operation on three people, don't forget, and so they'll need time to prepare for that, and in the meantime we're all going to need food, water, sleep...' she tailed off, realising how improbable it sounded. The plan would never get off the ground.

'I can't possibly bring Allan and Susan into this insane situation!' he cried weakly, his lower lip trembling. 'You'll never let them leave here alive!'

'You *will* bring them in – and as quickly as possible, or else I'll revert to plan A and *she* dies.' Victoria waved the knife in Stevie's direction. 'So you'll make the call as soon as you've composed yourself, and I'll find somewhere to keep you all until they arrive and I have everything set up.'

Her icy tone brooked no argument.

Blunstone looked lost and utterly defeated. Then something seemed to occur to him.

'The only room lockable from the outside is the library,' he said flatly.

His tormentor giggled. 'How very Agatha Christie! Then the library it shall be.'

Chapter 71

Layla crouched down and switched on the living-gas fire, which brought an instant glow and some welcome heat into the chilly, wood-panelled library.

Her movements were sluggish; she felt fuzzy-headed and weak with both hunger and fear.

Blunstone sat, hunched, in one of the two fireside armchairs, staring at the floor. An hour earlier, he had made the call to Edinburgh with a knife at his throat, his voice shaking with suppressed emotion. It was an emergency, he had told Allan Cameron, his anaesthetist. Layla's mother had been taken seriously ill in the States and she needed to have the operation reversed as soon as possible, so that she could travel to California to be with her. He and Susan Murray should leave first thing in the morning and be prepared for surgery in the afternoon. As he'd rung off, he'd nodded curtly at Victoria, his dark-ringed eyes full of resentment. 'They'll be here by nine-thirty am,' he'd said in a monotone.

'Good,' she'd said cheerfully, holding her hand out for his phone.

She had then made James and Layla haul Stevie, still gagged and bound to the heavy dining chair, up to the library. It had been hard going, but they had eventually managed.

Next, after patting down both of them and confiscating Layla's mobile, Victoria had escorted them to the downstairs cloakroom for 'comfort breaks', holding each of them at knifepoint while they waited their turn outside the door. '*You* can pee in your pants,' she had informed Stevie viciously.

Back in the library, the three of them had watched as she'd rummaged through the professor's desk drawers and removed a pair of scissors and a small, dagger-shaped letter opener. On his direction, she'd also found the room's old-fashioned ornamental key, which she then used to lock them in. At no point had she taken her eyes off them or turned her back.

'I'll return soon with refreshments,' she'd called through the solid oak door. 'Be glad there's such a thing as the twenty-four-hour supermarket. Don't go anywhere, folks!'

Her mocking laughter had receded towards the front of the house. A few minutes later, above the incessant patter of rain on the tall windows, they'd heard the faint roar of the Aston Martin's engine as the car set off at speed along the drive.

Now, Buller, who had been sniffing at the foot of the locked door, padded towards the fire's comforting warmth and plumped himself down on the rug with a contented harrumph.

For his human companions, however, the situation was far from cosy.

Layla was startled out of her stupor by Stevie's indignant squeals. She got to her feet, hurried over and removed the ball gag.

'About time!' Stevie shouted. 'Why were you fannying around with the fire, you idiot?'

'If you don't want me to replace this gag, you'll stop being so rude,' retorted Layla, anger clearing the fogginess from her mind.

She sat down in the armchair opposite the professor's. 'We need a plan,' she said to him, but he didn't take his eyes off the floor.

'Too right, we need a plan,' screeched Stevie. 'That Kiwi bitch is not getting hold of my body!'

She started struggling with her bonds again. 'We could break a window and escape that way... and you can use a piece of glass to cut through these bloody cable ties.'

'And what good would escaping do us, exactly?' James looked up at her bleakly. 'She'll only track us down.'

Layla couldn't help but agree. 'No, we have to find a way of overpowering her, and then we can hand her over to the police. They'll never believe her tales of body-swapping, if she's daft enough to tell them. She'll be done for kidnapping, housebreaking and attempted murder, and they'll put her away for a long, long time.'

'Huh! If I have my way, she won't live to see another morning,' Stevie said, her stark words sending a chill through Layla's bones. 'At any rate, you can still smash a window and cut these things off.'

James looked horrified at the prospect and after a moment, Layla said quietly: 'No, Stevie. We can't risk antagonising her by setting you free. And we're not arming ourselves with glass shards, either, in case you had that in mind. She's highly intelligent and is likely to check the windows before she comes back into the house. We need to bide our time and find the right opportunity to bring her down while she's off her guard – and preferably without having to kill her. I really don't fancy doing time for murder, if this all goes pear-shaped.'

She smiled bitterly. 'And anyway, for what you've done to us – *and for threatening to kill me* rather than let her have your body – you don't deserve to be released.'

Stevie's howl of rage had Buller jumping to his feet again. He growled low in his throat and wouldn't stop.

'UNTIE ME!' the Australian screamed over and over, rocking and bucking as she had done in the kitchen.

James put his head down again and, undaunted by the racket, seemed to retreat into a world of his own.

When she could bear the din no longer, Layla strode over to Stevie and replaced the ball gag. 'I warned you,' she hissed at her, turning on her heel and throwing herself back into the armchair. She was relieved that the dog's growling had stopped, but saw that he remained on alert. It gave her an idea.

'Maybe we could somehow get Buller to attack Victoria?' she suggested.

'Impossible!' snapped the professor. 'He's a great big softie. He'd never attack anyone, no matter how fiercely he growls at them.'

And he went back to his dark reverie.

Deflated, Layla stared into the flickering flames, her heart heavy with dread. A profound sense of loneliness stole over her as she realised that with Stevie's dangerous instability and the professor's apparent surrender to their fate, she now had only herself to rely on.

Chapter 72

But James surprised her. Without warning, he leapt to his feet and began pacing the long room, muttering to himself and running his hands through his already-dishevelled hair. His buff-coloured trench coat billowed around him as he swept past the antique bookshelves Layla had so admired on her first visit, which now seemed light-years ago.

She stared at him, half-fearing he was about to go off the rails; half-hoping he was hatching a plan.

Victoria had been gone around forty-five minutes. In the interim, Stevie had quietened down, but continued breathing heavily, a murderous look on her face. Buller had glanced first at his master and then at Layla and when neither of them responded, had settled back on the rug and shut his eyes.

Now, all three of them were watching Blunstone, waiting to see what he would do next.

Nothing they could have imagined would have come close to what he did.

After several minutes of his pacing, a car's engine roared outside, heralding the return of their captor. The sudden sound galvanised the professor into action. Darting towards a bookcase on the room's outer wall, he pressed one of its carved decorative roses. To the utter astonishment of his audience, the entire volume-filled façade swung forward on a hidden hinge, revealing an old wooden door.

Layla jumped up and laughed aloud, watching, entranced, as the professor unlatched it and, with difficulty, pulled it open.

A secret passage: the ultimate country-house cliché! she marvelled, childishly thrilled, despite the circumstances.

But the laughter died on her lips at the sight of his stricken face as he turned to her from the black maw of the newly-exposed doorway. His voice was tremulous as he said: 'Oh, Layla... my dear. I am so sorry, but I can't and won't go through with this farce. Take care of my darling boy. You'll find me at the place he is named after.'

And then he disappeared into the darkness.

Panic gripped her, rooting her to the spot. The room began to close in around her and a high-pitched whine filled her head, echoing Stevie's shrill cries behind the gag.

Moments later, the library door crashed open and Victoria made an aggressive entrance, knife held firmly in front of her.

Her sharp, predator's eyes immediately took in the scene. With a screech of indignation, she hurled herself towards the secret entrance, only just managing to skid to a stop before crossing the threshold. Layla, her faintness displaced by a spike of adrenaline, edged up behind her, holding tightly to Buller's collar. Through the doorway, she could just make out the upper stone steps of a roughly-hewn staircase that descended into the black void beyond.

Victoria screamed with rage and whirled around before Layla could even think of trying to overpower her.

'Where does this lead?' she yelled at her. 'Where has he gone? ANSWER ME!'

The small woman's fury was truly terrifying. She stamped her feet and tore at her hair, reminding Layla of the tiny horror that was Rumpelstiltskin in the Brothers Grimm fairy tale.

'I-I don't know!' she gasped, shaking her head in disbelief. 'He's only just this minute opened the door. We had no idea it was there!'

307

With another howl, Victoria launched herself through the portal and Layla could hear the muffled thud of her boots on the stairs.

She turned to look at Stevie, who, wide-eyed and struggling again, was squawking at her with increasing frustration. Then Layla did something she would come to regret: she freed her body-swap buddy, believing that the two of them would have a better chance of restraining Victoria whenever – and wherever – they caught up with her.

Releasing Buller, she dived towards the modern leather desk chair, hefted it above her head and hurled it at the nearest window. With an almighty crash, the tall, narrow pane shattered outwards, leaving one or two lethal-looking shards stuck in the frame. Next, she tore off the waxed jacket she still wore, wrapped a sleeve around her hand and tugged at one of the shark's-tooth shards until it broke off. Working frantically, she used the makeshift knife to saw through the plastic ties binding Stevie's hands and feet. Then she untied the gag.

Gasping with the effort, she watched the Australian try to stand, fail, and sit back down again with a thud.

'My feet are numb!' Stevie wailed, adding urgently: 'Quick, you get after them; I'll follow you as soon as I can move.'

Layla pulled on her jacket again. Summoning a latent bravery she knew was more Stevie's than her own, she approached the doorway and, with Buller at her heels, plunged into the black and baleful environment that was Cairnacraig House's most successfully-kept secret.

Chapter 73

She would have had to turn back, had it not been for Buller. The instant she started down the passage's stone steps, the blackness enveloping her brought a feeling of disorientation.

But the Labrador didn't falter, using his nose and night vision to lead the way while remaining close enough to Layla to be a barely-visible but reliable guide.

She hoped Stevie would have the sense to look for a torch or flashlight before following them.

The mercifully-short staircase led down to what felt like a blank wall. But this presented no problem to the dog, who turned left and then left again before setting off in a straight line, through a tunnel whose rocky sides Layla could touch with both hands.

She soon discovered that the ceiling was low, forcing her to stoop a little as the two of them progressed cautiously along what felt and smelt like a floor of musty, packed earth.

'Okay, we're heading east,' she told herself, desperate to maintain some measure of control.

With the tantalising scent of his master so fresh in the tunnel, Buller ploughed on steadily, panting excitedly. The feel of his fur at her fingertips was of great comfort to Layla, who was only just managing to keep claustrophobia at bay.

'That's right, Buller – *good* boy,' she breathed over and over again as they penetrated deeper and deeper into the murky black hole, towards goodness knew what.

Chapter 74
Victoria

Fuelled by fury and led by the narrow beam of her smartphone torch, Victoria hurried on through the tunnel, her thudding footsteps echoing off the rocky walls.

Despite her insane rage, a part of her was thrilled by the unexpected turn of events which had revealed this secret underground escape route straight from a smuggler's yarn. As far as drama was concerned, she couldn't have asked for a more appropriate scenario.

But it was *not* part of the plan.

She guessed that the tunnel must lead to the sea, which lay roughly a quarter of a mile east of Cairnacraig House. That wasn't far, but the pressing gloom and rocky uniformity of the passage made it a long and infuriating digression from her meticulously-laid timeline.

'He MUSTN'T get away!' she screamed, throwing herself onward, her phone held aloft like a talisman which created, rather than warded off, weird shadows that leapt and capered around the torchlit walls like demons released from their subterranean cells.

Chapter 75
Stevie

The fiendish shapes unfurled themselves again for Stevie, whose delayed progress through the tunnel was aided by a flashlight she'd found in the under-stairs cupboard. She held it high as she sped silently along, out of breath already, but determined to close the gap between herself and the others.

In her right hand, partially wrapped in a dishcloth, was the long glass shard Layla had dropped in her haste to follow Victoria.

Chapter 76
Victoria

Hearing his laboured breathing only a short distance ahead of her, Victoria grinned broadly. The old duffer had slowed down.

She nearly fell as the ground beneath her feet dipped steeply and unexpectedly, but she managed to regain her balance just as the shrieking protest of old wood reached her ears.

Had he come to the end of the tunnel?

This was confirmed by a funnelled blast of cold, wet air, which was abruptly cut off by a resounding slam, followed by silence. Two seconds later, she skidded to a halt in front of a small wooden door in the shape of a Gothic arch. There was a key in its heavy mortis lock. Breathlessly, she grasped the tarnished brass handle and hauled the door open, once again allowing the unruly elements to bluster through the dark passageway.

Clutching her phone, she pushed herself out into the storm-soaked easterly wind, blinking hard to clear her vision. She nearly screamed as she realised that the door opened on to a narrow, rocky ledge positioned halfway up a graduated cliff. A couple of steps farther and she would have fallen headlong and most likely broken her neck.

Her heart hammering, she whipped her head back and forth, searching for a sign of the professor. Yes! There he was, clambering up a pile of rocks to her right, heading for the clifftop, which was barely a ragged outline against the louring night sky.

She almost had him!

Chapter 77
Layla

Sticking close to Buller and singing breathlessly to herself to ward off the heebie-jeebies, Layla wondered if the nightmarish darkness would stretch on forever.

James must know this passage well, she thought, feeling ridiculously hurt that he hadn't told her about it either during her post-operative sojourn at the house, or at least as soon as they'd found themselves locked in the library. It was no coincidence that he'd suggested the room as their temporary prison, she now realised. He must have had some kind of escape in mind. *So why didn't he tell us what he was planning?*

But having seen the despair on his face and heard his parting words, she could only surmise that he really had reached the end of his tether and was intending to commit suicide at the nearby Bullers of Buchan.

'Oh, let's try to go faster, boy. We must stop him!' she cried to the dog, who obligingly increased his pace to a steady trot.

'Layla!' The faint sound of her own voice pulled her up short. Buller, who had continued on for a few yards, returned to her side, nuzzling at her hand as if to drag her away from the distant cry.

'Stevie!' she shouted back, relief flooding her. Despite all the grief the woman had put her through, she felt almost light-headed with gratitude that she wouldn't have to tackle whatever lay ahead, on her own.

'Stevie! We're here. We'll wait for you!'

Chapter 78
Victoria

'*Stop! Stop, you stupid bastard!*' Victoria howled, as she slipped and scrabbled up over the jagged, wet rocks. She had already cut her hand badly and the blood dripped, unheeded, marking the zig-zag path of her clumsy ascent.

Ahead of her, near the clifftop, she could just make out the shape of James Blunstone stooping to fill his coat pockets with what looked like loose lumps of stone.

'DON'T YOU DARE!' she roared, incandescent with rage as the realisation of his intention dawned on her.

The professor reached the top of the cliff, his tall figure shrouded by the light-coloured raincoat which no longer flapped in the wind. Then he disappeared from view.

'He hasn't done it; he hasn't done it,' she told herself manically, as she struggled up the last few feet of the climb.

He hadn't. He was now hurrying along an overgrown clifftop path which wound its way southwards. Soaking strands of wild grass whipped at her legs and the wind tormented her mercilessly, as she followed him as quickly as she could along the unfamiliar, treacherous terrain.

She stopped when she realised he had led her on to a slim strip of turf-covered rock, with a dizzying sheer drop on either side, which curved back on itself towards the land.

Her civil engineering work had taken her to many precarious places high in the sky, but never without a harness and never on a dark and stormy night. But Blunstone was making surprisingly good progress, hastening along the two-hundred-foot-high, circular causeway as if they were in balmy broad daylight. When he was roughly opposite her, hundreds of yards off, his dim figure turned towards her, as if making certain she could see him. Then he vanished again, behind what looked like a large clump of marram grass.

Furious, Victoria crouched down and began to crawl along the narrow strip, reducing the amount of body mass the raging wind had to buff against. Chancing a look down to her right, she saw to her amazement that she was suspended above a terrifyingly-deep, sea-sculpted hollow, carved-out over millennia. It was breathtaking, even in the dark, as the roaring, churning ocean far below emitted an eerie grey-green glow stippled by foaming white breakers.

She stopped in her tracks, mesmerised by the colossal power of the maelstrom beneath.

A high scream broke the spell. She looked up sharply in time to see, on the far side of the megalithic hole, a flash of beige hurtle down into the depths.

'NOOOOO!' she bellowed up at the cold, starless sky.

Chapter 79
Stevie

Stevie was now seriously out of breath, her small frame infuriatingly exhausted by her frantic run through the tunnel.

I can't live like this; I need *to get my old body back*, she thought angrily as she homed in on the siren sound of her Australian accent hailing her from deep in the gloom.

A few seconds later, the flashlight illuminated her own glorious figure standing just ahead. Layla was blinking furiously, blinded by the sudden illumination. Beside her, Buller began to growl.

'Shut that brute up, or I'll slit his throat,' she grunted, slowing to a halt a few yards in front of them and bending double to catch her breath.

'Buller, be quiet!' Layla commanded, and the dog fell silent, though his hackles were still raised. She looked at the glass shard with disgust, but said nothing.

'Good. Any sign of them?' Stevie gasped, rubbing at a stitch in her side.

'No, but we need to keep going. He's going to jump off the Bullers and we have to stop him. Come *on*, Stevie!' Layla sounded frantic and her eyes were full of fear. She and the dog turned back to the dark hole ahead.

'I can't help it if your bloody body isn't up to the task,' snapped Stevie, furious at feeling so weak. Taking a deep breath, she summoned all her strength and followed behind them, holding up the flashlight.

Within a couple of minutes, they could hear and feel a howling draught whirling past them, raising clouds of fine dust from the earthen floor.

'An open door!' shouted Stevie, finding her second wind, and pushing past them to take the lead.

Sure enough, the flashlight revealed an arch-shaped hole in the wall: a portal exposed to the elements. As they reached it, they could see the danger ahead and slowed down enough to be able to step gingerly over the threshold and on to the stony ledge.

Stevie looked over the edge and saw that the cliff below was not sheer; bristling with long grass and tattered shrubs, it graduated in a long curve towards the angry sea, which pounded on a small beach far below. A narrow, meandering pathway on her left descended to the hidden cove, but there was no sign of anyone down there.

'The Bullers are up and off to the right,' shouted Layla above the gale.

'I know! I've been there before, remember?' Stevie yelled at her, thinking: *When I saved your life, you stupid bitch*.

She began to shuffle along the wet and slippery ledge, her heart sinking as she realised that climbing the enormous pile of boulders that lay to the south was their only way up the cliff. With an impatient sigh, she wrapped her glass weapon fully in the dishcloth and slipped it into her jacket pocket.

'Hurry!' insisted Layla behind her. 'We haven't a moment to lose!'

As the three of them scrambled up the rock pile, Buller surprisingly sure-footed for all his stockiness, Layla shouted: 'Hey, look!' Drawing closer, Stevie saw a trail of dark spots.

'Blood,' she cried.

The grisly sight spurred them on and before long, they were standing on the clifftop path, peering across at the Bullers.

Thanks to Stevie's twenty-twenty vision, Layla was the first to spot the far-off hunched figure silhouetted against the sky. She grabbed Stevie's arm and pointed, and the three of them set off again, both women trying not to stumble on the sodden, bumpy path leading towards The Pot.

Chapter 80
Layla

As they drew closer through the storm-lashed gloom, Layla clutched at Stevie's arm.

'It's her!' she wailed into her ear. 'And there's no sign of James!'

Stevie shrugged her off violently. 'Jesus Christ; let go!' she yelled, barrelling forward on to the precarious path that formed the time-eroded rim of The Pot.

'Come back, Stevie!' Layla cried, hanging on to Buller's collar for security as much as for his own safety. But the Australian ignored her and she knew she could not possibly follow her. One near-miss was enough for a lifetime.

Instead, sobbing with fear, she crouched beside the dog and scanned the area as best she could for any hint of the professor's whereabouts. He was nowhere in sight.

Chapter 81
Stevie

The Kiwi had her back to her, rocking herself like a bloody baby and bawling up at the sky.

Stevie edged forward. She slipped the muffled shard from her pocket and deftly re-wrapped it to protect her hand and expose its razor edges. A white-hot rage had seared all fear from her mind. The nightmarish drop on either side of the path meant nothing to her.

Then she was on her: left arm wrapped around the bitch's chest; right hand holding the jagged fragment to her throat.

Victoria's startled screech was whipped away and lost to the elements.

'*Where is he?*' Stevie roared into her ear, not caring if she deafened her.

Soundlessly, the New Zealander pointed into the massive whirlpool that roiled below. Stevie blinked away the driving rain and peered down into the ocean-carved cauldron. Releasing her left arm, but with the knife still at Victoria's throat, she picked up the flashlight she'd dropped during the ambush.

Instantly, its powerful beam illuminated a buff-coloured coat, which must have snagged on a ledge halfway down the guano-streaked cliff. A memory-flash reminded her that Blunstone had been wearing the coat open when he'd escaped from the library. He must have either fallen out of it, or released himself from it, after it caught on the rock.

Rage and terror ripped through her as the full horror of her predicament sank in.

'Look what you've done, you EVIL BITCH!' she screamed.

Victoria gazed up at her and laughed, her upside-down face sinister in the murky darkness. '*You're* the evil bitch, remember?' she shouted, her blood-red mouth twisted in an ugly sneer. 'Okay, so the fool has foiled my beautiful plan, but you've still ended up *trapped for life* in someone else's body. *Nothing* you can do to me will change that!'

With a howl of fury, Stevie slashed the shard across her throat and tossed her, like an unloved rag doll, into the eternal tumult below.

Chapter 82
Layla

Speechless with horror and still clutching Buller, Layla watched her own body murder Victoria and hurl her into the churning crucible.

Does that make me *a murderer?* she wondered wildly. *They're* my *hands and they've just killed someone.*

Her shock-induced philosophising faded when she saw Stevie striding towards her along the causeway. The thought of running away never occurred to her, so rooted with fear was she to the sodden turf. But she managed to get to her feet shakily as the Australian drew nearer and her eyes widened in horror at the sight of the now-bloody shard the woman still had in her hand.

Seeing where Layla's frightened stare was directed, Stevie flung the weapon high into the air and watched as it arced and plunged towards the sea.

'*Don't – say – anything,*' she hissed, as she pushed past her and began to head back the way they had come.

Layla ignored her. 'Is he dead?' she shouted after her. 'Is he?'

Stevie whipped around, her dark hair plastered to her head, her eyes as flat and empty as those of a mannequin. 'What do *you* think?' she said sarcastically. Then she shrugged and added: 'It's over. Enjoy my body. I'm off.'

And she turned and ran, a small silhouette fleeing along the windy clifftop as if pursued by Dracula himself.

Paralysed with shock, Layla screamed after her: 'STEVIE! Don't go – there's something I need to tell you! *Something you really have to know!*'

But her words were sucked away by the storm and Stevie didn't look back.

Sensing her distress, Buller began to whine. But it wasn't until he started barking excitedly that she looked down to see what was wrong.

The big black dog was staring at something in the distance, back in the direction of the Bullers.

She followed his gaze and saw a lone figure making its way around the lip of The Pot.

The professor!

But he was thirty seconds too late.

Epilogue
Eighteen Hours Later: Cairnacraig House

Layla's Log

I'm writing this in the library, which only a short while ago was my prison.

The storm has finally died down; James has taken Buller for a late-night walk, and I'm alone in the silent house where my destiny was unnaturally altered in April this year.

I'm no longer addressing my log to Stevie: I have nothing to say to her right now.

She has vanished, stealing my life away *entirely unnecessarily*.

Last night, when I realised James was still alive, I let Buller run to him while I tore after Stevie, screaming her name over and over. But by the time I'd picked my way back down over the rocks, she'd already entered the secret passage and locked the door behind her.

I sat on the ledge and howled. James and Buller found me minutes later and the three of us had no choice but to climb back up the cliff and make our way overland, to Cairnacraig House. I ran ahead, but it was too late. She'd found the keys to the Mini and had driven off. James eventually discovered his own car keys, along with both of our phones, in a kitchen drawer.

Of course, we raced back to Aberdeen; first to Fittie, then to my home, but there was no trace of her, apart from the parked Mini and a hastily-written note she'd left on my kitchen table.

'*Don't try to find me,*' it read. '*There's absolutely no point. You got the best part of this body-swap shit, so consider yourself lucky.*'

And that was it.

As we sat, exhausted, at my table, our futures in ruins, James told me his story.

He had timed his escape to coincide with Victoria's return, guessing she'd be so incensed that she'd follow him without a thought for Stevie and me. He didn't mind the dark, as he knew the layout of the tunnel intimately, having spent many hours wandering back and forth, marvelling at the amount of time and skill that must have been employed in constructing it – probably when smuggling was at its height here, in the eighteenth century. There was no record of its true history, but it was his theory that some former – surely eccentric – gentleman of the house had spared no expense in ensuring his wine and spirits cellar was kept well-stocked at an illicit price.

'I would have told you about the secret passage before, but I was so immersed in the operation and its aftermath, that it slipped my mind,' he explained. 'I think I did hint at "bells and whistles" when I first gave you the grand tour, but I didn't elaborate then because I didn't want *her* to know about it.'

Up on the cliffs, he'd made sure Victoria had spotted him on the causeway, before hiding behind a high clump of grass and removing his raincoat. He'd filled the pockets with small rocks on the way. Hoping she wouldn't see him in his dark polo-neck and jeans, he'd crawled over to the edge of The Pot, pulled the bundled coat from under his jumper, screamed at the top of his voice and thrown it in. Then he'd crept back to his hiding place.

'I hoped upon hope that she'd believe I'd killed myself: it was the only way I could think of to scupper her plans for the operation,' he said, his voice barely more than a whisper.

'I also prayed that you and Stevie would manage to follow us and overpower her before she went completely berserk and returned to kill you both… it was a very clumsy plan,' he concluded miserably.

I didn't let him off the hook. His 'clumsy plan' had resulted in catastrophe.

'I wish you'd told us what you had in mind. We really thought you had committed suicide! That's why Stevie murdered Victoria and ran away! You didn't have to be so bloody convincing,' I raged at him.

He looked stricken and said nothing in his own defence.

But then I had to confess my own guilty secret: the one I had tried so desperately to share with Stevie when I realised she was deserting me.

'What finally persuaded me to participate in your project was finding out, early in the new year, that there was a chance that I could be in the early stages of multiple sclerosis,' I told James, unable to meet his gaze.

'The test wasn't conclusive, and I was too cowardly to have it repeated before our operation, but the symptoms I was experiencing do explain why Stevie has found my body so hard to deal with. I blame myself for not telling either of you the truth.'

He was silent for a long time and then said sadly: 'We have both done things we regret. The hardest thing is going to be how to learn to live with them.'

But this is not how it's going to end.

After returning to the professor's house and having had a few hours' broken sleep and another long discussion, we have decided that there's a very faint chance that all is not lost and that the project – and our lives – can be salvaged.

We're going to look for Stevie.

I want my body back, regardless of the risk of degenerative disease. I want my old life back: my home, my family, my work and my future prospects, whatever they may be. And it's not just because I miss them terribly; I have a growing fear that the longer I live as an imposter in this body, the more I risk being affected – *infected?* – by the part of Stevie's subconscious that got left behind. She has proved herself capable of murder, and so who knows what other dark desires and impulses are lurking deep in the recesses of the brain that plays host to my consciousness? Will they start to surface, as some of her dreams and memories have already done? And will I be able to control them if they do?

I don't want to be in a position to find out.

James will finance our search. It's going to be a hellish challenge. I'm sure that if we ever do find Stevie, she'll be overjoyed to discover that he is alive. But she's going to make it hard for us to track her down. After murdering Victoria and believing that there's no going back, she will be doing her utmost to escape detection.

Victoria...I feel sick at the thought of what's happened to her. We haven't reported her death and we don't believe her disappearance will be traced back to us. We can't get involved with the police – it's as simple as that. We can only hope that her body will be found and that she'll be given a proper funeral. Despite what she's done to us, I can't bring myself to hate her; the poor woman was completely insane. I keep wondering whether she has been washed out of The Pot and has drifted down to the Scaurs of Cruden. Perhaps her soul is waiting to rise for judgement, on Lammas Day. Knowing what we now know about consciousness, the concept of souls rising is no longer as fantastical as it sounded when James first told me the legend.

As far as James's colleagues, Allan and Susan, are concerned, he managed to head them off in the early hours of this morning, before they left Edinburgh. My mother's medical crisis had been a false alarm, so panic over, he told them. Then he asked them to remain on standby for the foreseeable future.

And as for the two of us: we will base ourselves here, at Cairnacraig House ('Ground Zero', as Victoria described it), while we search the world for Stevie. Whether we like it or not, for as long as she's on the run, James Blunstone and I are bound together in a self-inflicted exile from humanity: two desperate elements of an unholy trinity, seeking completion – and absolution.

Acknowledgements

This book is dedicated to my wonderful family and friends, all of whom have buoyed me up with their encouragement and interest throughout the writing and publishing process.

However, I would like to say a special thank you to a few of them in particular:

My parents, Bill and Dorothy Mackie, for inspiring my lifelong passion for reading.

My husband, Allan Montgomery, for believing in my dream of becoming an author.

My "muse", Kate Sutherland, for cheerleading this novel from its inception.

Fellow writer Shaunagh Kirby, for providing valuable advice on the plot.

Flora Wilson, for giving me that final push towards self-publishing.

PR supremo Morven Mackenzie, for spreading the word.

Star designer Mike Johnston, for creating such an atmospheric paperback cover.

And Jock, the terrier, for being my constant companion.

Finally, thank you for taking the time to read this book. I would love to hear what you think of it, so please get in touch. A customer review on Amazon would also be very welcome!

judymackieauthor@gmail.com
https://www.facebook.com/judymackiebooks
http://www.twitter.com/judymackiebooks

Copyright

17634825R00199

Printed in Great Britain
by Amazon